Distant Revenge

Edward G. Briscoe
Delores R. Johnson
Agatha D. Briscoe

Writers Club Press
San Jose New York Lincoln Shanghai

Distant Revenge

Published by Writers Club Press
an imprint of iUniverse.com, Inc.

For information address:
iUniverse.com, Inc.
620 North 48th Street
Suite 201
Lincoln, NE 68504-3467
www.iuniverse.com

ISBN: 0-595-09460-0

Printed in the United States of America

Part One

Chapter One

Dr. James Mercer, a prominent Washington Surgeon, felt good as he continued his leisurely jog along the nearly deserted path along Haynes Point. It was early in the morning. He could make out the faint smell of the cherry blossoms from the nearby tidal basin as he ran. A thin bead of sweat trickled down the front of his sweatshirt as he jogged. He had been running as a form of exercise for over three years and the scenery along the jogging trail had not lost its appeal. Off to the right, across the Potomac River, he could see the passenger jets as they took off and landed at Washington National Airport. Off to his left, he could see the hills of the Anacostia section of Washington. Haynes Point nestled between the confluence of the Potomac and the Anacostia rivers. It had been built in the early thirties from land, which was largely swampland. Like most of Southwest Washington, the land had been marshland and plagued with mosquitoes until the Army Corp's of Engineers went to work on the area.

He settled into the rhythm of his run. He was not scheduled to operate until ten o'clock that morning and he was enjoying this quiet time. It was a little after six thirty in the morning and there were only a few joggers out on the path. He made a turn as the War College came into view. The sun was just beginning to light the eastern sky as he ran.

Dr. Mercer had lived in the Washington area for almost twenty years. He had attended medical school at Georgetown University. The young medical student had so impressed his teachers that he was offered both an internship and residency training at the hospital complex. He had stayed on staff at the completion of his surgical residency and had built a solid reputation in the eight years that quickly passed. He had married early in his medical school stay. This marriage had almost resulted in his not being able to finish the four years. He had been blessed with twins his third year of medical school. The birth of the twins occurred three months after the death of both of his parents. They died in an automobile accident on a fog-shrouded Virginia highway. He became the caretaker of his two brothers and young sister and the father of twins all within the space of six months. His wife Margo, who had worked as a surgical nurse, was unable to return to work due to complications from the protracted labor and the need to stay at home to care for the twins who had been born six weeks prematurely. Had it not been for the help of a wealthy classmate, he would have had to end his studies until he was financially able to bear the many burdens.

He continued his exercise. He occasionally checked his pulse rate as he ran. He loved the cleansing of the soul which jogging allowed him. Pictures of the twins flashed before him. They would both be finishing their second year at Bennington College in a few months. They were both honor students and planned careers in the television industry. He thought about the upcoming case, which he would perform later that morning. He had become known throughout the Washington, Maryland and Virginia area for his expertise in performing complex pediatric surgery. He was on staff at many hospitals in the metropolitan Washington area. He operated frequently at the National Children's Center located in northwest Washington. In addition, he regularly volunteered time at the Howard University Hospital Center. This predominantly black institution was pleased to have his expertise added to that of the many fine surgeons who staffed the center.

He was nearing the halfway point of his early morning run when he heard the footsteps of another jogger approaching from his rear. He moved slightly over to the right side of the path to let the other runner pass. As the man approached the doctor, it became apparent that this was no ordinary jogger. Clenched in his right hand was a ten-inch long stiletto. The last thing that Doctor Mercer saw was the top of the Washington Monument. The stranger had plunged the stiletto deep into the doctors' back. Rapidly withdrawing the glistening blade, he plunged the knife time after time into the body of the dying man. With a swipe of his arm, he hurled the weapon into the nearby river and trotted off.

Ten minutes later, a female government worker out for her early morning walk saw a man lying on the pathway. She thought at first that the form on the ground might have had a heart condition. As she approached cautiously, she saw the gradually enlarging pool of blood. Her screams echoed through the spring morning. It took almost ten minutes to summon help, but the surgeon had suffered multiple wounds and nothing would bring him back. A hastily summoned ambulance crew shook their heads as they surveyed the carnage.

The homicide detectives arrived in their unmarked cars and set about reviewing the crime scene. The gray-haired man carried no identification. This was all too common in assaults involving runners. They seldom carried wallets, which would have contained identification. Due to the lack of identification, the body was transferred to the D.C. morgue where identification was not made for almost three days. His grief stricken wife was led from the dilapidated building housing the morgue. She was helped into a waiting car, which was driven by a friend of the family. Her sobs could be heard as the car drove slowly away.

D.C. police assigned several of their best men to investigate the murder of the well-known physician. There were no clues at the murder site. Although divers were sent to search the inky depths of the river, they were unable to retrieve a murder weapon. Interviews with clinical associates and friends offered no clues to the killing of this happily married family man. His associates were stunned and well over one thousand mourners attended the funeral services at the National Cathedral.

Detective Alphonso Smith was the lead detective assigned to the case. He wiped his brow as a young reporter continued to grill him during a press conference. This was the third conference in as many weeks and the police were making little progress in apprehending the murderer. "Detective Smith, why is it taking so long to develop leads in this case?"

"We have not been able to find one witness or even a motive. All we know is that he was taking his early run and was attacked by one or more assailants."

"Can you be sure that there was more than one assailant?"

"The autopsy results indicate that there was most probably only one perpetrator."

"Why do you say that?" the young reporter questioned.

"I'm not at liberty to give you all of the details and the autopsy report is not final. But the preliminary findings indicate that one weapon was used. The doctor was struck from behind. The motive is unclear since he was not carrying anything of value. He didn't even have a fanny pack. We checked with his wife and she agreed that he never wore a fanny pack or carried a wallet while jogging."

"Do you think this was a random act?" The reporter from the Washington Post queried.

"We just don't know at this point."

"What are you doing to make the park safe for joggers?"

"As you may or may not know, the park is actually under a dual jurisdiction. The Park Service and the District of Columbia share responsibility for patrolling Haynes' Point. My understanding is that the Park Service has beefed up its mounted patrols, but you will need to confirm that with them." The detective wiped has brow with a well-used handkerchief. "Folks, I'd like to wrap this up and get back to the case at this time. Thank you for your patience. We'll keep you informed of any further developments in this case."

With that, he left the room and headed back to his office while the reporters milled around jotting notes and rewinding tape recorders. The TV news reporters hurriedly gathered up their equipment and darted out in search of the next story.

Chapter Two

Dr. Stephen Mossler had finished his evening rounds on the pediatric unit at Cedars Sinai Hospital. He stood by the nurse's station engaged in an animated conversation with Sarah Jamerson, the head nurse.

"I will probably discharge Mary Holmes tomorrow. I think she can be followed as an out-patient."

The red-haired nurse smiled. "I think you made a save on this one, Steve. Lord knows, she was a pretty sick cookie when she was admitted."

"This is one of the worse cases of Lyme Disease that I have ever seen. I'm really glad that that resident raised the possibility of Lyme Disease. I hadn't really thought about it. That's medicine for you. Sometimes it's better to be lucky than good."

They both laughed. They had been working together for almost ten years. When he first joined the staff at the hospital, Sarah had been only two years out of nursing school. She had finished nursing school at George Washington University in Washington D.C. Dr. Mossler had trained at Georgetown University. They were both familiar with the city of Washington and this commonality drew them together. They had dated on several occasions, and secretly, Sarah had hoped for a blossoming of the relationship. It was during one of these early dates that the young physician had confided to her that he was gay. She was stunned at first and deeply hurt. She valued him as a good friend and the two of them remained close. He became her confidant as she moved through her many failed relationships. Her commitment to the tiny children who were her charges left little time for romance.

They still continued to see each other throughout the years. She was his companion when he needed an escort for the many hospital social activities. She kept his secret well. Their careers continued to advance.

She was promoted to assistant head nurse and then to head nurse. For his part, he built a thriving Pediatric practice with a sub-specialty in Pediatric hematology: the treatment of diseases of the blood in children. He had been offered the position of assistant chief of Pediatrics several months before, but had declined the position. He loved the clinical aspect of his practice and knew that the administrative demands of the offered position would require time away from his young patients. He had discussed this with Sarah. Sarah was the person who he knew he could trust, both to keep his secret and to give him sound advice when he faced practice related problems.

And so they were together this evening. He was about to return to his Marina Del Rey condominium and she was about to accept a date from one of the junior staff members. The doctor laughed as Sarah remarked about the difference in ages between herself and her prospective date. "None of us is getting any younger, you know. You have to make hay while the sun shines."

"Oh Steve, leave it to you to have a pat answer."

"Look Sarah, you don't even have to get dressed up. He's relatively new in town. Have him take you over to Westwood and have a relaxing evening."

"He had mentioned something about driving down to Redondo Beach, so I think I'll let him call the shots."

"That sounds good to me. I've got to run now, I'll see you in the morning," Glancing at his watch, the doctor smiled and headed down the long hospital corridor.

Finding the keys to the new Mercedes, which was parked in the Doctor's parking lot, he pressed the automatic door lock and wearily slumped into the driver's seat. This had been a long day. He looked forward to a cool drink and another quiet evening with Jonathan. Doctor Mossler had met Jonathan almost ten months ago. Jonathan was a pharmaceutical representative who had visited the doctor's office with a new medication. The two men had become instant friends and Jonathan had moved into the doctor's Marina Del Rey condominium several months later. The two had become lovers and were both careful to be discrete with their relationship. They drove out of town together on the weekends when the doctor was not on call. They often made the six-hour drive to San Francisco where Dr. Mossler had many friends and where the sight of two men holding hands did not provoke an angry response. He headed down La Brea Avenue, his thoughts turning to the upcoming convention in Las Vegas. He would miss Jonathan, but had convinced the younger man that he would be seeing many of his clinical associates who were unaware of his sexual preferences. Jonathan would be in New York that week, having opted to work at a medical convention in the city after quietly turning down the chance to work at the company's display booth at the Las Vegas medical convention.

He approached the Marina Freeway and sped up as he filled with the anticipation of being with Jonathan after a long day. He slid the magnetized parking card into the slot and waited as the gate slowly rose. His parking space was 1118. He pulled into the space and collected his briefcase from the passenger's seat. Keying the auto lock, he headed towards the elevator. He was unaware of the dark shadow that approached him. A hand was placed over his mouth and he felt a searing heat in his back as the intruder stabbed him. The briefcase flew from his hand as he attempted to remove the hand that covered his mouth. His mouth was filled with the warm taste of blood as he struggled to escape the stranger's grasp. The shadowy figure struck the doctor again and again until he finally released the lifeless body. The form sagged to the pavement of the parking structure.

In the apartment above, Jonathan paced. It was almost midnight. He had become used to the doctor's somewhat erratic hours, but usually his friend and lover called if he was going to be delayed. After another hour, he called the hospital operator and asked her to page Doctor Mossler. After a short while, the operator interrupted the call.

"Sorry sir, Doctor Mossler is not answering his page."

"Operator, can you put me though to the Pediatric Floor?"

"Just one moment sir, I'll connect you now."

"Pediatric Hematology, Mrs. Williams speaking. How may I help you?"

"Hello, Mrs. Williams, I'm trying to locate Doctor Mossler. This is one of his friends. Is he on the ward by any chance?"

"No, he was here earlier. I'm sure of that because I saw him talking to the head nurse."

"Oh, you must mean Miss Jamerson. Is she there?"

"No, she left about two hours ago."

"Thank you. I'll call around. I'm sure I'll catch up with him."

"Is it an emergency? I do know that Doctor Smothers is handling Doctor Mossler's calls."

"No, there's no emergency. I'm sure that he will turn up shortly. Thank you for your help." Jonathan went to the doctor's desk and fingered the large Rolodex. Finding Sarah Jamerson's number, he dialed. A somewhat groggy voiced Sarah answered the telephone. "Hello Sarah, this is Jonathan. I'm a little worried about Steve. He still hasn't come in yet."

"He left the hospital almost three hours ago. We were talking just before he left. He didn't mention any other things he had to do. I got the impression that he was going straight home."

"I'm a little worried. He always calls when he's going to be delayed."

"He may have stopped off for a bite to eat. He has been working really hard. He has some pretty sick kids who he is taking care of now and he has really been putting in some long hours."

"I'm sure he'll be along any moment now, it's just…It's just so unusual. Maybe I'm worrying a little too much. I'll fix myself a good stiff drink and just relax."

"Give me a call when he comes in."

"But Sarah, it's so late. I wouldn't want to disturb you."

"That's all right, I probably won't be able to get to sleep anyway. Just call me when he comes in."

"I'll do that Sarah and thanks so much for being a friend."

Jonathan poured a large glass of Scotch and paced the well-carpeted floors of the condominium for the next forty-five minutes. He went out onto the balcony that overlooked the darkened marina and the Pacific Ocean beyond. Although the unit did not face the street, he was alarmed as he heard the sound of sirens, which entered the street and seemed to stop in front of the building. He dressed hastily and took the elevator to the lobby of the complex. He was unprepared for the scene that greeted him. There were several police cars and an ambulance blocking the street. Off to the left, by the entrance of the parking structure, were several more police vehicles, their flashing lights cutting a swath through the light fog that drifted in off the ocean. A small crowd had gathered. Women, who lived in the building, several with their hair in curlers, joined the group. He saw a neighbor and moved towards him.

"What is all the commotion about?"

"They just found someone murdered in the parking garage."

Jonathan felt his legs tremble as he fought to breathe. He knew deep down inside who the victim was. He made his way towards a young police officer who was holding back the growing crowd.

"Excuse me, officer. Do they know who the person is? You know, the one who is inside the garage? Is it a male or a female?"

"It's a male. They haven't told me anymore than that."

"Can I go in?"

The officer shook his head. "I'm afraid not sir. This whole area is a crime scene now. Our orders are to keep out on-lookers."

"But...But you don't understand. My roommate is long overdue from his rounds at the hospital and I want to make sure that it isn't him."

"I'll go get my sergeant and see what he thinks. Just wait here. I'll be right back."

He returned a few minutes later with a rotund black man. He was wearing the gold stripes of a L.A. Police sergeant. He stopped in front of Jonathan.

"Good evening, I'm Sergeant Murphy. Officer Guthrey tells me that you may know the victim. Would you like to take a look? We have his wallet, but a definite I.D. would help us get started. I must warn you sir; it's not a pretty sight."

Jonathan nodded slowly. The chill of the ocean breeze blew against the beads of perspiration which had formed on his uncovered brow. He felt even colder as he was led into the garage. The area normally received very little sunlight and tended to be several degrees cooler than the outside air. The normally reduced tones of the garage were punctuated by moments of brightness as police photographers began to take pictures of the carnage.

Jonathan felt weaker as they moved through the parking garage. He knew that Steves' space was number 1118. His pace quickened as they approached the parking space. He now knew the reason that his friend and lover had been late. Stretched out beside his glistening Mercedes lay Steve's body. The blood, which a short time before had been his life-force, continued to ooze from his lifeless body.

Sergeant Murphy turned towards Jonathan.

"Could this possibly be your friend?"

Jonathan did not hear the officer's words. He had fallen to his knees, his body wracked with sobs. "It's him...My God, it's him. Steve. Oh Steve. What have they done to you?"

He felt a policeman's hand on his shoulder. Jonathan shook with grief. After several minutes, he lifted his pain filled body slightly and leaned against a car that was parked in the adjoining stall.

"We are going to have to ask you some questions Mr....I'm afraid I didn't get your last name."

Jonathan looked up. "I'm Jonathan Jobranski. Doctor Mossler was my roommate." He sobbed uncontrollably. "I was waiting up stairs for him to come home and I was afraid he might have had a flat tire or an accident, but not this. Not this."

"We can talk to you here or it might be better for you if we conducted our interview upstairs. This is going to be a very busy place for the next several hours and we can spare you the trauma of watching our officers work."

"Yes...Yes...Come on, we can go up to the condo." The stunned blond man led the two officers and they took the elevator to the eleventh floor apartment.

As they entered the condominium, Jonathan turned slightly towards the older of the two detectives. "I'm afraid that I didn't catch your names."

The older man reached out and shook Jonathan's hand. "I'm Detective Robinson and this is my partner, Ed White."

"I'm pleased to meet the both of you, but I only wish it was under different circumstances. Have a seat...have a seat. I'm going to use the bathroom and I will be right back."

The two detectives sat down on the over-stuffed couches. They glanced about the tastefully furnished room. They noted the expensive paintings and the bronze statues, which contributed to the feeling of opulence. The older man nodded towards the younger, as a smile spread over his worn face. Their inspection was interrupted by the sounds of Jonathan vomiting in the closed bathroom door. It was almost ten minutes before Jonathan rejoined them in the living room. His eyes were reddened and he was sweating profusely.

"Are you all right Mr. Jobranski?"

"I'll be O.K. in a little while. It's just that this is such a shock."

The ringing of the telephone in the kitchen jarred their conversation. Jonathan excused himself and walked unsteadily towards the kitchen.

"Oh Sarah, you won't believe what has happened." His body was again enveloped by sobs. "Steve is gone. He's gone. They found him in the parking garage. Someone murdered him. Yes...Yes, I'm with the detectives now." There was a pause. "Yes...Yes. Just tell the front desk people who you are and they will let you come up to the condo. I'll tell them that we are expecting you." He hung the telephone back on the receiver and rejoined the detectives.

"Mr. Jobranski, when did you last see Doctor Mossler alive?"

"I saw him this morning."

"Did you talk to him at all today?"

"No. I was in Long Beach all day visiting clients and I never got the chance to call him."

"How long have you known the Doctor?"

"For about a year. I met him when I visited his office to sell him a new blood product."

The detectives looked puzzled. "You see, I am a pharmaceutical representative and my job is to keep doctors like Doctor Mossler up to date on the new products which might enhance the care of their patients. As such, I travel a lot and I meet many doctors at conventions."

"How long have the two of you been sharing the apartment?"

"For less than nine months. Steve and I had become close friends and he asked me to move in with him."

The older detective cleared his throat. "Did you two have any other type of relationship?" The detective was obviously ill at ease.

Jonathan nodded his head. "Yes, we were lovers. I loved Steve with all my heart. He was good to me and for me. We loved each other." With the last word uttered, he broke into hysterical sobbing. He regained his composure after some minutes had passed.

The younger detective took notes as they talked. "Did the doctor have any family in the area?"

"No, his father passed away while he was a freshman in medical school and his mother died a year later. It was a terrible shock. He almost dropped out of medical school. He told me that a classmate helped him financially and he was able to finish. He never talked much about his family. He was an only son and he was always afraid that his parents would find out that he was gay. He hid this from his parents while he was in college and with their passing, he never felt the need to openly talk about his sexuality."

"Did he ever tell you anything about his benefactor."

"No, he was particularly close-mouthed about his college and medical school friends."

"Did he have any enemies that you knew about?"

"No, he was the kindest person on earth. His patients and their families adored him. Why, half the things that you see in this condo are gifts from patients' families. He was devoted to medicine and to his patients. He didn't flaunt his homosexuality and very few of his colleagues knew about his being gay. I can't think of a single person who would want to harm him."

The interview continued for another forty-five minutes before being interrupted by the sound of the doorbell ringing. Jonathan opened the door and hugged Sarah who had obviously been crying. He introduced her to the two detectives who wrote down her name and address. They excused themselves and promised to keep the two friends abreast of the results of the investigation.

Inside the apartment, the two friends talked until dawn began to light up the ocean. While they talked, the investigation team sifted through the meager evidence in the parking garage. The two detectives worked well into the morning hours. They had both been impressed with the grief shown by Jonathan and although it was early in the investigation, they were both convinced that the murder was somehow related to the fact that Doctor Mossler had been gay. Months passed and the murder of the amiable physician remained unsolved.

Chapter Three

Dr. Kevin Pointer had looked forward to this break for weeks. He was finally going to have four days away from his practice. An associate had agreed to cover his practice for the long holiday weekend. His associate would not only cover the holiday, which was observed on Monday, but had agreed to take over the entire patient schedule for Friday. This meant that he could sail for four days. The doctor was an avid sailor. He had purchased his boat three years ago after finalizing his divorce from his wife Pamela. His ex-wife and three children had moved back to Oakmill, Pennsylvania. He still kept in touch with his children and the four of them spent much of the summers sailing the many waterways that formed the Seattle area.

He was planning to sail up the Strait of Juan De Fuca the next several days visiting a friend who lived in Port Renfrew. This was a tiny town, which was located on the southeastern side of Vancouver Island. The next day, if weather permitted, he was planning to sail further up the coast of the island to Vargas Island. He had invited Dan Smith and his wife Mary. Marjorie Holcolm would complete the foursome. Marjorie was an Intensive Care nurse who had been dating the doctor for almost ten months. The younger nurse had been instrumental in helping the doctor overcome periods of depression brought on by his bitter divorce and by the absence of his three children. Dan Smith was a young surgeon who Kevin had met when Kevin was first opening his practice. The two doctors often assisted each other in performing complex pediatric surgical procedures. They had developed a deep friendship and Dan and his wife had remained loyal to Kevin during the stormy divorce period.

Kevin lived in a suburb of Seattle called Waterview. Perched on a high hill, the town had a commanding view of Puget Sound. He had been forced to sell his former residence in order to satisfy the terms of the divorce decree. He had saved his money and after two years he had found a three-bedroom condominium in the Waterview Towers. He had spent a great deal of time and money tastefully furnishing his new apartment, taking care to keep the furnishings compatible with anticipated visits of his children. The months following the divorce and the departure of his former family for the East Coast had been very lonely for the doctor. He had used his medical practice as a crutch, spending long hours working in the operating rooms of the several hospitals where he was a staff member. He went out of his way to assist other surgeons when they were operating. He was always available to cover the practices of the other surgeons. He took an active role in the teaching of medical students. He rarely vacationed. He grudgingly took vacations when he felt his skills being eroded by the long hours he was spending in his medical practice.

While visiting Tortola in the British West Indies, he was introduced to sailing. Several of his friends had persuaded him to join them on a bare boat charter and he was smitten by the sport of sailing. Upon returning from his vacation, he began to devour all of the books he could find which contained information on boats and on sailing. He spent all of his free weekends visiting the many boat shows and water-based events which made the Seattle area a boating paradise. He began to subscribe to magazines such as "Yachting" and "Boating." He realized that he had found a way to fill the void. It was not long before he began to look in earnest for a sailboat. He read the classified advertisements and boating sections from all of the area newspapers. He talked to boat dealers and salesmen and he spent time visiting many of the marinas that dotted the shores of Puget Sound.

At last, he found his love. She was a fifty-one foot Pearson ketch-rig motor sailer with a 109 horse power auxiliary engine. It had berths for six persons. Because it was ketch rigged, the sails were more easily managed by a smaller crew and as the doctor's knowledge of sailing increased, he was able to sail the boat by himself on those many occasions when he wanted to be by himself. He had a large steering wheel in the cockpit at the back of the vessel. The boat offered good visibility as he maneuvered it through the often-crowded waterways.

He was able to find a marina that was located about twenty miles north of Seattle near the town of Edmonds. He spent many of his weekends on the boat using the marine operator to answer any pages that he received. He was happier than he had been in a long while. He spent hundreds of dollars and many hours installing new instruments and many gadgets in his new hobby. His friends knew that if he did not answer his telephone at home, he was on his boat.

He dated Mary Holcolm intermittently. He was unprepared emotionally to make any sort of commitment. She understood and enjoyed his company. She had been raised on the seacoast of Maine and was an accomplished sailor. It was her knowledge of sailing that had drawn the two together. She often accompanied Kevin as he visited the many boat shows and marinas prior to his purchasing of the boat. He renamed the boat "The Spirit." He did this partially because of his understanding of how much the divorce had taken from his own spirit. The second reason involved his realization that when the boat was under way, the boat itself seemed to possess a spirit. He loved his boat almost as much as he loved the practice of medicine.

He had decided that he would stock the boat on the night before the group's departure. This would save them several hours the next day. It was almost nine o'clock before he finished hospital rounds and shopping for the provisions, which he knew would be needed. He listened to a cassette as he drove North on Interstate Five towards the marina at Edmonds. He exited the freeway and turned West down the dirt road, which lead into the Marina. A fog had drifted in from the Puget Sound and the visibility was reduced. This caused him to slow the car. He turned into the large marina driveway and parked near the slip in which sat "The Spirit." It took him almost thirty minutes to unload the boxes of supplies and he also had brought his carry-on bag, which contained everything he would need for the next several days.

The marina was deserted. The yellow lights, which were mounted on stark aluminum poles, gave eerie shadows as the fog continued to drift in from the Sound. A muffled clanging came from the rigging of the moored vessels as a slight breeze tapped their lines against the many masts. Kevin busied himself stowing the many items in their assigned places. He poured himself a large glass of Scotch and relaxed on the cloth-covered seat in the main salon.

He dozed off and was awakened sometime later by an increased rocking of his beloved boat. He thought that he heard footsteps on the deck above him. He sat up on the chair and looked about the cabin. He must have been mistaken he thought. That was probably a prop wash from a passing vessel. A few minutes later, he again heard what he thought were light footsteps on the deck. There was no mistaking the sound this time. He stood up in the salon and headed aft towards the hatch which led to the deck. As he slid the hatch opened, he called out. "Is anyone there? How can I help you?" As the hatch was fully opened, he found himself staring upwards towards shoes and dark pants. The rest of the person's upper body was hidden in the swirling fog. That was the last thing that he saw. There was an orange glow as the bullet left the nozzle of the silencer-equipped weapon. The first bullet entered the doctor's face just above his left eye. His already dead body twitched as five more bullets were fired, all finding their mark. A streak of blood marked the doctor's slide to the bottom of the cabin steps. The shadowy figure stepped back and melted into the swirling fog.

His lifeless form was found early the next morning by Dan and Mary Smith who arrived about eight A.M. When they received no answer from within the cabin, Dan stepped through the still opened cockpit hatch and saw the carnage within the salon. He stepped back into the cockpit and gently pushed Mary towards the stern of the boat.

"We had better call the police!"

"What's wrong, Dan?'

"Something terrible has happened to Kevin. Don't look honey. Quick! We have to find a telephone." Running back up the marina dock, they entered the clubhouse and hurriedly dialed 911.

Within ten minutes, several squad cars roared into the marina, their large tires throwing up showers of gravel as they stopped abruptly at the dockside. Two officers approached the Smiths who were huddled together.

"Are you Doctor Smith?"

"Yes, we're the Smiths."

"So it was you that the dispatcher talked to?"

"Yes, it was us. Something terrible has happened to our friend."

"Why don't you show us where his boat is moored and we'll take a look."

Dan led the way as they headed towards "The Spirit." The four of them walked slowly down the dock. The fog was beginning to lift and as Dan glanced around he noticed that a Seattle Ambulance and three more police vehicles were pulling into the marina parking lot.

"Why don't the two of you wait here and my partner and I will look around."

Both policemen pulled their guns from their holsters and climbed on board the darkened vessel, which rocked gently in the morning swell. They returned moments later to the couple who had been joined now by Majorie Holcolm. She was sobbing quietly as Dan attempted to give her the details of the grisly find. The police spoke in quiet tones as they explained the results of their brief search of the boat.

"We didn't want to look too closely because this is a crime scene and the area is small. We will call Homicide and they will come out and go over the area with a fine-toothed comb. In the meantime, we need to get a statement from each of you. It's sort of chilly out here so why don't we go into the clubhouse?"

Kevin's stunned friends followed the officers into the clubhouse. On the way, the policeman barked out orders to several of the other officers.

They were joined about an hour later by two Seattle Homicide detectives. The senior officer introduced himself to the group.

"I'm Seattle Homicide detective Leron Baker and this is my partner Edward Garcia. We handle cases in smaller jurisdictions such as Edmonds even though, technically they have their own department.

I know this must be quite an ordeal for the three of you but we have to ask you quite a few questions."

He nodded towards a group of chairs, which were arranged in front of an unused fireplace.

"Why don't we all get comfortable and we will try to get through this as quickly as we can?"

The members of the group arranged themselves in a circle around the lead detective and answered his many questions as best they could. The questions related to the morning's tragic events and each member of the group was asked about his or her relationship with the slain physician. Marjorie dabbed her eyes with a large red bandana as she gave her responses to the many questions concerning her relationship with Kevin. Dan recounted the growth of his friendship with Kevin and filled the detectives in on the professional background of the slain doctor. The interview lasted for almost two hours. By then the morning sun had began to burn away the fog that had covered the area.

Boat owners and marina workers stood around in small groups trying to get as much information as they could about the terrible event. A television truck and camera crew from Channel Four was soon joined by reporters from two other stations with their camera crews. Onlookers watched through the windows as the interviews continued. A policeman stood at the entrance of the clubhouse and refused entry to all who attempted to enter the facility.

It was almost eleven thirty when the questions stopped. The two detectives assured the grief stricken friends that they would keep them informed as the investigation progressed and promised to catch the murderer.

Dan had the telephone number of Kevin's ex-wife. The slain physician had a sister who lived in Maryland. She was his next of kin. It would be her task to make the arrangements for the funeral. The couple drove home slowly. He did not look forward to making the necessary telephone call.

The two detectives made their way towards "The Spirit." As they approached, they noted that several of the owners of vessels which were tied up in adjacent slips walked towards them. Several reporters joined them.

"Can you tell us what happened?"

"No, it's too early for that now folks. We haven't even been on the boat. All we know is that the owner of the boat appears to have been slain. We can't even give you his name until his next of kin has been notified. We'll have a full statement for you as soon as we know more of the details. We have a lot of work to do, so if you will excuse us, we'll get started."

A female reporter identified herself as Sheila Peterson of Channel Four News and began to ask questions, but Detective Baker dismissed her with a sweep of his hand and stepped into the cockpit of the boat. He spoke to a sergeant who was standing nearby. "I want these people, including the members of the press, moved back to the end of the dock. This is a crime scene and I don't want them messing it up."

The older policeman nodded and began to move the on-lookers back. Several of the on-lookers protested that they were the owners of boats that were tied up adjacent to "The Spirit", but the policeman ignored their protests.

The detectives spent the better part of the afternoon going over the interior of the vessel. Members of the evidence team were kept busy collecting items, which might aid the investigation. The team was able to recover four cartridge cases. Police divers were sent into the chilling waters to search for a possible weapon but their efforts were unrewarding. The initial feeling of both officers was that this was an attempted robbery that had somehow gone horribly wrong. This thought lingered with both of the men despite the fact that the doctor was still wearing his brand new Rolex watch when his body was found.

The headlines in the Seattle newspapers the next day read, "Seattle Doctor Gunned Down on Yacht. Robbery Suspected." The investigation moved slowly along.

Detectives Baker and Garcia worked methodically on the investigation. They were able to find out most of the routine matters such as educational background and professional affiliations without any degree of difficulty. They knew that Kevin had a sister in Maryland and she was able to fill them in on much of his family background while she was in Seattle for the funeral. Their parents had been killed in an airplane accident while Kevin was a freshman in medical school. Their father had not been a believer in insurance and thus the brother and sister were left with the barest of financial assets. The parent's home had been heavily mortgaged and there were numerous bills, which depleted the estate. Katherine had been a freshman in college at the time and was forced to drop out of school for a semester. It was during this time that Kevin told her that he had recently been able to make a loan from a friend. The amount of the loan was enough to provide both of the children with enough money to complete their studies. Kevin had never told her where the money came from. He kept the source a secret.

The detectives were puzzled by this unexpected source of money. They talked together as they sat in the detective headquarters' office.

"You know Lee, there's something that just doesn't really fit here. Where does a medical student get that kind of money from?"

"You're looking at maybe a hundred thousand dollars or more. He was going to Georgetown and that ain't cheap. She was at a state school, but she still had a hell of a lot of living expenses. She was smart but I talked to the financial aid officer. He pulled her records and she only got about five thousand dollars in financial aid per year which left her with a seven thousand dollar a year nut."

"It doesn't add up, Eddie...It just doesn't add up."

"You bet your ass, it doesn't add up. What friend is going to loan another friend that kind of money?"

"We pulled the good doctor's bank records for the past ten years and there is not one transaction which would indicate that he was paying back some kind of loan."

"And you know that nobody gives you that kind of money."

"I think we need to call the Feds in on this one."

"I think you're right. I'll make some calls."

"I'm beginning to see drugs written all over this thing. I can just smell it. How many times do you find a robbery victim hit six times? Maybe somebody wanted the doctor gone."

"You know that I've had a feeling that something wasn't quite right about this from the first day. How many times do you and me come up with a complete blank?"

"Yes, we have a couple of shells with a couple of smeared prints, but nothing else. Ballistics called the other day and said that they were sending the casings to Washington. Maybe they can do something with the prints. Our boys drew a blank. They were able to lift partials, but they were unable to get any matches."

"You know that this case is kicking our butts?"

"Yeah, it's a toughie but we'll get to the bottom of it. We always have."

They presented their findings at the weekly headquarters' meeting. The next days' headlines in the Seattle papers read, "Police Link Slain Doctor to Drugs." The department was besieged with irate telephone calls for the next two days. Outraged professional colleagues spoke out in support of the slain surgeon. They pointed out his involvement in community activities including his anti-drug work. There was just no way that his killing could be drug related. This could not possibly be a gang-type hit. The doctor was too well known and too open in his activities.

The Seattle Police Department called a press conference and denied that there was any evidence connecting the brilliant doctor to drug related activities. They were unsure just how the information had been leaked from the conference, but wished to assure the medical community and the community at large that the doctor had been killed during an attempted robbery. The pressure to solve the case, mounted on both detectives Baker and Garcia. No new leads were found. The FBI began to quietly work on the case, doing extensive background checks into the activities of the slain doctors' medical school days. There was still no positive match of the smudged fingerprints. The case continued unsolved.

Chapter Four

Dr. Catherine Brinks had been busy for the last two days. She had spent the better part of that time working desperately to save the lives of several children who were on the Pediatric Ward at Oakland Children's Hospital. Her duties as Assistant Chief of Pediatrics at the Hospital often required her to work long hours, but the past two days had been different. She had been involved in the inspection activities of the Hospital Accreditation Committee and the better parts of each day were spent answering questions posed by this group. The committee visited every hospital in the United States on a regular basis and a bad report from this organization could result in the hospital losing the Federal funds upon which the facility depended for it's survival. As the Assistant Chief of Pediatrics, Dr. Brinks was also in charge of the teaching of medical students and young doctors in various stages of their medical training. In addition to these duties she had her own active pediatric practice to conduct. The doctor had always lived her life at a hectic pace. This explained the fact that she had never married even though she was stunningly beautiful and had had many suitors. She just never had the time for a family of her own. Her pediatric patients and medicine were her life.

She had graduated from Georgetown University and received her specialty training at the Stanford Medical Center in nearby Palo Alto. She had been offered the opportunity to join the staff at Oakland Children's Center. She loved the San Francisco bay area and she accepted the offer. Dr. Brinks was a pediatric neurologist. She specialized in conditions which affected the nervous system of children. She was a brilliant clinician who was regularly sought out for consultations not only in the San Francisco area but also from around the country. She had subsequently turned down many offers to join the staff of other institutions. She turned these offers down preferring to stay in Oakland where her tiny charges lived.

It was a late July evening as she drove her car up the winding and dimly lit street called Saroni Drive. Saroni Drive circled through an area of Oakland known as the Montclair section. This area was occupied by many of Oakland's most wealthy families. Several of her clinical associates lived in her neighborhood. Homes rarely went on sale in this area. It was one of the most stable areas in the Bay Area. This was why she had hurried to the realtor's office the minute she had heard one of her colleagues mention that there was a "For Sale" sign on a house several blocks from his home. She had fallen in love with the house during the visit with the realtor and she had made an offer at the full asking price. The owners had accepted her offer within twenty-four hours and within ninety days she had closed escrow and moved in.

She lived alone. She had a cat named Lu Lu. The cat was her companion. The cat often rode with her as she toured the Bay Area. Doctor Brinks had no family other than her cat and the many patients. Some of her tiny patients called her Auntie Catherine as she feverishly worked over them in an attempt to save their lives. Her father had raised her by himself. He had suffered a massive heart attack while she was a junior in medical school. He had passed away three hours later, leaving mountains of debt that wiped out his meager estate. She could still see his face as she glanced into the coffin. He had been a shipyard worker who had saved all of his meager earnings to send her to college. When she had been accepted to medical school, he had taken an additional part-time job and he sent her twenty-five dollars every week until the week he died.

A light fog drifted through the eucalyptus and pine trees as her car continued up the winding road. The lights of her car cut an incandescent swath through the darkness. Drops of condensation from the lofty trees struck her windshield as she continued up the road. No cars passed her as she drove. She rounded a final corner and saw the reflector that bordered her driveway. She pulled into the driveway and parked the car.

It took her several moments to gather all of her belongings from the car. Like many physicians, she practically lived in her car, often applying make-up or munching on a bagel as she drove from place to place in her frantic race with death. Doctor Brinks fumbled through her handbag for her house keys. She inserted the key, but noticed that the door was unlocked. She thought for just a moment and then remembered that she had left the house hurriedly early that morning when she was called out to see a sick child at the hospital. She entered the darkened house and called out to her cat.

"Lu Lu. I'm back. I'm home. Lu Lu. I'm home."

These were the last words she spoke as a gloved hand covered her mouth. She tried to scream as a stiletto was plunged into her side. She attempted to flee the searing heat of the blade but the more she struggled, the more she was struck. She collapsed forward into the foyer. A pool of blood began to flow from her body. In the kitchen was the body of her beloved cat, Lu Lu. The intruder had slit the throat of the once lively animal. As the killer was preparing to leave the house, the telephone began to ring. The sound of the telephone startled the man. He stood very still. As he waited, the answering machine played its message and then recorded a message from Melissa Dobbins, a close friend of the physician.

The hospital staff was somewhat alarmed when the doctor did not make her appearance at rounds the next morning. Dr. Brinks was known for her punctuality and she had never missed morning rounds. When calls to her home went unanswered, one of the nurses called the Oakland Police Department. She related the staff's concerns and requested a patrol car to visit the Doctor's home.

The policeman pulled his vehicle into the driveway of the house and upon climbing the stairs, he felt that something was terribly wrong. The front door was wide open and an upturned shoe lay in the edge of the foyer. He drew his pistol immediately and ran back to his vehicle. Clicking the button on his radio, he immediately called for back up. The early morning quiet of the neighborhood was soon shattered by the sounds of police cars and an ambulance. When several more cars had pulled into the driveway, the officer again climbed the stairs and with his weapon at the ready entered the quiet building. Several other policemen followed him and together they searched the entire house. It was obvious to the officers that the doctor had been dead for quite some time. Her outstretched hands were mottled and her limbs had already begun to stiffen.

It took almost an hour for the Homicide team to arrive. Several members of the news media who had heard the broadcasts over police scanners that they carried in their cars preceded them. The forensic team was kept busy until early that afternoon. The members of the team who were used to seeing human savagery at its worst were stunned by the fury of the attack and noted that the cat had not been spared. It was late afternoon when permission was given by the coroner's office to remove the body of the beloved physician.

Her stunned co-workers gathered in small groups in the hospital corridors and at nurse's stations and talked in muted tones. Several were seen to be crying openly. The Channel Nine News carried a two-minute piece detailing the facts as known at that time. The next day, the Oakland Tribune ran a banner headline. "Oakland M.D. Slain in Montclair."

As small as many of Doctor Brinks' patients were, they seemed to realize that something was wrong. She had always come to see them. Where was she? Parents tried to explain to the young ones that the good doctor had gone to heaven. Well over two thousand mourners filled the church and churchyard for the funeral ceremonies.

Merlin Dobson, Chief of Homicide Detectives of the Oakland California Police Department, had been a member of the city's police force since 1968. He had taken the Police Academy Examination in the spring of that year shortly after his return from the U.S. Marine Corps. He had served two tours in Vietnam while in the Marine Corps. His military experience had served him well as he patrolled the streets of Oakland. He rose quickly within the police ranks and was soon assigned to the Homicide Detective Division. He was known throughout the department as a no-nonsense officer who had compiled an amazing record by solving seventy percent of the cases he was assigned to. Eight more years passed and he was promoted to Chief of Homicide Detectives.

At the wheel of an unmarked police vehicle, he was headed toward the Montclair section of Oakland. He was very familiar with this area which butted against the foothills. He also knew that finding the addresses of residences in the area was difficult due to the fact that many winding roads traversed the area. He saw a television station truck a short distance ahead of his vehicle and decided that he would follow the truck. The road climbed slightly as he drove. At approximately seven hundred feet above sea level, the Montclair section was known for its foggy nights and chilly temperatures. On occasion, it had even snowed lightly in the area.

Detective Dobson had been called about 9:00 a.m. that morning. One of the two detectives assigned to the case wanted him to review the crime scene. The case involved the murder of a thirty-five year old pediatrician, Dr. Catherine Brinks. The doctor's body had been found earlier that morning when concerned friends and co-workers asked the police to drive by the doctor's residence to see if anything was wrong. Something was terribly wrong. The first policeman on the scene had found the mutilated body of the doctor. She had been stabbed multiple times. There had obviously been a struggle, but the doctor stood little chance. The intruder had obviously surprised the victim. A further search of the tastefully furnished house had turned up another victim–the doctor's cat! The cat had also been stabbed multiple times and its throat had been cut. These were the sketchy details given to Detective Dobson before he left headquarters.

He watched as the television truck was waved to the side of the road by a uniformed police officer. He passed the truck and pulled up in front of the house. This was difficult because there were many vehicles blocking the road. The narrow roads in the area did not lend themselves well to off-road parking. As a result of this, the entire road had been closed off. A large Channel 16 news truck was parked off to the left side of the barricade. Detective Dobson nodded towards a uniformed officer who immediately recognized him. The officer lifted the yellow crime scene tape and nodded back. His face was grim. At about this time a tall red-haired female emerged from the house and stood on the front porch. She smiled as she recognized Dobson.

"Hello, Jonetta. What do we have here?"

"You're not going to believe it, Merl. We though we just had a routine robbery attempt gone bad until we found something interesting."

"Yeah? Don't keep me in the dark. What did you find?"

"Come on in and take a look." She motioned to him. "It's one of the weirdest things I've seen in quite a while."

He knew that Jonetta had been a member of the police force for over ten years. He followed her into the kitchen of the house. They avoided the crime scene investigators as they moved through the house. Spread on the kitchen floor was the lifeless body of the victim's cat. Splotches of blood on the kitchen wall seemed to indicate that the animal had been thrown against the wall before being mutilated.

"This is an interesting thing, Chief. If you look closely you can see a tiny group of blood splatters leading from the kitchen to the downstairs."

"You don't think that they came from the cat?"

"I would bet a days' pay that the cat struggled with the intruder while he was being mutilated and that the cat managed to get few licks in before he went to cat heaven."

Kenneth Porter, a young black detective who had been standing in the kitchen and listening to the conversation, laughed.

"I'll bet that this poor little bastard used up all of his nine lives last night."

The female detective looked at him, a smile forming as she did so.

"Oh, Kenneth, that's sick. You know, that's sick."

"I think we need to bag this little bastard and have the crime lab folks examine his claws. He may have gotten a piece of the perp."

The young detective laughed.

"I'll have to remember that one for sure. A piece of the perp. It sure has a ring to it."

His face grew stern for a moment. "You know we're dealing with a real sickie here? I mean, what kind of person kills the victim's cat? I could understand a dog maybe, but what the hell was the cat going to do?"

"I'm sure that we will find that out when we catch the guy."

Glancing at his watch, Chief Detective Dobson gingerly walked down the stairs towards the foyer. When they reached the front porch, he turned towards the other detectives and said, "If I were you, I would keep the bit about the cat under wraps for now. We need to see what other leads the forensic boys turn up. I'll be in my office if you need me. Why don't we plan to meet in my office around nine tomorrow so that we can brainstorm this mess a little?"

The detectives both smiled and Dobson made his way towards his unmarked vehicle.

Over the course of the next several weeks, the team of detectives conducted a thorough investigation of the evidence as it was collected. The doctor had suffered injuries to multiple organ systems of her body. The coroner was particularly disturbed by the ferocity of the attack. Detectives Coppedge and Porter talked at length with members of the coroner's team. They came away from these talks convinced that the doctor had not been killed while surprising a burglar in the midst of a break-in. The unknown assailant had entered the residence with one thought in mind; to deliver harm to the physician.

Scrapings from beneath the slain cat's claws were found to be consistent with human skin and blood. The tiny spots of blood on the floor were not of the type found in cats. Grouping and typing of the blood splatters proved that they were not of the same type as Doctor Brinks. The team continued with their search for the killer. They conducted interviews with a number of Dr. Brinks' peers, friends, and neighbors, but found no real clues to the slaying. The investigation continued.

Chapter Five

Leesburg Psychiatric and Neurological Center was located in the complex of buildings that had been formerly known as Leesburg General Hospital. The center was known as L.P.N.C. to those who worked there. Leesburg Hospital had occupied the site for almost forty years. As the sixties approached, the hospital had fallen on hard times. The Leesburg Hospital Board had reluctantly sold the hospital to American Psychiatric Centers, the parent company of L.P.N.C. The facility had reopened its doors in early 1972. The institution served as a psychiatric referral center. Physicians in the greater Leesburg area used it as an inpatient facility for their severely mentally ill patients.

The town of Leesburg had a population of thirty thousand. Another thirty thousand people lived in the surrounding countryside. The town was located on the banks of the Lehigh River. The surrounding countryside was known as the Pocono area. There were many resorts scattered through the mountainous terrain. The city of Philadelphia was a two and one half hours drive to the south. The town of Oakmill was approximately a one hour drive to the northeast.

At first the psychiatric center had done well. As years passed there was increasing competition for its patient load. More and more psychiatric patients began to be treated on an outpatient basis. Newer psychotropic drugs limited the duration of hospital stays. The center had begun to cut medical staff. The center also began to cut medical corners. As these changes were made the level of patient care declined. Patients and their families complained to their referring physicians. The number of referrals began to drop. With the decline in referrals came a further drop in revenues. More reductions in staff took place as staff left under their own volition. Conditions within the facility worsened in a never-ending spiral.

Into this set of circumstances on a bright fall day in 1980 came a patient who was admitted with a diagnosis of severe depression. The plan was to hospitalize the patient for a short while. However, once inside the facility, his depression deepened and his stay continued. It was almost ten years later that plans were finally made to release him from the facility. This release was not necessarily due to the fact that his depression had been cured. The Leesburg Psychiatric and Neurological Center was due to close its doors two weeks after he was released. The patient was still a sick man.

Chapter Six

Client number 107 had been hospitalized on the advice of his treating physician. The patient had begun his long spiral into his dark depression after a family tragedy. While he had been hospitalized, the psychiatrists at L.P.N.C. had tried numerous forms of therapy including electroshock therapy and newer drugs. All attempts at group therapy failed. His downward spiral continued. The patient seldom left his room. He mingled with the other patients only at meal times. He frequently missed meals.

He would brighten up considerably when his wife came to visit. She lived in the town of Oakmill, which involved a two-hour round trip for her. She visited her husband faithfully for the first three years he spent in the facility. At that point, her own tragedy overtook her and her visits to patient number 107 stopped.

Claudette Jones worked for a small computer company in the town of Oakmill. She had worked there for almost twelve years. She had gotten the position after finishing her requirements for her associate degree in data processing at the nearby College of the Poconos. The school was a junior college, which attracted its student body from many of the area families who could not afford to send their children off to the major schools that were located in Philadelphia. Many of the students finished their requirements and transferred after two years to regular four-year colleges, but Claudette had decided to find a job.

It was while attending the school that she met her husband-to-be, Samuel. He was a nursing student who had ended up at the College of the Poconos after a two-year stint in the army. While in the army, he had spent a tour of duty in Vietnam. He had been a member of the Airborne Rangers and had often operated far behind enemy lines. His military service had left him deeply scarred. With the help of Claudette, he was able to begin his transition back into civilian life.

They had dated for a year. They married when both were in their last year of college. Stacey was born ten months after the wedding. Life was good. Samuel passed his nursing examination and was hired as a floor nurse at Oakmill General Hospital. He worked the night shifts at the hospital. He was able to care for the baby while Claudette worked the day shift. Claudette's mother lived in Oakmill and she was always willing to help with the care and feeding of her only grandchild. The family lived for a while with Audrey Donatto, Claudette's mother. The couple was soon able to put enough money aside for a downpayment on a small bungalow. Samuel used his veterans' benefits to make the purchase and the family moved six blocks from Mrs. Donatto's house. She continued to visit them on an almost daily basis. Things went well until Stacey got sick.

Stacey Jones was an adorable three-year-old child. Her parents and Mrs. Donatto took turns spoiling her. She thrived on their attention. She was showered with toys and had just received a new bicycle two days before she was taken ill. She had training wheels attached to the new bicycle but these did not prevent her from taking several spills as she rode her new bicycle through the neighborhood. Her illness began early that morning. She refused to eat her breakfast. It was Saturday morning and both of her parents had the day off.

"My tummy hurts, Daddy. My tummy hurts."

Samuel and Claudette had planned to drive up to Lake Pocono for the day but these plans were shelved as Stacey began to run a fever. Samuel tried his best to nurse the child but by three o'clock that afternoon, it was obvious that the child needed to see her pediatrician. Dr. Waterman was Stacey's pediatrician, but like many of Oakmill's populace, he had opted to leave the confines of the town for the cool waters of Lake Pocono.

Two hours after being paged, Dr. Waterman returned the call.

"Dr. Waterman speaking. Oh yes, Samuel what's going on?"

"It's my little girl, Doc. We hate to bother you, but she seems to be really sick."

"No bother. Why don't you meet me in the emergency room in forty-five minutes?"

Upon seeing the child, Doctor Waterman knew that something was wrong. The child, who was normally cheerful, was listless. The child's temperature was 104.6 degrees. After examining the child, Dr. Waterman approached the couple.

"I think she just has a summer virus, but she seems a little dehydrated. Her white cell count is elevated which doesn't quite go along with a viral illness and she is a little bit anemic. We'll look after her for you. Oh yes, I would like to introduce you to Doctor Brinks. She is one of our pediatric residents. Doctor Brinks and Dr. Stephen Mossler are pediatric residents from Georgetown University who are spending the summer here at Oakmill General. They will help me with Stacey's care. Now I'll excuse myself so that I can talk to the admitting department. As soon as we know which room Stacey will be admitted to, Doctor Brinks will come back to the waiting area and you can go up to the room with Stacey."

Samuel nodded. "That sounds good to us. You don't think it's serious?"

Dr. Brinks and Dr. Waterman shook their heads simultaneously. Dr. Waterman smiled.

"It's just a summer virus."

Stacey was finally admitted to the pediatric floor. While her parents watched at her bedside, she continued to weaken. Doctors Mossler and Brinks visited the child's bedside several times during the next several hours.

The young physicians were part of a four-member team, which had been sent to Oakmill General Hospital to spend their first year of pediatric training. The idea behind the exchange involved the need for the residents in training to learn more about medicine in relatively isolated communities. The other two members of the team were Dr. Kevin Pointer and Dr. James Mercer. These two physicians were surgical residents who hoped to specialize further. They both wanted to be pediatric surgeons.

The four physicians had been classmates at Georgetown University and welcomed the chance to escape the confines of the Metropolitan Washington area. Dr. Mossler wanted to specialize in pediatric hematology. The final member of the team was Catherine Brinks. Her future interest was pediatric neurology.

She was the youngest of the four doctors. The three men tended to be very protective of her. She was stunningly beautiful and treated each of the three men as brothers. She had never dated any of the three. There was a quiet bond of friendship among the four.

Dr. Brinks was particularly concerned as she sat in the Doctor's lounge drinking her third cup of coffee. Stephen Mossler, who was known as Steve to all of his close associates, had just joined her at the small table.

"How's your shift going, Cathie?'

She looked up. There was a look of concern on her face.

"Oh, I don't know Steve. That little kid in 208 has me worried. Her attending thinks that she has a viral illness, but her abdomen is awful tender."

"It may just be adenopathy. Any history of trauma?"

"I didn't really ask. I think I will ask some more questions when I go back upstairs. Something just isn't right. I think that she has something more than a summer virus."

"You know how these attending docs are if they don't have an answer."

"Yes, there isn't that much summer flu in the world."

The other doctor smiled. "Well, I've got to see a few more patients. I'll look in on Stacey when I'm up on the ward."

Stacey's condition continued to worsen as the hours passed. Dr. Brinks telephoned Dr. Waterman who chided her for her concern

"Relax, she'll be alright in the morning."

But morning never came for Stacey Jones. Steve and Catherine called their fellow residents at about one-thirty. After introducing themselves to the parents, the two doctors examined the child. They explained their concerns to the worried parents. Further questioning revealed that the child had taken several falls from her new bicycle in the days leading up to her illness. A CAT scan could be ordered but there was not time enough to call in the CAT scan technician and the radiologist. Doctors Pointer and Mercer recommended immediate abdominal exploration. They conveyed their feelings to Dr. Waterman who reluctantly agreed to the procedure.

Due to the isolation of Oakmill General and due to the fact that it was a weekend, it took almost two hours to call in the operating room team. In the meantime, Stacey was prepped for surgery as her grief-stricken parents stood by her bedside. At four thirty that morning, she was wheeled into the operating room. Twenty minutes later she was dead.

Upon making the incision into the child's abdomen, the two young surgeons were greeted by a gush of blood. Further exploration of the child's abdomen revealed that she had suffered a ruptured spleen, the result of her several falls from her brand new bicycle. The two surgeons worked hastily as they tried to stem the flow of blood. The anesthesiologist at the head of the table frantically pumped in uncross-matched blood which had been hastily obtained from the blood bank. Their efforts were in vain. The diagnosis had been overlooked for too long. Stacey Jones was gone.

The four friends met in the surgical lounge ten minutes after the child had been pronounced dead. A shaken Dr. Waterman appeared five minutes later. Dr. Pointer explained the abdominal findings to the stunned group. Doctor Waterman asked that they inform the parents, as a group, of the child's demise. The five saddened figures walked towards the pediatric ward and the waiting parents.

The looks on the faces of the doctors said all that needed to be said. Claudette Jones began to wail. She collapsed into the arms of her husband who cried openly. The young doctors explained their findings during the operation and left after several minutes. Dr. Waterman was left to explain the events to the grieving parents.

On a quiet hill in the Pocono Mountains on a hot August day, The Jones family watched as their child was laid to rest.

Chapter Seven

The weeks immediately following Stacey's death were a blur for Samuel and Claudette Jones. Stacey's grandmother, Audrey, was hospitalized with chest pain. The doctors soon released her after determining that her symptoms were due to anxiety. The grief of the two parents was bone deep. Samuel refused to eat and Claudette required sedation by her family doctor. Dr. Waterman called several times to express his sympathy and remorse. Well-wishers visited the tiny bungalow. Stacey's unused bicycle sat in the tiny garage. Samuel was unable to return to work. He had suffered too much at the hospital. One month after the death of her only child, Claudette returned to her job at the computer company. She found that she was unable to work full time and she was placed on part-time status. The bills from the hospitalization of their lost child began to arrive slowly. The funeral expenses added to the couple's debt.

Samuel spent many hours of many days locked in Stacey's bedroom. He ate only once a day and then sparingly. His weight dropped and an unhealthy pallor enveloped his face. At Claudette's insistence, he reluctantly visited Dr. Oaks, who had been his doctor for several years.

Dr. Oaks called Claudette one evening and voiced his concerns about her husband's mental state. Claudette listened, but refused to have Samuel admitted to Leesburg Psychiatric and Neurological Center. She tried her best to pull her husband out of his worsening depression, but at last she realized the futility of her efforts. She knew that all would be lost if she did not follow the advice of Dr. Oaks. Reluctantly, she finally agreed to Samuel's admission and she packed him a small suitcase.

Samuel was emotionless as an orderly led him through the arches of what had once been Leesburg General Hospital. Leaves were showing the first hint of autumn change. Samuel spoke only a few words as he answered the admitting clerk's questions. He seemed to shuffle as he was led down the long corridor to the room which would be his home for the next ten years.

Samuel settled into the quiet routine of the center. His first months at the institution were filled with many evaluations and conferences with members of the psychiatric staff. He answered their many questions but refused to discuss the death of his daughter. He related his military background and talked openly of the dangers he had encountered and survived. He recounted the many dangerous missions performed by the ranger units to which he had belonged. It took several months before he was able to even speak about the fact that he was married. This, despite the fact that Claudette visited him every weekend. Although Samuel's mood seemed to brighten somewhat after each of her visits, by the next day he would resume his silence.

He was often seen seated by the side of his bed, arms wrapped tightly around his body. Samuel seemed lost within himself. He had to be urged by the members of the nursing staff to perform the most basic of personal tasks such as showering. Although he stayed almost exclusively to himself, he was often seen reading a well-tattered bible.

Mrs. Donatto often accompanied her daughter on the visits to see Samuel. She soon dissolved into tears as she watched his health deteriorate. After three months at the center it became obvious to the medical staff that Samuel was suffering from more than a depression.

It was on a cold early winter morning that Sam's case was presented to the Multi-disciplinary staff conference. This body included Samuel's general practice doctor, several psychiatrists, members of the nursing staff, two social workers, and several other caretakers. Their task was to map out a treatment plan for each of the patients at the institution. The agenda included complete medical and social histories of each of the patients who were being presented at the conference as well as clinical updates on the management of their condition to date. These conferences were, by their nature, lengthy. The presentation of Client 107 took six hours.

Dr. Oaks, who had been Samuel's General Practice Physician, was the first to speak. He read his patient's complete medical history. He stated that Samuel had been in good medical condition until Stacey got sick. He elaborated on the attempts that had been made to avoid hospitalization and on the failure to manage his patient on an outpatient basis.

Mrs. Bates, who was the chief social worker at the institution, followed him. She presented his social history including his military record. Claudette had found a copy of Samuel's military service folder while she was cleaning out a spare room at the house. This record added much to the conference. While in the military, Samuel had been seen by the base psychiatrist on two occasions. These visits had occurred during an interval of six months in 1971. The soldier had been diagnosed as possibly suffering from a mild case of post traumatic stress syndrome. However, his condition was not severe enough to warrant restriction from duty. He had been given several prescriptions for anti-depressant tablets. He had continued to take the medications on an intermittent basis until his discharge from the military. Mrs. Bates then discussed Samuel's history during the interval which led up to his enrollment at the College of the Poconos. She listed his hobbies as hunting, fishing and collecting knives.

She was followed by two of the psychiatrists who were consulting on the case. The two men disagreed on the exact diagnosis of Samuel's condition. Their exchange was lively.

"I think I agree that Mr. Jones has elements of a depressive disorder, but I think that he is also exhibiting many of the symptoms of paranoid schizophrenia." The speaker was Dr. Chad Eaglin. Dr. Eaglin had been on the staff of the hospital for three months and due to this fact, many on the committee tended to agree with the opinion of Dr. William Casey who was one of the older staff members.

Dr. Casey rose slowly from his chair and moved towards the front of the conference room. Clearing his throat, he began. "I agree with Dr. Eaglin that this patient is showing signs of depression, but I have talked with the patient for several hours. At no time during my interviews has

Mr. Jones exhibited any of the characteristics which one would need in order to entertain a diagnosis of Paranoid Schizophrenia. I have not found any evidence of inappropriate symbolism or evidence of delusional thought pattern. I will admit that his affect is flat and that he may have some degree of autistic absorption with his inner thoughts, but this man has been though quite an ordeal."

Dr. Eaglin interrupted him. "I have spent more time with Mr. Jones than any of us here except the nursing staff. Let us not lose sight of the fact that depression is present in almost all cases of Schizophrenia. Depression is part of the disease and not the disease. I will stick to my earlier diagnosis. I think that Samuel Jones is suffering from Paranoid Schizophrenia."

Dr. Casey smiled at the younger man. "While I may respect my colleagues opinion, I don't agree with it and I am sure that time will prove my diagnosis to be the correct one."

The conference continued until late that afternoon. The members of the committee decided that Samuel Jones would be given types of therapy reserved for those patients who were only suffering from major depression. As time passed and Samuel's depression did not lift, the diagnosis given by Dr. Eaglin was accepted by the hospital staff.

The patents at L.P.N.C. were relatively isolated from the events of the outside world. Their access to media such as television was severely restricted by the hospital staff. Few read the newspapers. One day as Samuel was thumbing through a two-month-old "Oakmill Herald" which had been left in the patient's lounge by a visitor, he glanced at the obituary pages. His eyes closed for the briefest of moments as he read. "Local Physician Passes. Dr. Thomas Waterman, an area physician for over forty years, passed away on Thursday. He was the victim of an apparent heart attack." The article continued with a history of the doctor's medical training and listed his hospital affiliations and surviving family members.

Samuel looked out of his window at the darkened Pennsylvania countryside as a light snow began to fall. He remembered Dr Waterman. He had been the man who used the words, "a summer virus." He had been

Stacey's doctor. Along with those other four doctors who were only at Oakmill General for training, he had taken Stacey away. A tear coursed slowly down his cheek as he read the rest of the doctor's obituary. He would never forget the five doctors, nor would he forgive them for taking away his little girl.

Samuel's stay continued into the next year. He made little progress towards recovery. Events continued in the outside world. Claudette fell seriously behind in the bills and one year after Samuel was admitted, the bank foreclosed on their tiny bungalow. Now Claudette was no longer able to sit in Stacey's room. All of her child's belongings as well as the rest of the family's possessions were packed up and stored in a leaky shed behind the home of Mrs. Donatto. Claudette moved into her mother's house.

She kept the news from her husband.

Claudette could tell that her husband's illness was worsening. He would begin each of her visits by asking questions about Stacey. How was she? How was Stacey doing in school? How did Stacey like the piano lessons? Did Stacey like her new puppy? Claudette voiced her concerns to the staff members and she talked at length with Dr. Eaglin who was now the primary psychiatrist assigned to her husband's case. She signed the papers, which gave the hospital permission for her husband to under go electroshock therapy. She saw little improvement after the first series of electroshock treatments.

She continued to visit her husband every week but her husbands' illness was beginning to take its toll on her. She began to drink and her job performance declined. Her co-workers were supportive at first. They knew that her life was in turmoil. After a while it was clear to the managers of the small company that she would have to be fired. Reluctantly, almost three years after Samuel had entered L.P.N.C., her company gave her a severance check. She did not tell her husband that she had lost her job.

Mrs. Donatto returned to the small house one evening after attending a Bingo game and found her daughter's lifeless body stretched across her bed. On the nightstand were several bottles of prescription drugs. The frantic old women called 911 but she had been away too long. Claudette Jones was dead on arrival at Oakmill General Hospital. By coincidence, she was examined in the same emergency cubicle where her beloved daughter Stacey had lain barely three years before.

The funeral was held on a stark winter day. Samuel, accompanied by a caseworker, seemed barely aware of what was happening. He looked about furtively at the few mourners, mostly Claudette's co-workers and a few of her mother's friends. The only person he seemed to recognize was his mother-in law. In his mind, he seemed to think he was at Stacey's funeral. He couldn't understand why Claudette wasn't there. He asked Mrs. Donatto "Where is Claudette?"

Mrs. Donatto, consumed with grief, could only sob uncontrollably. In a few short years, she had seen her family disintegrate, first with Stacey's untimely death, then Samuel's breakdown, and now her only daughter was gone. The old woman could not bear to explain what had happened to Claudette. This made him even more confused.

As the mourners proceeded to the gravesite, their footsteps crunching in the icy ground, Mrs. Donatto realized that now she and Samuel only had each other. It would be very difficult for her to make the trip to the mental hospital to visit him, but she resolved to try as often as she could. It would be difficult not only physically, but also emotionally for them both. Maybe with time she could help him understand that Claudette, too, was gone.

Upon his return to L.P.N.C, Samuel was even more withdrawn for some time. During Mrs. Donatto's first visit, she had tried to explain gently that only she would be coming to see him now. He nodded absently. As she talked, he remembered the cold winter day of the funeral and realized why Claudette wasn't there. Mrs. Donatto spared him the details of Claudette's death, simply saying that she fell ill, but by the time the paramedics arrived it was too late to save her.

"Too late" echoed in Samuel's mind. Those were the same words that the doctors who let Stacey die had used. "Too late. Too late." he muttered again and again.

Over the next several years, Mrs. Donatto's visits became less frequent as her own health declined. Her visits and letters were Samuel's only contact with the outside world. In this way, she became more attached to her son-in-law. He was now her only family. The relationship was good for both of them. His psychiatrist, Dr. Eaglin, encouraged Mrs. Donatto in her efforts to maintain contact with Samuel.

Dr. Eaglin, being a progressive therapist, sought out new treatments aggressively. Samuel's condition gradually improved over the succeeding years as the doctor tried various drug therapy advances in addition to counseling sessions. He remained, however, severely depressed and was still delusional.

During his eighth year of treatment, Samuel progressed to taking part in some of the group activities at the hospital. He was observed holding short conversations with several of the other patients. There was a Vietnam veteran who was hospitalized in the same section as Samuel. They began a friendship based in part on their shared war experiences. However, his prognosis and need for continued in-patient therapy remained unchanged.

Chapter Eight

By the end of Samuel's tenth year, changes in the mental health care industry conspired to affect Samuel's stay at L.P.N.C. The hospital was nearing bankruptcy due to increased costs and declining revenues. The numbers of patients had shown a steady decline, as more outpatient therapy became the norm. Samuel's caregivers began to take steps to prepare him for release to the outside world. His social worker assisted him in securing disability and Veteran's benefits so that he would have a source of income. She arranged for him to live with Mrs. Donatto. The old woman welcomed this relief to her loneliness and increased isolation due to advancing arthritis.

Dr. Eaglin arranged for outpatient care with a clinic in Oakmill. As he held his exit interview with Samuel, he emphasized the need for Samuel to continue his medications and outpatient therapy to Mrs. Donatto and Samuel. The doctor had become the most knowledgeable person about Samuel and his demons, besides Samuel himself. He felt uneasy at the necessity to release this patient to the outside world without any continuing mental health care. He knew too often compliance was very difficult to maintain and that often the small gains made during hospitalization were erased as the patients re-entered their old environments. As he bid Samuel and his mother-in-law goodbye, he silently prayed that Samuel would beat the odds and continue to progress.

Mrs. Donatto led Samuel through the arches of the entryway of the Leesburg Psychiatric and Neurological Center. Clutching his bag of meager possessions, Samuel boarded the bus for Oakmill and his return to a world that he hardly knew. Mrs. Donatto took the seat beside him. As the bus drove away, Samuel looked back at what had been his home for the last ten years. He was filled with both excitement and anxiety as he left L.P.N.C. Samuel looked out at the rolling countryside and noted that many changes had occurred while he was hospitalized. A new shopping center occupied what had once been a rolling meadow. Fast food signs lined the highway. His outdated and ill-fitting clothing pressed against his body. His belt squeezed around his waist, which had increased in girth over the intervening years. Mrs. Donatto had found what she thought were his best looking clothes in the possessions Claudette had left in the closet.

Her new responsibility weighed on his mother-in-law's mind as they journeyed in silence. As they approached the bus station in Oakmill, Mrs. Donatto began to come out of her own reverie.

"It's so good to have you home, Samuel. I'm going to take the best care of you that I can. I know I can't do everything Claudette would have done, but we'll get along. You just wait and see."

At the mention of Claudette, Samuel perked up. "When will I get to see her? And how about Stacey?"

"Now, Sam, you remember what happened to them both. Don't you? They're up in Heaven. It's just you and me now."

"Oh yeah. Sometimes I forget. When I do remember, it makes me...it makes me hurt. I'm sorry."

"Nothing to be sorry about, dear. Now come along, here's the cab to take us home."

They took the cab to Mrs. Donatto's small house. They were both tired after the emotionally charged trip home. After re-heating a small meal in the microwave, Mrs. Donatto showed Samuel to his new room and they both retired.

The next morning, Samuel seemed to be disoriented again. He wanted to go to his house.

"Oh, dear. We can't do that, Sam. I sold the house after Claudette passed away," she lied.

Samuel sat silently. Mrs. Donatto watched him carefully and tried to judge his mood. She was still apprehensive about her ability to deal with

Samuel. The nice doctor at the mental hospital had told her to take things slowly and if she was worried about Samuel to call the Oakmill Mental Health Clinic. She hoped she could handle everything.

Samuel did not leave the house for several days. One morning Mrs. Donatto awoke and called out to him. He did not answer. At first she was frantic but her concern evaporated when she looked through the kitchen window. Samuel was out in the backyard, rake in hand, busily working in the backyard. He was raking up the leaves that had accumulated as fall gave way to early winter in the Pocono countryside. She opened the kitchen door and smiled.

"Oh, there you are Samuel. Can I fix you a little something to eat?"

He looked at her, a look of recognition crossed his face, and he smiled.

"No, thank you, I fixed myself a little toast and coffee about an hour ago."

"Have you been up long?"

"Yes, I woke up about six thirty but I didn't want to bother you, so I came out to tidy up the yard a bit."

"Samuel, you know that you are never a bother. I'm so glad to have you home."

He smiled and returned to his work. Mrs. Donatto watched him through the kitchen window long after she had returned inside the cozy kitchen.

Samuel continued working for several hours. He collected the leaves in several large piles and burned each pile. The smell of the burning leaves floated over the neighborhood. When he had put the tools away, he walked slowly back into the tiny house. Mrs. Donatto sat in her tattered recliner watching a soap opera. She was so absorbed by the television that she did not hear Samuel enter the room. She appeared somewhat startled as he spoke.

"We need to visit the bank this afternoon so that I can open a new bank account. My disability checks will be coming to this address. The social worker at the hospital made all the arrangements for me. I will need an account."

Mrs. Donatto arose slowly from the recliner.

"I'll freshen up a bit and we can be on our way. There are some more clothes out in the shed if you would like to bring them in. You've gained a bit of weight, but I think that most of them might still fit you. Look through them and if you decide that you want to go shopping after we leave the bank, we can go to Wal-Mart."

Samuel nodded and walked outside towards the small shed that stood at the edge of the property. He returned sometime latter carrying several children's dresses. He held them out to his mother-in-law.

"I'll take these to Stacey when I see her."

The older woman was distraught.

"Oh Sam, you must have opened one of the wrong boxes. Here, let me put those away for you."

Samuel clutched the dresses closely to his chest. The old lady made no effort to take them from him. They stood for a moment in an awkward silence and then Samuel handed the clothing slowly to her. She took them from him and headed off towards the bedroom. She returned moments later clutching her handbag. She found her house key and said nothing further as Sam followed her out to the garage where she kept her car. The car was a five year old Subaru which, despite its age, had less than ten thousand miles on the odometer. Mrs. Donatto seldom drove far. She started the vehicle and they were soon on their way. Samuel looked out of the side window and said little as they rode.

The car slid into the parking lot of the First Ponoco Savings and Loan Bank. Mrs. Donatto was recognized by several of the customers who were waiting in line. She spoke to them and introduced Samuel to an elderly lady who was filling out a deposit slip.

"Agnes, you remember Samuel don't you. He's my son in-law."

Agnes Milharty smiled.

"Why of course I do. How are you, Mr. Jones? It is so nice to see you again. We are really glad to have you back at home. We are so glad that you are better now. I hope that we will see you in church one of these Sundays."

Samuel smiled awkwardly and looked at the gray-haired old lady. His face was somewhat grim but he finally broke into a wide grin.

"Do you still make those German chocolate cakes like you used to do?"

The lady laughed.

"I still do and if I have time, I will bake you a great big cake and drop it off at the house for you and Audrey. I'm so glad that you remembered my cakes after all these years."

Mrs. Donatto and Samuel moved to the 'New Accounts' section of the bank and began to talk to the clerk.

The young lady smiled. "O.K. Mr. Jones, just fill out these papers and all I will need is a driver's license and one other form of identification and we'll be all set."

Samuel looked at the clerk; a look of puzzlement filled his brow.

Mrs. Donatto was the first to speak. "I am afraid that his driver's license may not be up to date."

In the meantime, Samuel had produced a tattered card from his pocket. The clerk glanced at what once had been a pristine card. She looked up, her eyes moving first from Samuel and then to Mrs. Donatto.

"This expired seven years ago, Mr. Jones. Do you have your new card?"

Mrs. Donatto spoke quickly. Tension filling her voice as she spoke.

"He hasn't had time to apply for his new driver's license yet. He's only been home for a few weeks."

The young clerk looked at Samuel.

"Have you been out of state?"

Samuel fidgeted as he looked around the bank.

"Yes...Yes, I've been away."

"I'll be right back." The young clerk smiled nervously as she shoved her chair back from the desk. She hurried off and was soon seen in an animated conversation with an older man who was dressed in a dark business suit. She pointed towards the couple several times as they talked. The clerk, accompanied by the banker, approached Samuel and

Mrs. Donatto. The banker held the old driver's license as he spoke. Recognition filled his face.

"Why, hello Mrs. Donatto. This must be Samuel Jones, your son-in-law?"

"Yes, yes Mr. Denkins, I'm so happy you remember us."

"I do...indeed I do. And how are you feeling, Mr. Jones? It has been years since I last saw you. How are you feeling?" He repeated. "How are you feeling?"

Samuel rose slowly from the chair and shook the man's outstretched hand.

"I'm getting better sir. I'm getting better."

The blue-suited man handed the card to the young clerk.

"The license won't be a problem, Miss Hearns. I have known Audrey almost all my life and she is one of our finest customers. Miss Hearns will take good care of the both of you and if there is anything that I can do for either of you, just let me know."

"Thank you. Thank you very much."

"I will look forward to talking to you again."

The banker smiled and headed back towards his office. The clerk began typing the account application.

The couple left the bank forty-five minutes later. Samuel carried a new bankbook and a pack of temporary checks. Mrs. Donatto spoke first as they entered the car.

"Now that wasn't too bad, was it? I think that while we are out, we should go to the Motor Vehicle Department. You will need to get a new license so that you can write checks."

There was a long line in the Motor Vehicle office. When Samuel presented his worn and out-dated license to the woman who was manning the counter, he was given a small booklet and told to return in three days to take the written test. There would be no need to take the driving part of the test. Samuel and Mrs. Donatto returned home and he spent the next several days reading and memorizing the questions in the booklet. They returned three days later, he passed the test, and four weeks later a shining plastic card arrived in the mail. Samuel gazed at the picture emblazoned on the tiny card. The face that gazed back at him was older than he remembered it and his hair was turning gray, but he was pleased with the result. He was beginning to re-enter the world.

One cold December morning, Sam asked Mrs. Donatto if he could borrow the keys to her car. She hesitated for a moment and then handed Samuel the keys.

"I just want to go out for a little ride," he assured her.

He was gone for almost two hours. He returned with a pile of sporting magazines and a box of candy for his somewhat startled mother in-law.

"Oh, Sam, you didn't have to buy me anything."

"No problem at all," he replied. "You have been awfully good to me. I'm thankful for all that you are doing for me. I'm thankful that I can take myself to my clinic appointments. I don't have to walk across town and you don't have to miss your soap operas. I'm thankful and I wanted to give you a little present."

Mrs. Donatto smiled as she opened the box of chocolates.

Samuel spent several days reading in his small room. Christmas was rapidly approaching and the couple visited several of the nearby malls. The old lady could not help but notice the look of sorrow that Samuel wore as he watched the excited children dart to and fro about the mall. He was spending more and more hours riding about the countryside as time passed. His mother in-law never asked him about his travels but was always somewhat relieved when he returned safely.

Christmas was a quiet time in the small house. A snowstorm blew in from the west and blanketed the area with two feet of windblown snow. Samuel purchased a small tree and the two lonely people decorated the tree with ornaments from a small box that Samuel had found in the garage. Mrs. Donatto cooked a large turkey and as the snow continued falling, they ate at the small table in the kitchen. Halfway through the meal, the old lady noted that her son in-law had tears in his eye. She reached gently across the table and rested a wizened hand on his arm. He coughed slightly.

"I really miss Stacey and Claudette. I really miss them."

Mrs. Donatto smiled faintly as she patted his arm. "I miss them, too, Samuel. I miss them, too."

"Do you think that they will ever come back?"

"You will see them in heaven, son. You will see them in heaven."

Chapter Nine

The winter snows in the Pocono mountain area were frequent that year. Samuel was limited by the weather. He often took short rides through the town. On many of these trips he found himself circling Oakmill General Hospital. Often with the car engine running in an attempt to ward off the chill, he would sit for hours parked near the entrance to the emergency room. He would watch the ambulances arriving and departing. He would watch the cars as they drove into the often ice-covered loading area. He would watch as parents arrived, some carrying tiny infants seeking medical treatment at the hospital's doors.

On other days he would visit the graveyard where Stacey and Claudette lay side by side. Mrs. Donatto had waited several months before showing him the cemetery with the two bronze markers. When the weather permitted, he would remove the tiny frozen bouquets from each of the gravesites and replace them with new flowers that were often frozen by the time that the sun rose over the frozen Pennsylvania countryside. He often wept as he retraced his footsteps over the crunching snow.

He read sporting magazines and when not reading, he often joined Mrs. Donatto as she watched television in the living room. He cleared the snow from the sidewalks that fronted the house and cut firewood for the fireplace. There were many evenings that passed with the fireplace glowing brightly and the two people slumped in their seats as the television droned on. At last, one or the other of them would awaken. After turning off the television, he or she would awake the other and they would mumble their sleep filled goodnights as they headed for their separate rooms.

February was mild. There was only one major storm that blanketed the area. Soon the snow began to melt slowly. Samuel began his pattern of taking longer trips. Although he still spent many hours parked near the emergency room and longer hours at the still frozen cemetery, the length of his trips increased. He was very careful not to miss his appointments at the Oakmill Mental Health Clinic and he still took his medication when he remembered to take it. He found that one of the medications made him very sleepy. This had not been a problem while he was hospitalized, but it became a problem as his trips lengthened. By omitting a tablet from one bottle each day, he was soon able to determine which bottle of pills made him sleepy. He stopped taking the pills contained in this bottle, although he did not give this information to Dr. Eaglin at the mental health center. He continued to refill all of his prescriptions in case the doctor checked with the pharmacist.

One day he surprised Mrs. Donatto by telling her that he wanted to go to a gun show in Philadelphia. She was somewhat hesitant, but after a short discussion and warning him to drive carefully, she agreed. He packed a small well-worn bag and was soon driving through the mountainous terrain towards Philadelphia some two and one half-hours away. He rented a room at a small motel on the outskirts of the large city and spent the next day visiting a gun show at the Philadelphia Convention Center.

The exhibit area of the convention center was filled with hundreds of people. Some talked with the exhibitors about the newest productions in camping and hunting apparel. Others fingered shiny new rifles and handguns. There were many booths that showed exhibits of hunting knives and self-defense weapons. In small rooms adjacent to the main exhibit area, there were classes on the varied aspects of hand-to-hand combat as well as classes on deer and duck hunting.

Samuel approached a booth that was occupied by a tall blonde man. The man had a military bearing. He offered his hand to Samuel.

"Hello, I'm Sergeant Miller. Retired United States Military. Would you like to look at our display?"

Samuel smiled and the two men spent the next fifteen minutes discussing the variety of para-military weapons that made up the display.

Samuel did not purchase any of the products, but he left the booth with a handful of printed materials and the business card that was embossed with large gold letters. "Eugene Miller. Sgt.U.S. Army Retired."

Samuel spent the rest of the day roaming the large exhibit halls and attending several lectures. He returned to his motel late that evening after eating dinner and going to a movie. It was the first time he had gone to see a movie at a theater in over ten years. He called Mrs. Donatto to tell her that he would be back in Oakmill the next day. The return trip was uneventful. He spent the next several days in his room reading the many materials that he had collected at the convention.

Winter began to relax its grip on the Pocono area. Spring was on the way. The snows continued to melt. It was still too early for the trees to begin to bud, but the temperatures began to slowly rise. Samuel had not made any trips since returning from Philadelphia, so Mrs. Donatto was not surprised when he told her one early Monday morning that he was going to drive down to the Washington D.C area to attend a sporting show at the Washington Convention Center. He assured her that he would return on Wednesday so that he would be able to keep his appointment with Dr. Eaglin on Thursday. He again packed his small bag and drove off in the Subaru. Mrs. Donatto watched from the front porch as the little car turned the corner and was soon lost from sight.

Samuel drove east until he was able to reach Highway 70. In less than six hours he was approaching the outskirts of Washington. He found lodging at a hotel located near the Potomac River and paid in crumpled twenty-dollar bills for two nights' lodging. He spent the rest of the day visiting the Whitehouse and the Washington Monument. The sports show was not due to open until the next morning. He walked around the Tidal Basin and looked at the cherry trees that lined the Tidal Basin. The trees were beginning to bloom. Their sweet fragrance was in the air. The petals from the trees drifted across the area like the snowflakes that Samuel had just experienced during the long winter. Washington, being further south than Oakmill, was weeks ahead in welcoming the return of spring.

He had breakfast at a small restaurant that overlooked the Potomac River with East Potomac Park and Haynes Point beyond. He waited until nine o-clock and then asked the bellman for directions to Georgetown University.

He drove up Wisconsin Avenue. The traffic was very congested. People strolled the widened avenue. Quaint shops and open-air markets lined the crowded streets. Students with their brightly colored Georgetown University sweatshirts sipped expresso coffee and talked in huddled groups. Many stood near the entrances to the small cafes and held conversations with their friends who were seated at cloth covered tables. Students carrying heavy book bags hurried down the cobblestone side streets. A warm spring sun lent its rays to the congested scene.

Samuel turned on to Prospect Street and was able to find a parking space, which was just being vacated by an elderly woman driving a large red car. He maneuvered the small Subaru into the space noting that there was plenty of room. He walked west towards the main campus. At the campus gate he asked the guard, a small portly black man, for directions to the main library. The guard smiled and gave Sam a small campus map, onto which the guard had marked Sam's route in red ink.

Samuel strolled across the main campus. In the tower, a bell tolled the hour. There was an increase in the number of persons hurrying about as classes changed. Samuel followed the map which the guard had given him and ten minutes later, he found himself in front the main library. He entered the building and approached the desk. A young woman who was obviously a student smiled at him.

"Good morning, sir. How may I help you?"

Samuel looked around the large room. "I hate to bother you, but I'm working on an article on the university and I need to get some information on graduates from the medical school. I wonder if you have any yearbooks or information that might help me."

The student thought for a minute and then punched the keys of a small computer that sat on her desk. She watched the screen intently as it flickered. She smiled as the machine answered her question.

"Yes, I think this might help you. In addition to yearbooks, we have a journal that documents all of our graduates from the eighteen hundreds. They are still working on it. The graduates before 1800 may be missing, but I think this will be just the type of material you are looking for."

She then punched anther computer key and a printer came to life. Several minutes later, Samuel was on his way up the stairs to the section of the library carrying the books that he needed. The library was massive and it took him almost thirty minutes to find the books he was looking for. He seated himself at a well-worn oaken table and spread the books out before him. There were several yearbooks and a large new book entitled, "Georgetown University Graduates 1950-1985." The yearbooks included both medical school and liberal arts graduates. He scanned the newer book first and jotted notes on small pieces of paper as he read. He was looking for four names. He found all four of the names. In addition to the years of graduation, there was a small biography on each person. Also listed for many graduates were both home and office addresses and telephone numbers.

Brinks, Dr. Catherine E; BS '72, MD '76;
r. 311 Saroni Drive, Oakland, CA 94611 (415) 666-3499
Office: Oakland Children's Hospital, Oakland, CA (415) 444-2349

Mercer, Dr. James S; BS '72, MD '76;
r. 801 I St, S.W., Washington, DC 20001 (201) 555-2948;
Office: 3100 DuPont Circle, #10, Washington, DC 20001 (201) 555-9900

Mossler, Dr. Stephen L; BS '72, MD '76;
r. 4504 Marina Way #1118, Marina Del Rey, CA 90293 (213) 651-0001;
Office: 5914 La Cienaga Blvd. #248, Los Angeles, CA 90036 (213) 689-8877

Pointer, Dr. Kevin H; BS '72, MD '76;
r. 1208 Spinnaker Way, Waterview, WA 98683 (206) 445-2234;
Office: 1809 Fifth Street, Seattle, WA 98677 (206) 455-0777

He wrote slowly, not wanting to miss a bit of information. When he had finished, he surveyed his list. He smiled. He had the information he was looking for. He placed the book at the edge of the large table and picked up the book, which had the large gold letters on its face. "Georgetown University. Class of 1976."

He turned the pages, his hand shaking slightly as he turned. One by one, he found the pages that contained the pictures of the four people he was looking for. Their images smiled at him from the pages. He wiped a tear away. These were the four people who had taken away his Stacey. These were the four people who he had never forgotten. He would never forget these four people or his little girl.

He left the library and walked slowly across the campus. As he walked, he was deep in thought. He now knew that Dr. Mercer lived in Washington D.C. Samuel plotted as he walked. He was so engrossed in his thoughts that he walked headlong into a student who was riding his bicycle across campus. The bicyclist, and the backpack that the student was carrying, landed on the grass by the pathway. Samuel was apologetic as he helped the student collect his scattered valuables. The student was angry at first but when he noted the intentness on Samuel's face, he righted his bicycle and rode off across the campus. The student looked back at Sam several times, as he rode away.

Samuel drove aimlessly around the Washington area for several hours. He returned to the Convention Center and bought a ticket for the Gun show. He left the center several hours later. In a bag, which he clutched tightly by his side, was a ten-inch long shiny stiletto that he had purchased from a salesman who manned one of the self-defense booths. He drove back to the motel that he had checked out of early that morning and, again paying with crumpled twenty dollar bills, reserved a room for another night.

He called Mrs. Donatto and told her that he would be staying in Washington for another night. He said that he was enjoying the sightseeing and would not be back in Oakmill until late Thursday. He asked her to reschedule his appointment with Dr. Eaglin. Mrs. Donatto's voice had a worried tone as she spoke with her son in-law. Samuel continued his assurances and then he hung up the telephone. He sat by the telephone for several minutes and then placed a small tourist map which he had bought in the motel lobby before him. He noted that the address of Dr. Mercers' home was only a short distance from the motel.

Samuel awoke at four o'clock the next morning. He showered and was soon ready to check out of the motel. He gave the front desk manager the room key and was soon seated in the Subaru. On the front passenger seat, he placed the newly purchased stiletto and the tourist map. He started the car and drove slowly towards the address, which was printed on the notes that he had taken the previous day. He found Southwest S Street after driving only about a half mile. He cruised slowly down the block, noting the numbers as he drove.

Eight O One-S Street was a town house. It sat on a corner of a row of similar houses. The area was not unlike many of the areas on the southwest Washington area that had undergone re-gentrification during the early nineteen seventies. During this time, black tenants had been enticed to leave the rundown area. Many of the former tenants were relocated in housing projects located near the periphery of the city. Many others just simply left, their whereabouts being unknown. With the tenants removed, the contractors moved in. Many of the rundown buildings had their insides gutted and rebuilt. New occupants, mostly white middle and upper class people, were offered the refurbished homes. With their proximity to government offices, the restored homes offered all of the conveniences of city living. There was no longer a need to commute to the government buildings along the crowded traffic corridors.

Samuel parked the Subaru about one hundred yards from the townhouse. He waited quietly. Fifteen minutes later, a slightly graying man clad in a jogging suit came out of the townhouse. Samuel began to sweat profusely. The person Samuel saw was a little heavier than the picture which had been in the yearbook and his hair was beginning to gray at the temples, but it was the same man. Doctor James Mercer, one of those people who had taken Stacey away.

The man started the car and drove towards Maine Avenue and the waterfront. Samuel followed at a discrete distance. The man did not seem to notice that Samuel was following his car. Ten minutes later, the silver car had entered East Potomac Park.

This spit of land, which was man-made during the reclamation projects on southwest Washington areas' marshes, jutted out between the confluence of the Anacostia and Potomac Rivers. Its circumference was almost three miles. A well-used jogging path circled the entire park, turning back upon itself at a point called Haynes Point.

The doctor parked his car near the entrance to the park. Samuel was sure that the man intended to jog the complete circumference of the park, returning to his car when finished. Samuel drove slowly by the doctor. He was involved in completing his stretching exercises and did not seem to notice Samuel's car.

Samuel pulled to a stop on the north side of the park. He was less than twenty yards from the jogging path. He trembled as he switched off the Subaru's engine and waited. He reached across the front seat and fingered the glistening blade of the stiletto. His head was pounding. He had not taken his medication for two days. He had wanted his thoughts to be clear. He looked in the mirror from time to time, noting the joggers as they approached. As it was very early in the morning, there were only a few joggers on the path. He saw, off in the distance, a tiny figure approaching from the rear. The figure was clad in a green running suit. The color was the same color that Doctor Mercer had been wearing. The figure approached. He was less than a quarter of a mile away now. Samuel felt his heart pounding. The figure moved closer. Samuel gripped the stiletto. When the figure was one hundred yards away, the blackness in Samuel's vision increased.

What seemed like moments later, the blackness cleared. The stiletto was gone. Samuel looked around him. The sun was higher in the eastern sky now. Samuel noted that his shoes were wet and small bits of grass clung to the wetness. In the distance Samuel noted a small crowd and police vehicles. The lights of an ambulance glared in the early morning light.

Samuel was very dizzy. He managed to start the car and drove towards the exit from the park. He slowed as he passed the small crowd that was gathering. He saw that the paramedics and police were kneeling beside the lifeless figure of a man clad in a green jogging suit. He continued on and saw a highway entrance sign, which read 295 North. He followed the signs and soon merged into a lane marked I-495 West. He drove west and then recognized the road, which he had driven down just three days before. By the middle of the afternoon, he was parking the tiny Subaru in the garage of Mrs. Donatto's house. He felt tired. More tired than he had felt in quite some time.

Chapter Ten

As Samuel walked into the small house, he noticed the loud sound of the television. He called out to Mrs. Donatto, "I'm home."

Not getting an answer, he walked into the living room where he assumed she had fallen asleep watching the afternoon soap operas. Something didn't look right as he approached the recliner. He called out again, and still got no response. A thin column of saliva had found its way down the front of her tattered housedress. Her head was titled unnaturally to the side. The remote control lay on the floor at the foot of the recliner. Her lifeless eyes peered at the television. Her hands were deeply mottled. He gently touched her wrist. The skin was cold. He shook the stiffened body. Racing to the telephone, he hurriedly dialed 911.

He stood on the porch as he heard the approaching sirens of the rescue squad, which was quickly followed by a patrol car. The first police officer arriving at the scene questioned Samuel.

A paramedic approached them, shaking his head slightly. "She's been gone for quite a while."

The officer nodded towards Sam. "This is her son-in-law. He's been away for four days. He said he talked to her last night and she sounded fine."

The paramedics made several telephone calls. Two hours later, the body of Mrs. Donatto had been removed from the house and taken to the Oakmill Mortuary and Funeral Home. After the mortuary attendants had taken the body away, Samuel sat at the kitchen table and wept. God had swiftly and surely punished him for what he had done in Washington, D.C. Now he was truly alone.

Sometime later that evening, Samuel remembered that his mother-in-law had a large metal box in the house where she stored important papers. He found the box and set the papers in neat piles on the kitchen table. He read each of the documents. She had several insurance policies and a deed. There was a large envelope with an Oakmill attorney's name on it. Samuel suddenly felt very sleepy and without taking off his clothes, he soon fell asleep across the bed in his tiny room.

He awoke the next morning and called the lawyer's office. Attorney Murph arranged for a meeting at his office at 1:30 that afternoon.

The telephone rang at about 10:30 that morning. It was Mr. James from the funeral home. They talked at length about the funeral arrangements. During the course of the conversation, Samuel mentioned that he had found several insurance policies. Mr. James asked him the amounts.

"There is one for two thousand dollars. And another one for five thousand."

The voice on the other end of the line answered "That should be plenty. Just bring the policies by and we'll make the proper arrangements."

"She told me she didn't want a lot of fancy doings when she died."

"No problem, we'll follow her wishes."

Samuel mentioned that he would come by after seeing Mr. Murph, the attorney, that afternoon.

Mr. James spoke. "No problem at all. We'll be here until 6:30. Do you know where our place is located? It's right on the corner of Sixth and Main."

Samuel assured Mr. James that he would come by later that afternoon.

Samuel met Mr. Murph in his office downtown that afternoon. Mr. Murph was an elderly man who had been practicing law in Oakmill for almost fifty years. He stood up as the young secretary ushered Samuel into his office. He walked from behind the desk with some difficulty, clutching a large gold-tipped cane. Samuel shook the old man's gnarled hand.

"You must be Mr. Jones. I'm so sorry about Audrey. She was my classmate back when Oakmill School had 15 students. I've done all of her legal work for years. Have a seat. Have a seat." He pointed an arthritic finger towards an ancient leather chair.

Samuel sat down. As he leaned back in the chair, he looked about the old man's office. There were shelves from floor to ceiling, containing faded books. Behind the desk, was a wall bearing the attorney's yellowed diplomas and several pictures, obviously taken when he was a much younger man.

Opening a folder, the old man cleared his throat. "Well, young man, there are a few things I need to tell you. About six months ago, Audrey came in and had me make a few changes in her will. Being that you are her only kin, she wanted to do right by you. She had the house and a couple of small lots in the hills. She was a very thrifty woman and managed to save a little money. Some of it's in CDs and that kind of thing. She had me set up an account at the First Pocono Savings and Loan Bank for you two months ago. She put most of her cash in that account and stipulated that it be delivered to you upon her death. It'll take about a week to get a check in the amount of ten thousand dollars to you. Is that OK?"

Samuel was speechless. A tear rolled down his cheek as he nodded. Finding his voice, he said, "I never knew. I never knew. Why did she leave all that money to me?"

"Well, I can't say exactly, but I do know she was very fond of you. It broke her heart to see how you were devastated by your little girl's death. Plus, she always said how good you were to Claudette and the child. In many ways, you were the son she never had. Now, what would you like me to do about the property? She left all that and the car to you, too."

"I don't know. I need time to think."

"Yes, yes. There is no hurry. Take your time. If you decide to sell any of it, we'll execute a Power of Attorney, and I'll handle all of the details for you. In the meantime, I'll get the car registration changed to your name. It's been paid off quite a while now, so you'll get the pink slip. And I'll call you when the check is ready."

Samuel stood and shook the old man's hand. "Thank you for everything."

Five days later, Mrs. Audrey Donatto was laid to rest on an early spring morning in the Poconos. The mound of fresh brown earth stood beside the gravesite, which was immediately adjacent to Stacey and Claudette's graves. The Subaru and four other cars followed the long black hearse. The four other cars were filled with elderly mourners. Several had to be assisted to the gravesite. The pastor from Mrs. Donatto's church read a few words and the small group dispersed.

A few of the mourners visited the quiet house. They reminisced as they sipped tea and ate the small repast prepared by some of Audrey's closest friends. Agnes Milharty had baked a large German chocolate cake. After a short while, the group departed. Samuel was left alone. He gathered up the soiled dishes and washed them in the sink. He turned on the television in the living room and sat on the couch. Mrs. Donatto's empty recliner stood alone.

Samuel spent the next several days reading magazines. While cleaning up Mrs. Donatto's room, he noted that she had several stacks of outdated travel magazines. However, he could not remember her ever taking a trip. One of the magazines extolled the virtues of the foothills of the Sierras. There were several towns mentioned in the article, including one called Placerville. The town was located near the site of the original gold discovery. The article continued with descriptions of the hunting, fishing, and gold panning opportunities in the area. After much thought, Samuel decided that he would move his meager belongings to California. There was nothing holding him in the Poconos anymore.

The next day, he visited the graveyard. He brought fresh flowers and sat by the graves of the three members of his family. He talked to them at length about his upcoming trip and promised to return to see them often. An observer would have thought that he was holding a conversation with someone beneath the sod. He often paused, nodded, and used hand gestures.

Several days later, he received a call from Mr. Murph. "Hello, Samuel. I'm just calling to tell you I have the check ready." They made arrangements to meet that afternoon.

Samuel told Mr. Murph of his plans to go out West. He had decided to sell Mrs. Donatto's house and lots, but he would keep the Subaru. "I'll need about a week to clean up the house and get her things moved out. I'll donate them to the Goodwill."

The old man stood and handed Samuel an envelope. He placed a trembling hand on Samuel's shoulder. "Don't worry about a thing. You've been through enough. I'll take care of selling the property for you. Just drop me a line once you get settled, and I'll arrange to get the proceeds of the sales to you. It probably won't be that much money, so spend what you have wisely."

The old man and Samuel walked across the office floor. Samuel turned towards the old man. "I can't begin to thank you. I just can't begin to thank you."

"No need, young man. You've been through a lot."

Once outside, Samuel looked at his watch. He had fifteen minutes to make it to Dr. Eaglin's office. The receptionist ushered him inside. He spent the next half-hour detailing his plans. The young doctor voiced his concerns, but reluctantly agreed. From a list on his desk, he gave Samuel several names of associates he knew on the West Coast, one of whom practiced in the Placerville area. He also wrote a prescription for a six-month supply of medication for him and cautioned Samuel to continue his medications.

The next several days were spent packing. He made arrangements with Goodwill to pick up the furniture and household effects. Several days later a van arrived with the Goodwill Industries logo emblazoned on its side. Within two hours, the three men who had arrived in the van had cleared the house of its meager contents. They next turned their attention to the items in the garage and small shed. Samuel watched them as they worked. One of the heavily muscled men was about to add a box to the moving dolly. He turned as he felt Samuel's vise-like grip on his biceps.

Samuel shook his head from side to side. "Not that box. I want to keep that."

The man placed the box on the rapidly emptying floor of the garage. Samuel knelt and partially opened the box. Inside were several of Stacey's faded dresses and a small collection of her toys.

The movers continued with their work.

The heavily muscled man asked Samuel. "What about this old bicycle?"

Samuel looked at the rusting bicycle, which still had its training wheels intact. His eyes misted as he said, "That's OK. You can take that."

The man rolled the rusting bicycle with its cobweb filled spokes and flattened tires down the driveway. He lifted the bicycle and handed it to another man who was in the back of the truck. There was little left when the large blue truck drove away.

Samuel went back inside the house. He began to load his few possessions into the Subaru. He had cashed the check early that morning at the bank. He put the stack of bills in a small cardboard box, which he slid under the passenger seat of the car. All that was left for him to do was to drop off the house keys at Attorney Murph's office and to pay one last visit to the cemetery. Within an hour, the small blue car headed south along the winding Poconos roads. Samuel drove until he saw the Pennsylvania Turnpike. He took the turn-off that pointed to the west and headed for the California foothills.

Part Two

Chapter Eleven

The whitecaps blew from the churning seas as the small boat fought its way to the southeast. There was a noticeable list to the portside of the ship as she slugged through the rain swept ocean. The ship was a sailing whaler. It was a three-masted bark, built some twelve years before in New Bedford. The foremast was only half its height, the top one-half having been snapped in two as the brave ship had been battered by the hurricane. The storm had caught the ship in its grasp two days after the ship had left Kingston, Jamaica. The foresails were torn and pieces of sail flapped in the easterly wind. The tiny ship's timbers groaned as she pitched and rolled. Pieces of rigging trailed behind the ship. She mounted each new crest and continued on her journey towards the southeast.

The name on her once proud stern proclaimed for all to see, "The Confederate". The vessel had left Kingston less than three days before. Her destination had been the North Coast of South America. She had been one day out of Kingston when the skies to the east began to darken. The winds increased and within twelve hours the ship was held prisoner by the vicious hurricane. It was mid July1862.

It had been a long voyage for the tiny vessel with her crew of thirty and the one hundred and fifty souls who were crammed below decks. The smell of human waste coupled with the smells of vomit drifted up through the hatch. The weather did not permit the passengers to emerge from the crowded spaces below. The seas and the ship's movement made the cooking of any type of food impossible. Many of the passengers had not eaten since the tiny ship was one day south of Kingston. Many of the small children below decks as well as many of the older passengers had succumbed to the heat. The crew, for fear of flooding, could not open the hatches. Soft moans and the sounds of hymns being sung filled the passageway.

Below decks six members of the crew, their clothing blackened and drenched with sweat, took turns squeezing the bellow's pump that spit the brackish water that continued to flow into the ships innards.

The plight of "The Confederate" had started almost three years before. In 1860 a group of slave states had called a convention to discuss secession from the Union. South Carolina had been the first state to take the bold step of seceding. In the months that followed other states had followed. In the spring of 1861, the first shots had been fired as Confederates attacked Fort Sumter. On April 13, 1861, Fort Sumter had surrendered. The war was on.

Most of the passengers, who were crowded below decks, had at first not been bothered by the war. The battles were far to the north and the Confederate units seemed to be holding their own. The enormity of the war grew as loved ones said their good-byes and rode up dusty roads with the rapidly enlisted units. Life in South Georgia and Florida continued much as before the war. The farmers continued their efforts to coax the earth into discharging a harvest. The farmers redoubled their efforts to increase crop yields. Vegetables replaced cotton as hungry troops increased the need for supplies.

Things took a turn for the worse in February of 1862. Jefferson Davis was inaugurated as President of the Confederacy and three days later, on February 25, Nashville fell to Union forces. Nashville was the first Confederate State capital to fall. Things had taken a turn. Union gunboats began to tighten the noose on New Orleans. On April 28, 1862, Admiral David G. Farragut sailed up the Mississippi and demanded the surrender of New Orleans. This city, which had been considered an international city, surrendered. Although it would be several days before Union troops entered the city, the Confederates had lost a major prize.

These events were not unnoticed by a small group of men who lived in the area surrounding Tallahassee. Several days after receiving news by rider, they scheduled a meeting. The men had been friends for many years.

The rider from Mobile had not brought good news. The war was starting to turn. The enthusiasm was waning.

The five men met in the home of Lineus Johnson. He, like his brother-in-law Abner Broussard, was a wealthy ship builder and ship owner. The two men had built a small fortune building and contracting out the vessels needed to ship the crops, which the surrounding farmers raised. They transported hundreds of thousands of bails of cotton to European markets. The increased level of battle and the Union blockades had had a profound effect on the incomes and the lives of both of these men. They were concerned and their faces mirrored their concern. Three other men joined them. Abraham Gulliver and James Garrison were wealthy planters from southern Georgia. Cornelius Doubleday owned three mills, all within a thirty-five mile radius of Tallahassee. Cornelius was married to Melissa Garrison, a cousin of James.

They met at "Sea Lanes", the large white mansion owned by Lineus Johnson. The mansion stood on a bluff overlooking the city of Tallahassee. Servants hurried about carrying platters of steaming food for the visitors who, they had been told, were important people. The men arrived at intervals during the late afternoon. Cornelius Doubleday had ridden for two days on horseback after receiving a note carried by a sweating black slave. The slave had been given a new mount and hurried back south with the reply. Cornelius would be present. James Garrison had ridden from his home in Calvary, Georgia. He had sighted several columns of Union soldiers on the way down to Tallahassee, but had managed to avoid being seen by them. Abner Broussard had ridden from his farm near Panama City.

Night was falling and a humid breeze blew across the porch when a slave summoned them to dinner. They chatted as the servants brought the various courses and kept their wineglasses full. After dinner, the men walked slowly into the large library at the end of the house and assembled around a large sturdy table that was piled high with maps and documents.

After sipping from large brandy snifters and smoking large cigars, the men removed their coats and the discussion began.

Lineus stood at the head of the table. "We all know that the war is going poorly. My question is where do we stand and what do we intend to do? You know that I support the Confederacy, but I'm beginning to worry about the war and about my family." He then sat back in the richly upholstered chair.

Cornelius Doubleday was the next man to speak. "I am pretty damned worried, myself. The mills are only operating at thirty percent of their capacity. All the available ground is being planted with staples. The troops need to be fed. I'm shipping more corn than I ever did but the cotton gins are idle. What with having to feed all the slaves and share croppers, it's rough and getting rougher."

Several of the men at the table nodded as he spoke. Abraham Gulliver stood and paced about the room as he spoke.

"I have been talking things over with Martha and with...with taxes and the crops being paid for in Confederate Dollars, I'm in a bad way. Why just last week, I had to sell off twenty slaves. I have never sold my slaves before. You come to my plantation and I take care of you and yorn until you go in the ground. That's the way that it's always been with me, but no more. I've even been thinking about selling my holdings and going out West. The places won't do me no good if the Yankees burn them. Hell! With New Orleans gone, I can't ship nothing. I really don't know. I really don't know." He poured another drink of brandy from the large decanter.

One by one each man voiced his concerns with the way the war was going. A terrible turn had befallen the Confederacy. It was Lineus Johnson who put forth the proposal, which kept the men talking into the early hours of the morning. The Eastern sky was beginning to lighten when the group of men pushed their seats back, promising to resume their discussions in the early afternoon. Two elderly white-haired black men entered behind the group and began to clean the smoke filled library.

The men resumed their negotiations early the next afternoon. The talks continued into late that night. On the morning of the third day, the plan was finalized. They would begin to sell off their holdings. They would leave caretakers and managers with the holdings that they were not able to liquidate. They would accept payment only in gold, even if this meant taking a financial loss on the dealings. They would each be allowed to bring ten slaves. The elderly and infant slaves would be left in the care of the managers. They would sell off any excess slaves not needed to run any property or plantations left behind. They would take breeding stock, both human and farm animals. The choices must be critical. Abner Broussard would quietly lay up a vessel and they would leave for the northern shore of South America in six weeks time. The ship would leave on the last day of June and as there was a great deal of danger involved, the departure date was definite. They would gather at Apalachicola Bay two days prior to the intended departure. They each were sworn to secrecy. Those loyal to the Confederacy, as well as Union sympathizers, were apt to turn them in to the authorities if the plan or the participants became known.

The group had chosen Apalachicola Bay due to its remoteness and due to the fact that it was sheltered from the Gulf of Mexico by Cape St. George and Cape San Blas. The bay was located approximately seventy-five miles southeast of Tallahassee. It was in a fairly remote area and a ship hidden there would not likely be seen by Union patrol boats. The surrounding area, although marshy, was dotted with sandy areas that would offer little difficulty when the wagons with their loads traversed the area. The next few weeks were spent attending land sales and making lists of slaves, household effects, and finally a passenger list. When finished, there would be almost two hundred souls on board the tiny vessel.

In order not to attract attention from their neighbors, members of each man's family left in small groups and headed for the rendezvous point.

Abner Broussard had made arrangements for one of the captains of a three masted sailing bark to hide the ship at the edge of the mangrove covered waterway until all was ready for boarding. The captain, who had been in the employ of Abner, was given permission to bring his own family members, as well as the families of crewmembers, on board. The Captain was also promised three hundred dollars in gold coins if he managed to complete the voyage with the vessel and its cargo intact. Each of the twelve crew members was offered fifty dollars in gold coins to help them get settled in the new land.

Each of the men made the necessary arrangements, telling inquisitive neighbors and business associates that they were moving to southern Florida to wait out the war. The managers and caretakers were given advances and advised that the employers would be back within six months. Groups of family members and slaves left each of the great houses at intervals. As the families had often traveled about before the war, their departure raised little interest. Livestock and wagons carrying the minimum of household effects left and traveled south by circuitous routes. The groups met at a small coastal village called Eastpoint and traveled by small boats, keeping well inshore so that they would not be spotted by the occasional Union patrol boat which swept the area. One by one, the groups began to assemble on the shores of the large bay. They camped and waited for the remaining members and their supplies to arrive. The sandy soil was not as easily traversed as the planners had thought, but sweating slaves, aided by the members of the ship's crew, coaxed the last of the creaking wagons and the braying livestock towards the ship which lay anchored thirty yards offshore. The last group to arrive was the Garrison group. They had come all the way from South Georgia. They had been forced to detour around several groups of Northern soldiers. Members of the groups hugged each other. Several of the women cried hysterically. They had been worried that the ship would sail without them.

The families looked haggard from their journey. Several of the smaller children were ill, but there was not a moment to lose. The captain wanted to sail with the morning tide. The afternoon and evening was spent loading supplies, household effects, and livestock into the holds of the ship. Those animals, for which there was no room, were turned loose into the verdant Florida bayous. Tiny boats rowed by crewmen and slaves made many trips across the blue water of the bay. Last to load were the family members and the slaves. At seven the next morning, as the sun pierced the fog filled Florida sky, they sailed. The bark, sporting her new name "The Confederate", hoisted sail and moved slowly down the bay rounding Cape St. George and turning South-south-west into the blue-green waters of the Gulf of Mexico.

Chapter Twelve

The plan was to stay far out in the middle of the Gulf of Mexico, staying well west of Florida. News had reached Tallahassee several days before the party left that there was fear that the Union Navy was planning to attack Tampa. Mobile, Alabama had also come under enemy bombardment. The captain knew that by sailing in the middle of the Gulf, he would, with luck, be able to avoid the ships of the Union Navy. Little did the group know, but on June 30, Tampa would come under attack.

Two days after leaving the bay, they spotted a ship on the horizon. "The Confederate" altered her course to the west and the masts of the distant ship disappeared below the horizon. The winds were almost constant from the east. The little ship, although loaded to the gunwales with cargo and humanity, plowed through the warm gulf waters.

After sailing for almost six hundred miles, the lookouts spotted the distant shore of the Yucatan peninsula. The quartermaster turned the bow of the ship towards the east and within a day and a half, the southern coast of Cuba appeared. The ship hove to off the beautiful coast and a crew was sent ashore for freshwater and fruit. They returned several hours later, having encountered a Spanish patrol, which had fired on them. One of the sailors was slightly injured in the incident.

Putting aside plans for further visits to Cuba, the ship turned south and three days later, lookouts spotted the northern-most of the Cayman Islands. They circled the largest of the three-island group, but could find no entrance though the great reef, which encircled the main island. They turned towards the east. Progress was slow. The winds were almost head-on. The vessel was forced to make frequent tacks in order to maintain headway.

Days later, they saw the green shores of the island of Jamaica. After another day's sailing, "The Confederate" was safely anchored in Kingston Harbor. Crewmembers, accompanied by several slaves, went ashore to replenish supplies and fresh water. The crew returned four hours later. Four of the slaves had disappeared into the thick jungles, which grew up to the edge of the town. Efforts to chase them down had been fruitless.

There were several other foreign ships anchored in Kingston Harbor. The captain, along with several leaders of the expedition, rowed over to the closest vessel. They spent several hours discussing the best sailing routes to South America and problems "The Confederate" might expect to encounter. Weary passengers filled the upper decks of the ship, enjoying the tropical sun. Many of the teen-aged passengers swam in the warm tropical water. Three days later, "The Confederate" weighed anchor and slipped from Kingston Harbor. Her crew was relaxed. They were well away from the war zone and the danger from Union Navy capture had passed. South America was less than a two-week sail. Excitement gripped the passengers. They were on their way to a new land.

"The Confederate" headed South-south-east and moved slowly along. All went well until the ship was two days out of Kingston. Dark clouds appeared on the eastern horizon. The wind began to increase. The captain reduced sail and turned in an effort to run before the impending gale. Little did he know, but this was to be more than a gale. A fierce hurricane was bearing down on the over-laden vessel. "The Confederate" had sailed into the path of a raging storm. This was the time of the year when savage storms, birthed on the East Coast of Africa, prowled the Caribbean waters. The storms sank hundreds of ships and devastated islands that were in their path.

The storm increased in intensity. Below decks, passengers screamed as they were tossed about in the darkness. Huge water casks rolled about in the hold of the vessel, destroying her balance and threatening to erupt through the side of the ship. On deck, voices were drowned out by the howling wind. The rigging shrieked in the wind. Rigging was torn apart by the wind and sails were shredded. The ship entered the eye of the hurricane and the passengers thought that their many prayers had been answered. This was not to be. Two hours later, the winds returned, their intensity seeming to have increased.

Three crewmen were swept into the howling sea as their mates struggled for handholds on the slippery deck. Below decks, several passengers were crushed as cargo shifted. The smell of excrement and vomiting filled the air. Frightened children clung to frightened adults. There was an explosion as the foremast splintered and fell into the ocean. Flailing rope trailed from the fallen mast. The first officer warned the captain that the ship was taking on water through several areas in the hull. Men, including the most able-bodied slaves, were hurriedly sent below decks in an effort to plug the leaks.

With the passing of the eye of the storm, the winds changed direction and blew from the southeast. The tiny ship was helpless and began to move to the northwest. Hours passed and the desperation increased. The ship's decks tilted to the port side and huge waves made their way unhindered across the sloping deck. Several more crewmembers were swept overboard. Quietly at first and then more perceptibly, the winds began to slacken. The rain, which had been continuous, gave way to intermittent squalls. The seas, while still churning, were lowered in height. No longer did the waves tower above the mast. Was salvation at hand? The captain met with the leaders and advised them that the condition of "The Confederate", although grave, was not as desperate as it had been. The leaders nodded in agreement and went below decks to inform the huddled and terrified passengers.

The skies lightened and the tropical night gave a hint of moonlight as the vessel struggled south. Morning found the vessel under bright skies. Remaining crewmen, assisted by slaves, began to clear the ship of debris and to care for the injured. Twenty-six passengers and ten crewmembers had perished in the storm. There was a funeral service held in the mid-afternoon and the bodies of the victims were lowered over the side of the ship. Relatives cried tears of anguish as their loved ones were buried in the sea. The stricken vessel plowed on, its forward progress slowed by the storm damage. Lookouts were sent aloft to look for land.

The sun was just emerging from the eastern horizon when an excited slave began shouting. "Ah see land! Ah see land!"

He pointed to the South. Within two hours, the outline of an island appeared. Checking his charts, the captain determined that this must be one of the islands in the Lesser Antilles. A quartermaster took a quick fix of the sun and determined that the ship was too far west and too far north for the island to be one of that group. The ship sailed closer and four hours later was circling a large island. In the distance could be seen a ridge of mountains. Palm trees and breaking waves marked the shoreline. The ship began a series of tacks. There was a large reef that seemed to encircle the entire north shore of the landmass.

Moving further east, the lookouts spotted a large break in the coral reef. Beyond the break lay a sheltered harbor. The ship tacked and sailed through the reef and into the shelter of the harbor.

Discussions were held and it was decided to beach "The Confederate." Night was approaching as the ship ground to a halt fifteen yards from the beach, her keel firmly trapped by the sandy bottom of the bay. Crewmembers were sent aloft and the sails were lowered. The tiny ship leaned towards her right side. Passengers scurried on deck and a prayer service was held. Weakened voices joined in the singing of hymns. "The Confederate" had survived the storm. It was mid 1862.

Chapter Thirteen

Darkness was falling and so it was decided that the passengers would remain on board the ship until the next morning. A small landing party composed of slaves and crewmembers went ashore that evening and under the light of torches, began clearing a landing site. They worked far into the night. By morning, the tired passengers were eagerly lining the rails, waiting to be rowed ashore. It was decided to post armed guards around the perimeter of the camp. The leaders had brought an extensive arsenal of pistols and rifles as well as powder and musket balls. These were carefully taken ashore and stored in a cave, which was a short distance inland.

There were only one hundred and twenty people left when roll was called the next morning. Many of these were suffering from the trauma of the hurricane. Twenty of the group were slaves. Those people who were able to work began building the first crude huts. Little did they know that the camp would grow and one day be called Doloresville. The well-sheltered port would become a center of commerce for the island. Little did they know that cargo of another kind would one day lead to the island undergoing a civil war much like the one that they had sailed so far to escape.

The next several weeks were spent setting up the small settlement. There was abundant fresh water, although game was scarce. A hunting party happened upon a well-worn trail, which meandered off towards the interior of the island. There were signs that indicated that the trail had recently been used.

Three weeks after landing, the group's leaders met to discuss further plans for the settlement. After much discussion, they decided on a name for the island. It would be called New Savannah. The settlement that was slowly being carved out of the wilderness would be called Doloresville. The name was in honor of the oldest passenger who had survived the voyage, Dolores Johnson.

The issue of the slaves' status was argued for several meetings. After much debate, it was decided that due largely as repayment for their assistance on the storm-swept voyage, all slaves would enjoy the status of free men. They could own land, which was to be given them by grants. They could not, however, hold public office or vote. The twenty slaves reacted joyously when they received this news. They continued working for their former masters.

Survey teams were sent out to explore the island. They discovered a mountain range running through the center of the island. To the north was a high peak, which was covered by clouds. The land was very fertile, although the rainfall seemed to vary widely. In many ways, the island resembled the land they had just left. The southern portion of the island was more arid than the northern portion of the island. It seemed suited for growing cotton, should the population spread to the south. Other areas seemed able to support the growth of tobacco.

Several months passed before they contacted the first inhabitants of the island. A survey party scouting the northwest end of the island found a small town. The town's inhabitants greeted them in a friendly manner. The townsfolk were a mixture of people. Many of them looked Spanish and many of them were obviously Negro. There were also many that looked like Indians. The people in the town spoke a dialect that seemed to be a mixture of French, Spanish, and a scattering of words that were unknown to the visitors. Among the survivors of "The Confederate" were several families who spoke French and Spanish. Communication was therefore not difficult.

The people explained that in the distant past, their families had sailed to the island from the island of Hispaniola. They had done so to escape the harsh Spanish rule. People from the western end of Hispaniola who were fleeing fighting between the French and the largely African population later joined them. They found that the island which had initially been a French possession, had been abandoned by France as its problems in Haiti increased. After failing to prevent an overthrow in Haiti, the French had abandoned the island and moved their interests to islands such as Monserrat. The French did not want to overburden their supply lines by holding onto an island in the mid-Caribbean. The island, technically, belonged to no country.

The survey party determined that the island was roughly 3500 square miles and that there were several bays that were well sheltered. These bays could be put to use in the future, as commerce increased. They also found several villages on the slopes of the mountains. People who appeared to be Indians inhabited these villages. They encountered no more Europeans after leaving the first town.

Several years passed and the newly arrived Americans continued to develop the tiny settlement of Doloresville. The European population was augmented when a Danish sailing vessel, which had been caught in a hurricane, landed with one hundred fifty storm-wracked survivors. They were offered refuge and those who chose to stay were given land grants.

It was nearly five years later when a passing ship brought news that Lee had surrendered at Appomattox in April of 1865. The sailors brought tales of a devastated South. The survivors of "The Confederate" felt that they had made the right choice. By now, New Savannah was their home. They had toiled too long now, to return to a ravaged South.

Crops such as tobacco and cotton flourished in the rich island earth. Livestock multiplied and the population of the island grew. Commerce between the northernmost town and Doloresville increased. As the population increased, there was a need for governance. A series of meetings was held and after several months, a constitution was written and accepted by the members of both settlements. There would be free elections and all of the citizens of the island, including freed blacks, would be allowed to vote.

A militia was formed as well as a small police force. The town, which had been settled before the arrival of the Americans was, renamed Port

Leesville. A growing settlement on the Southeast tip of the island was called Port Allison. The western most town, which was nestled on the fertile slopes of the mountain range, was called Joansville. A large bay on the southwest of the island was called Port Ricardo. A wagon trail was cleared and circled much of the island.

Elections were held and the first president of the Island of New Savannah was James Garrison. Trinidad Sierramonte, a member of one of the first families from Hispaniola, was elected vice president. The thirty-man senate was elected and began to meet on a monthly basis. Among the bills passed, was a bill allowing for the collection of taxes. The taxes were to be used to further develop the infrastructure of the island. A group traveled to the Dutch island of Aruba and made arrangements to purchase several small sailing vessels. These were used to transport cotton and crops such as tobacco around the Caribbean, visiting such ports as Caracas and Maracaibo.

And so New Savannah entered the twentieth century. Several of the original leaders of that small group of people who had boarded "The Confederate" passed away. Families had been living on the island for three generations. There were numerous intermarriages. There were unions of the first American families with the Spanish and French families who had lived on the island before the Americans came. Former slaves married Indians and Spanish women. The population of new Savannah was multicultural and diverse.

The people lived together in harmony. The wealth was spread among many people. The wealthiest families were the Johnsons, the Gullivers, the Garrisons, the Broussards, the Doubledays, the Sierramontes, and the Bantoms. The last family, the Bantoms, was descended from Leroy Bantom who had left Tallahassee as a slave. He had thrived on freedom in New Savannah and had amassed a fortune by growing foodstuffs on his initial land grant. When the old man had died in 1901, he had almost nine hundred acres under cultivation. Members of his family had been elected to offiice in the 1904 election, an event the old man did not live to see.

The discovery of bauxite in the nineteen thirties did much to improve the economy of the island. A railroad system was built to transport the ore from the mountain mines to Port Leesville. Another line ran from Doloresville into the flanks of the central mountain range. Foreign workers, who were working at the mining sites, needed accommodations and soon several hotels were built. The United States of America, which had formally recognized the tiny country in 1917, built a small embassy. The embassy staff spoke highly of the beautiful beaches and pleasant tropical climate. With the end of World War One, tourists began to trickle into the country.

New Savannah continued to prosper. World War Two with its horrors spared the country. The country had declared its neutrality at the onset of the conflict and ships from many nations docked at both Port Ricado and at Port Allison. Baja Airport, which stood five miles outside of Doloresville, received daily flights from South America. German officers strolled the streets of the capital city. Their presence was seemingly unnoticed by the populace. American patrol vessels refueled at the large bunkers on the southern part of the island.

English was the primary language with Spanish being a close second choice. The population continued to worship at both Catholic and Baptist churches. The New Savannah currency of exchange was the Savannah Peso. Its value fluctuated, but was worth approximately one dollar U.S.

Things went well until the early nineteen sixties. Fidel Castro had recently overthrown the Cuban government and was interested in spreading his ideologies throughout the Caribbean. He sent emissaries to New Savannah. There were formal discussions but the Senate, backed by the president of New Savannah, saw no reason to change a political system which had worked so well.

In 1963, the islands dotting the Caribbean Ocean were beset by a drought that lasted for over two years. Agriculture was destroyed on many of the islands. New Savannah was not spared. For the first time in the history of the Island, it became necessary to import staples such as rice, coffee, and other vegetables. Many families suffered from the drought which seemed never ending. It was the winter of 1965 before rains fell on the parched slopes and plains of the island. Diminishing amounts of bauxite ore from the mines had compounded the financial damage from the crop losses.

A new and more devastating plague was about to consume the island. The plague was drugs. Members of the Sierramonte family started the epidemic. The family had maintained ties with relatives both in the Dominican Republic and in Columbia. A branch of the family had migrated to Columbia, after living for years in New Savannah. The family in Columbia had been embraced by members of the Colombian drug cartel and were deeply involved both in the cultivation of coca plants and the production as well as distribution of cocaine. They had approached Faustino Sierramonte, the patriarch of the New Savannah family, with a simple offer. Would he be interested in helping them ship certain packages through his shipping company in Port Leesville? The elderly man had thought little about the ramifications of the offer. He readily agreed. He had formed the company after World War Two and had added to his family's already vast fortune by shipping bauxite ore and molasses to other parts of the Caribbean and to the United States.

At first, the task was easy. Small airplanes began landing periodically at the airports in both Jackson and at St. John. The cargo was transferred to trucks and arrived several days later in Port Leesville. The cargo was off-loaded from the trucks and immediately loaded aboard ocean going vessels. Many of these vessels were destined for ports such as New Orleans or Miami. The crates were labeled "farm machinery". In some cases, the crates were labeled "leather goods". The small planes landed on a weekly basis at first, but soon the airplanes were landing on a daily basis. The size of the aircraft increased, as did their number. They soon began using Baja Airport. New Savannah customs officials were not routinely based at the island's two smaller airports. All freight entering Baja Airport was subject to customs inspection.

It was only a matter of time before the old man was confronted by a high ranking customs official who discussed with him the fact that a crate labeled "Leather Goods" had been found to contain fifty kilograms of cocaine. The senior man pretended dismay at first. After discussing the matter further, the customs official became an employee. Corruption had reached New Savannah.

Relatives from Columbia approached enterprising farmers, who were largely descendants of the island's first Indian families. Now that the drought was nearing its end, would they like to plant a replacement crop? Soon, the flanks of the mountains were dotted with coca plants. Higher up the slopes, small factories blossomed. Their pure coca product was packaged, labeled, and placed on Sierramonte vessels for shipment to distant ports.

The majority of the people did not condone the increased activity and involvement in the production and transshipment of drugs. Many were against the activity. Several Catholic priests spoke out, but their warnings went unheeded. Many thought that the activities would lessen with the death of the old man in 1967, but his son Fernando, who inherited the old man's fortune along with his drug connections, continued the practice. He involved judges and other leaders in the profits.

Drug enforcement agents from the United States visited the island on numerous occasions. They were amazed at the amount of drug activity. The President of the United States invited Malcolm Broussard, who was the president of New Savannah, to Washington to discuss the issue. When the talks proved unrewarding, the United States President took the first of many diplomatic measures. From May First 1967, all ships bearing New Savannah registry were barred from entering U.S. ports. He further banned all travel between the two countries. The staff of the U.S. embassy was recalled and diplomatic relations between the two countries was halted.

Chapter Fourteen

Eduardo Sierramonte was in the eleventh grade when the United States imposed its first set of sanctions on the island of New Savannah. He was the oldest son of Fernando Amando Sierramonte and Maria Vasquez Garrison. The couple had four other children. Katrina and Miguel were twins. They were four years younger than Eduardo. The youngest son was named Trinidad after his great-great-great-great grandfather who had once been vice-president of the young republic. The youngest child was Semalina, who was dark-eyed and mirrored the family's Spanish ancestry. Semalina was eight years younger than Eduardo. Trinidad was six years younger than Eduardo.

The five children lived on a large estate on the northeast side of Doloresville. The estate was some twenty miles from town and was perched on a bluff. The foothills of the central mountain chain formed the backdrop of the estate. Cattle, in large numbers, roamed the estate. The cattle were descendants of animals brought to new Savannah by the first settlers. The bulls were prized throughout South America. The children would spend many hours riding the ranges of the one thousand-acre ranch. They were being educated at St. Mark's Parish School, the school in which many of the island's elite families enrolled their children. There were dormitories for children from families who lived great distances away. The children were happy.

Eduardo was a member of the varsity soccer team and had won many honors for his excellence in his academic studies. He excelled in sciences and hoped one day to be a doctor. The parents loved all of their children, but they were proudest of Eduardo. They had nourished him the longest.

Each child had his or her distinct personality, but Eduardo was different in many other ways. He was aggressive and was at his best tackling another boy on the soccer field. He had one distinct flaw. He was easily slighted. When he considered himself slighted, his aggressive tendencies often displayed themselves.

Eduardo was in his room studying one night when his parents entered. A look of concern was etched on both of the parent's brows. Fernando Sierramonte was the first to speak. As Eduardo looked closely at Maria, he could see that his mother had been crying.

"Eduardo, please be seated. What we have to discuss with you tonight is of the gravest importance."

Eduardo looked at both of his parents.

"As you are aware, there have been activities going on in our country which have brought about negative reactions from several countries. The most severe reaction has been from the United States, which has banned our ships from entering their ports. They have banned all forms of travel between our two countries and have placed restrictions on many of our imports. The process is not one that will soon be reversed. Nor can the process be reversed. Unfortunately, my late father was at the basis of the problem and I inherited the problem from him."

"But what is the problem, Father? Why can the problem not be corrected?"

"The problem is drugs, Eduardo. Drugs are the problem. Unfortunately, our family is deeply involved. There are those who would kill us if we tried to back out of our dealings with them. I am not sure that we would want to back out. No matter what you may think, our economy is linked to drugs. The drugs have lessened our dependence on fat foreign tourists with their condescending ways. We no longer have to spend our lives digging rocks out of the ground. We are no longer looked down upon by the Americans with their hypocritical ideas. We did not teach the Americans to use drugs, Eduardo. We only catered to a demand."

Eduardo looked at his mother and then back to his father. "But how does this affect me? I sell no drugs. I study hard. I own no ships. I have never even been to America."

His mother spoke. "Eduardo, you are my oldest son. I want what is best for you. I know of your love for medicine. I think that someday, this will be all over and you can come back."

Eduardo was bewildered. "Come back? Where am I going? Come back? Where will I be?"

His mother sobbed and looked to her husband for the answer.

"My son, I have made arrangements for you to go to the Catholic school in the Dominican Republic. Father Sanchez is the headmaster and he is well connected in the United States. If you continue to do well in your studies, he has promised me that he will speak to the teachers at Georgetown University in Washington, D.C. He will arrange for you to get a Dominican Republic passport and if all goes well you can attend college and medical school there. The Jesuits run Georgetown. We have contributed well to them in the past."

There was silence in the room. Mrs. Sierramonte's sobs continued.

Eduardo looked up at his parents. He spoke at last. "Is this what you want me to do?"

"It will be better for you in the end. You will see. It will be better."

"But what about the others?"

"We will talk to the other children. They will understand."

His father then handed him a large manila envelope. "I have deposited five million American dollars in a numbered account in Georgetown, Grand Cayman. The money is yours to use as you please. It will help finance your education and will provide an avenue of safety should the need arise. It is a lot of money, but we have a lot more."

The three of them stood in the middle of the room. All three cried openly. Eduardo realized that he would be going and his parents realized that their son would be leaving.

Three weeks later, Eduardo boarded a small private jet. As the jet taxied along the runway at Baja Airport, Eduardo could see his father waving at the plane. It was the last time that he would see his father alive. His mother, as well as his sisters and brothers, had bid their farewells at home.

They could not stand the heartbreak of seeing him off at the airport. It would be over eight years before he saw any of his family members again. Tears filled his eyes as the plane climbed high into the tropical clouds.

Approximately one hour later, the outline of the island of Hispaniola appeared off to the north. The jet continued its southerly approach and gently touched down twenty minutes later at the airport in Santo Domingo. An elderly Catholic priest, who was dressed in a wrinkled black suit with a high white collar that was sweat stained, met him at the ramp. Father Sanchez had made all the arrangements and after walking though the customs area, they loaded Eduardo's four suitcases into the trunk of an old Chevrolet. It took the old man three hours to drive over the twisting roads.

At last they entered Puerto Plata. The town was situated on the northern coast and was ringed by hills. The bay of the tiny town was crescent-shaped and several tourist ships were moored at the docks. There was a large church that was nestled on a hill overlooking the town. There was a large school next to the church. A dormitory building completed the campus. To the north, Eduardo could see the waters of the Atlantic Ocean. Several nuns hurried across the campus. The students were all in the dining room having dinner when Eduardo and Father Sanchez arrived. Father Sanchez summoned a young priest who helped Eduardo move his belongings into a small room of the top floor of the dormitory. This would be Eduardo's home for the next two years.

Chapter Fifteen

Loneliness gripped the young student. He had studied hard while in New Savannah but he found that the faculty at his new school made even more demands on him. He missed his island home and family. As the eldest son, he was duty bound to carry out the wishes of both of his parents. He was active in sports and was able to win a place on the varsity soccer team. The soccer team members were a source of emotional support for the new student. He eagerly looked forward to the matches that the team played. The matches often involved trips to distant parts of the island.

The Dominican Republic occupied over two-thirds of the Island of Hispaniola. Haiti occupied the rest of the island. The island had been the site of the first European settlement founded by Christopher Columbus in 1492. It was very mountainous. The island had been the scene of much political intrigue. Rafael L. Trujillo had been the main political force on the island for thirty-one years. His regime had been overthrown in 1961. Since his overthrow, there had been an extended period of political uncertainty. This phase was winding down when Eduardo arrived.

Eduardo was able to see much of the island as the soccer team toured. The team played matches in such places as Santo Domingo, San Juan, and San Cristobal. Although English had been the primary language in New Savannah, the majority of the country's inhabitants spoke Spanish. Eduardo was proficient enough in Spanish to communicate effectively. His speaking skills improved dramatically as he conversed rapidly in Spanish with his teammates.

He spent the summer teaching English to students at the church-run school. He lived in the rectory with Father Sanchez.

The two spent many hours discussing the problems that would face Eduardo when he attended school. Although he would retain the

Sierramonte name, there must be no connection to the Sierramonte household that was connected with the drug cartel. He must never tell anyone that his real home was New Savannah. He was given the names of several men in the Washington area. If he ever felt that he was in great danger, he was to contact them. He must make no attempt to contact his family. All mail that he wished to send home must first be sent to Father Sanchez. The old man would in turn forward the letters using Catholic Church pouches, which were never opened by those seeking to fight the drug cartel.

The hot tropical summer passed quickly. One hot evening in late August, Eduardo loaded his baggage into the old Chevrolet that had first transported him to the school several years before. The two men spoke little as the old car moved slowly along the crowded island roads. Each was lost in his own thoughts. They stood together in the waiting area. The student and his mentor. At last, Eduardo's flight was called. The two men embraced and the student walked slowly up the ramp onto the waiting jetliner.

Chapter Sixteen

During the two years that had passed since leaving New Savannah, Eduardo's father had sent him a monthly stipend of three thousand dollars a month. Having no need to spend the money, Eduardo had instructed Father Sanchez to open a bank account in the student's name. The account held over sixty five thousand dollars when Eduardo completed high school. He had written Father Sanchez a check, which was enough to cover tuition, fees, room, board, and books for the coming year. Father Sanchez had sent a check, drawn on the church's account, to the Georgetown University finance department. For all intent and purposes, it appeared as though the church in Puerto Plata was sponsoring the young man's education.

Eduardo carried approximately nine thousand U.S. dollars with him as he sat in the seat of the jet. He gazed down at the dark ocean waters as they slipped beneath the wings of the airplane. He was lost in thought. Could all this be really happening? Was he really going to the homeland of the people who were attempting, in so many ways, to isolate his tiny country? He was too excited to sleep on the flight and he ate sparingly from the items on the small tray, which the flight attendant had placed on his seatback tray. He was finally able to doze. He awakened sometime later as the plane began its descent into the Miami area. The jetliner circled the city while in the landing pattern and Eduardo was amazed at the number of lights that twinkled below him. This was the largest city he had ever seen

He tried to maintain an air of calmness as he waited in the customs line. He looked around the large terminal as he waited. Finally, it was his turn to be questioned by the customs official. The agent was a large black woman who noted his passport and student's visa. She smiled. She pointed to an exit door and handed the documents back to Eduardo. He smiled and thanked her, then walked slowly through the door. The departure monitors directed him to his connecting flight and within an hour, he was seated in another airplane, on his way to Dulles International Airport, which was located just outside the Washington, D.C. area.

He chatted with a young female student from the U.S. Virgin Islands who was also on her way to Washington to attend college. The girl was returning to American University for her third year of pre-medical studies. She was very familiar with the Washington area and told Eduardo that she would be available to show him around Washington after he got settled at Georgetown. He thanked her and put her telephone number and campus address, which she had written on a small slip of paper, in his wallet.

The airplane finally began its descent towards the Dulles airport. Passing over the darkened countryside, Eduardo saw just a few twinkling lights. The other student explained to him that Dulles airport was actually located thirty to forty miles from the city. It would be necessary to take a taxi or bus in order to get into the city.

Eduardo was somewhat concerned, but his concern vanished as he walked into the waiting area. Standing in the middle of the waiting area were two students carrying a large banner reading, "Welcome Georgetown Students". Eduardo approached the pair and was given directions to a bus which would transport students going to the university. He collected his bags and soon joined a group of students who had arrived on various flights. Each was loaded down with the essentials they deemed needed for the coming year. The bus waited another half-hour and then began its one-hour trip to the campus.

The bus arrived at the campus gate and the driver directed the group of students to the arrival center. There, volunteers, who held long lists, met them. The names of arriving students were noted and accompanied by a volunteer, who was in most cases, an upper classman. They were escorted to their new homes. Someone had been kind enough to provide small carts and each student loaded his belongings on a cart and dutifully followed the volunteer who had been assigned to him or her. The students made a somewhat funny sight as they struggled across the humid and moonlit campus with their carts.

Eduardo was drenched with sweat when he slid the last of his luggage into the small dormitory room. He had been given a room on the third floor of a building that lacked an elevator. The volunteer handed him a stack of printed materials and told him to familiarize himself with the papers. The volunteer then left, bouncing the luggage cart down the stairs as he made his exit.

Eduardo noted that the small room had two beds. He had obviously been given a double room. His roommate would be arriving later. He stretched across the small bed and within ten minutes, he was fast asleep. The trip had been exhausting, both physically and mentally. He did not awaken until early the next morning. He awoke, still fully clothed, after hearing a knock on the door. He opened the door of the small room and gazed out at a group of people. In the middle of the group stood a tall boy who appeared to be the same age as Eduardo.

Apologizing for his appearance, Eduardo extended his hand. "Good morning, I am Eduardo Sierramonte."

"Hello. Pleased to meet you. I'm Manuel Augustino."

He then introduced Eduardo to his parents and sister. The family had driven down from New York City, where Manuel's father was a member of the UN Delegation from Venezuela. His father had been a prominent lawyer in Caracas before joining the UN Delegation two years ago.

They crowded into the tiny dormitory room and talked politely for almost an hour. Manuel was entering Georgetown as a pre-law student. He, too, was an accomplished soccer player. The family talked about their home in Venezuela and their adventures in New York City. Eduardo related the well-rehearsed partial truth.

"I am an orphan, but my father left me with a secure future. The Jesuits in Puerto Plato provided me an education and now I am here at

Georgetown. Everything is so different here, but it gives me great pleasure to meet you and your family, Senior Augustino." Seeing the close-knit family reminded Eduardo of the painful separation from his own family.

Taking the hurt in his eyes to be loneliness, Manuel's mother and father felt compassion for the young man. Glancing at his watch, Mr. Augustino said, "We have to run now. I have an appointment at the Embassy. I've made dinner reservations for 7:00 p.m. Eduardo, I'd like you to join us."

Eduardo smiled, "I'd be honored."

Manuel's family, accompanied by the two boys, climbed down the crowded dormitory steps and walked towards a Volvo station wagon loaded with Manuel's belongings. The two young men struggled during the next half-hour, making repeated trips up to the third floor. The remainder of the afternoon was spent unpacking the essentials and arranging them in the small dormitory room. Eduardo showered and lay across the small bed while Manuel did the same. They dressed and headed downstairs to wait for the rest of Manuel's family.

They had dinner in a quaint restaurant in the Kalorama section of Northwest. This was a section of the city in which many people of Spanish descent lived. The group talked at length about Washington and the adventure of living in New York City. They conversed in Spanish. Manuel's sister, Carmen, was a junior in high school and was interested in pursuing a career in medicine. The dinner lasted until well after 10 o'clock. The group bid its good-byes in front of the large ivy covered dormitory. Eduardo and Manuel were left alone to begin their college days.

Over the months, the two young men were inseparable. They both tried out for the Junior Varsity Soccer team. They both made the team and found that their leisure time was at a minimum. Time not spent studying was spent practicing soccer or participating in the many trips that the team made on weekends to play opponents. Eduardo particularly enjoyed the soccer team because it allowed him to see much of the area surrounding Washington, D.C. Games were played against colleges such as the University of Maryland, the University of Virginia, and the University of Pennsylvania.

Eduardo was able to contact the young lady who had been his seatmate on the flight from Miami. They dated sporadically. But the relationship never deepened due to the fact that Eduardo had many secrets and little time.

Eduardo received packets of letters from Father Sanchez on a regular basis. These letters were a source of both happiness and despair for the student. He was glad to hear from his family, but he missed them desperately. His loneliness was underscored by seeing the easy contact Manuel had with his family.

He was overjoyed when Manuel invited him to New York for the Christmas break. Being with the Augustino family was one of the best Christmas's he had had since leaving home. The family went out of its way to make sure he felt a part of their celebration. They enjoyed showing Eduardo the sights of New York City and the surrounding area. Never in his imagination had he dreamed of such a place. Even more than the sightseeing, he enjoyed being with the Augustino family. And they enjoyed having him. Over the years, Eduardo grew closer to Manuel and to the Augustino family, spending most of his vacations with them.

He spent the summers on his studies at Georgetown. He wanted to get to his medical studies as soon as possible. He reasoned that when he was finished, he could return to New Savannah and help his father and his country. He had many conflicts over his enjoyment of life in America and the worsening situation at home.

It was while at summer school taking an advanced Chemistry course that he became a friend with two other pre-med students. The first was Kevin Pointer. Kevin had grown up in Davenport, Iowa. His desire was to practice pediatric surgery. He was a top student in biochemistry and had toyed with the idea of being a research chemist, but a clerkship the previous summer had allowed him to work with doctors who were pediatric surgeons and he had fallen in love with the specialty. He talked constantly about advances in the field of surgery as a whole and pediatric surgery in particular.

The second young man was Stephen Mossler. Stephen was a bespeckled blond man, who was interested in being a pediatrician. He had had an uncle who was a pediatrician. The young student had spent every summer while he was in high school working in his uncle's office. He had no doubt that he would finally become a pediatrician. He was an excellent Chemistry student.

The three young men worked hard, pursuing the accelerated summer schedule. Their friendship blossomed and after the summer class finished, they continued to see each other on an almost constant basis. They were often seen accompanied by Manuel sipping coffee at one of the outside cafes that dotted Wisconsin Avenue. They would talk at length about their expectations in their chosen fields. Eduardo, for his part, was interested in becoming a specialist in Internal Medicine. Manuel would chide all three of them saying, "You should all be lawyers. That's where you could really help."

They would laugh and reply, "The world has too many lawyers, and not enough doctors!"

Kevin and Stephen were roommates. They shared a tiny apartment on N Street, not very far from the campus. Eduardo and Manuel would often visit the apartment when they grew tired of cafeteria food and wanted to cook their own South American and Caribbean dishes.

Eduardo was on the Dean's list during his entire time at Georgetown. He was able to complete his pre-med requirements in three years. He applied to Georgetown University Medical School and was accepted in the spring of his final year. He was overjoyed at his acceptance and immediately wrote Father Sanchez, who promised to convey the good news to Eduardo's parents.

Manuel, who still had another year of pre-law studies, did not want to lose Eduardo's company as a roommate. So the two young men began looking for an apartment to share. They would move in at the end of the

Spring Semester. The good news was heightened when their friends Kevin Pointer and Stephen Mossler also received news of their acceptance to Georgetown Medical School. They threw a large party at Kevin and Stephen's apartment. The party lasted into the wee hours of the morning.

As Eduardo's graduation approached, what should have been a happy time for him was really sad. He knew that his parents would not be able to attend. He had, however, persuaded Father Sanchez to make the trip to Washington, D.C. Eduardo met the old man at the American Airlines gate at Dulles International Airport. He was pleased to see his mentor, but was surprised to see how much the priest had aged during the last three years.

For his part, Father Sanchez was happy to see how much Eduardo had matured during his time in America. The two men embraced warmly. Father Sanchez wiped a tear from his cheek. "My son, my son. I'm so happy to see you. I bring greetings from your family. They are very proud of you. You know they would be here if they could, but things are not going well in New Savannah."

They conversed rapidly in Spanish as they waited for the priest's well-worn bag to come down the conveyer belt. Eduardo had borrowed Kevin's car for the occasion. He gripped the elderly man's arm and guided him towards a battered vintage Volkswagen that was parked in the airport lot. The old man was tired from his trip. He would be staying at the rectory with one of his friends, who was a teacher at Georgetown. Eduardo noticed that the old man was nodding off as the lights of Washington neared.

During the next several days, Eduardo, Father Sanchez, and Manuel spent hours seeing the many attractions of Washington, D.C. Eduardo was surprised to find that the Augustino family had made reservations and would be attending his graduation, this despite the fact that Manuel would not be graduating until the following year. Eduardo felt honored that they would act as his surrogate family along with Father Sanchez for this very special occasion.

The sun broke on a warm June day. The campus was filled with happy soon-to-be graduates and their families. Eduardo laughed, but deep down his family's absence limited his joy. He missed his family and New Savannah as he had never missed them before. All too soon, it was time to make the trip back out to Dulles and to help the old priest who was Eduardo's link to both family and homeland, board the jetliner bound for the Dominican Republic.

Chapter Seventeen

Eduardo spent several weeks visiting Manuel and the rest of the Augustino family in New York City. Accompanied by Carmen, the two young men visited sights such as the Empire State Building. Time was also spent riding the scattered subways and taking the ferryboat to Staten Island. They visited Coney Island and stuffed themselves with hotdogs and cotton candy. They roamed the streets of Greenwich Village and played chess with strangers who sat in the broad green parks. Too soon, it was time for Eduardo to return to Washington. He had many things to do in order to prepare for the coming school year.

As had been done during his undergraduate years, Father Sanchez arranged for payment of Eduardo's tuition and fees. The old priest's luggage had contained almost thirty thousand dollars in U.S. currency. The customs inspector had not even bothered to question the elderly priest. He instead, had noted his collar and stamped the priest's passport, making the sign of the cross as he did so.

Eduardo and Manuel had signed a rental agreement for a three bed room town house on Prospect Street. They had looked at an apartment at first, but after discussing the subject, had decided that both men wanted larger living quarters. Manuel was still in New York, so Eduardo used some of the money that Father Sanchez had brought for him to furnish the townhouse. He was sure that Manuel would be pleased with the results. The two friends talked excitedly almost every evening. Kevin Pointer and Stephen Mossler dropped in on several occasions to applaud the new purchases.

Eduardo was proud of the townhouse when the Augustino family arrived in late August. He excitedly showed them both floors of the house. He talked at length about the various improvements he had made, as they stood in the center of the large living room and toasted the new home of the two boys. After dinner, the Augustino family departed for New York City and Manuel began arranging his belongings. He was happy to be free of the crowded dormitory with its noisy undergraduate occupants.

Several more weeks passed and, at last, the medical school held its opening exercises. Eduardo, accompanied by Kevin and Stephen, sat in the large auditorium as the dean read his welcoming speech. Classes started the next day and Eduardo and his friends settled into the medical school routine. There were hours of lectures, followed by hours of laboratory studies, followed by long nights of reading. Eduardo found little time to spend with Manuel. Manuel was busy as well, studying for the Law School entrance examinations. The brilliantly colored leaves fluttered about the Georgetown streets as the students studied into the early morning.

September and October passed rapidly. October marked the mid-term. The examinations were difficult but all three of the friends did well. They were celebrating at Kevin and Stephen's small apartment when the telephone rang. The call was for Stephen. His face clouded as he listened to the voice on the other end of the line. He slowly replaced the receiver. Five minutes before, he had been enjoying the success with mid-term examinations. Now he sat down wearily on the couch and began to cry. His friends looked on astonished.

Eduardo was the first to speak. "Stephen. Stephen. What's wrong?"

"That call was from my mother. My father just had a massive heart attack and was rushed to the hospital. They don't expect him to live. My God...My God. What am I going to do?" He grasped both knees towards his body. Anguish was written all over his features.

Eduardo knew that Stephen's father ran a small farm machine business in Indiana. Although Eduardo had never met Stephen's parents, he knew that they were his sole support. Stephen's mother had taught in a small school until a heart problem had forced her to take a leave of absence. Stephen had barely qualified for financial aid due to his marginal scores on the entrance examination. Despite his high marks in course work, he had not impressed the computer that figured financial aid. His father's business profits allowed him to stay in school.

The three friends made hurried calls to the airlines. The next morning they drove a distraught Stephen to catch his flight to Indiana. After seeing their friend safely aboard his flight, they drove slowly back into Washington. Kevin spoke as he drove.

"I hope Mr. Mossler survives his heart attack. You know that the cost of sending Stephen to undergraduate school was hard for the Mosslers. They mortgaged everything they had. He was almost ready to give up on coming to med school but his father convinced him to try. And then when his mother got sick, it was devastating. He went to the Dean for financial help, but you know that can take months."

Eduardo was quiet. He was thinking about the money that his father had placed in the Cayman Islands for him. Was this a time to use some of the money? He would wait and see how things turned out for his friend. He would wait.

Things did not turn out well for Mr. Mossler. He died the same afternoon while undergoing emergency coronary by-pass surgery. Stephen returned to class one week later. He was deeply distraught. He would not be able to finish the rest of the term. He met with the Dean. His mid-term grades, although passing, were not high enough to warrant financial assistance. Perhaps it might be better if he took some time off and worked. He could return to school in one or two years and complete his studies. Stephen knew that it might take several months to find a job and that it would take much longer than one or two years to save up the required funds.

Eduardo was concerned about his friend. He invited him out to dinner the next evening. They sat in a restaurant that looked out over DuPont Circle. Eduardo listened as his friend spoke.

Stephen's voice cracked with emotion. "I have worked so hard Eduardo. I have worked so hard."

Eduardo moved closer to the table. "I may be able to help, Stephen. I have a plan. As I told you before, my late father left me well off. I have more than enough money. I can give you enough money to complete the rest of your studies."

Stephen stopped eating and looked across the table at his friend. "Do you know how much money we are talking about? It'll take at least one hundred thousand dollars for me to finish. We can't even work during the summers. There are clerkships planned for the next three summers. Besides. No one has that kind of money."

Eduardo continued chewing on a piece of bread. He added nonchalantly, "I do."

"And you would do this for me? Why?"

"You are my friend and you have been good with me. I am aware that many of the students do not take kindly to students from other countries. You and Kevin have been different. We have been friends since we met in the chemistry class. Yes, I would do this thing for you. I would not even ask for repayment. We are friends."

Tears rolled down Stephen's cheeks. He could not finish his meal. He looked about the restaurant at the well-dressed diners who continued their meals unaware of his plight.

"And how would you get that much money?"

"I have it and many times more. If you so desire, I will talk to my advisors back home in the Dominican Republic and they will make arrangements."

Stephen sat back in his chair, his unused napkin in his hand.

"I will have to think about it Eduardo. One hundred thousand dollars. I just don't know."

"We have a few more days left of mid-semester break. If you tell me your answer in a few days, I am sure the money will be here by the time next semester's fees are due."

Two days later, Eduardo had his answer. Stephen had an apologetic voice as he agreed to accept the funds. That night, Eduardo sent a letter to Father Sanchez along with copies of information he was sure that the Father would need to open a bank account in the Cayman Islands for Stephen Mossler. Two weeks later, a young priest who was visiting Washington from the Dominican Republic sought Eduardo out in anatomy class. He handed Eduardo an envelope on which was written his name. He instantly recognized the handwriting of Father Sanchez.

The instructions were simple; an account had been set up in a bank in Grand Cayman in the name of Stephen Mossler. When he needed money for tuition and other payments to the university, he was to contact Father Sanchez. Father Sanchez would then pay the university from a church account. He would replenish the church account by wire transferring funds from Stephen's account. If Stephen needed monies for living expenses, then Stephen was to go to his own bank, which was Briggs Savings and Trust, and they would initiate a direct wire transfer from the Cayman Islands bank into the student's personal account. In no event was Stephen to transfer more than five thousand dollars in any one month for personal use.

Eduardo had done some reading and knew that this was well below the threshold that alerted authorities.

Stephen was delighted with the news and thanked Eduardo profusely, promising to one day repay him. Eduardo smiled. "It is nothing my friend. Someday I may need your help and I am sure that you will aid me just as readily."

The winter cold gripped the East Coast. Christmas was near. The Augustino family had again invited Eduardo to New York. Manuel had purchased an old Ford and when classes finished two days prior to Christmas, the two friends hastened up the turnpike. Eduardo had brought little gifts for each of the family members. He eagerly awaited the arrival of each holiday.

Father Sanchez had written that all was well in New Savannah, although newspaper reports indicated otherwise. He had thought about his home and family a great deal during the holiday period but he knew that it might be as long as eight more years before he was finally able to return. He was deep in thought when Manuel interrupted him.

"Eduardo, what are you thinking about/"

"Oh, nothing Manuel, just about home."

"You mean the Dominican Republic or New Savannah?"

Eduardo was suddenly very alert. "What do you mean, New Savannah?"

Manuel glanced at his friend. "While we were moving some things at the townhouse last summer, a box fell open and there was a passport with your picture on it as well as your name. I could not help but see it. It fell on the floor."

Eduardo grasped Manuel's arm.

"You have told no one of this, have you?"

Manuel was grim-faced as he spoke. "Eduardo, am I not your friend? Why would I give your secret away? And who would I tell? Why would I tell anyone?"

Eduardo settled back. For the next two hours he talked about the path which had led him to Georgetown. He was able, at last, to talk to someone other than Father Sanchez. He was no longer an orphan raised by the church. He was Eduardo Sierramonte from New Savannah. He told Manuel all about the Island and his hope that things would be better. He talked about the distress the United States embargo was causing his country. He talked about how difficult it was to like Americans as individuals and yet to hate the American Government. The car continued through the wintry New Jersey countryside. Soon, off in a distance, the New York City skyline appeared. Eduardo was spent. His friend said no more.

Eduardo's Christmas was extra joyous. He had shared his plight. Loaded with Christmas gifts and fattened by Mrs. Augustino's cooking, the two friends returned to school eight days later.

The spring semester was almost finished when another of Eduardo's friends was beset by tragedy. Eduardo and Manuel were watching the news one spring evening, when news of a small airplane accident was shown. The small airplane had been on its way from West Virginia to

Washington D.C. when a violent spring thunderstorm sent the small Cessna spinning into the face of a nearby mountain. The passengers had not yet been identified but the aircraft was registered to Authur Pointer of Charlestown, West Virginia.

Manuel continued watching the screen. "Say, Eduardo, isn't Kevin from West Virginia?"

"No, I know he was raised in Iowa, but his family moved to a place called Oakmill in Pennsylvania. I know his father is a pilot. No. It couldn't be. Probably someone with the same last name. Besides, the plane was from West Virginia".

The telephone rang about thirty minutes later. It was Stephen. Had they been watching television? Kevin's father owned the plane. Stephen was trying to find Kevin to tell him the news. Kevin had gone out on a date and was not expected back until later that night. Stephen would call them as soon as Kevin returned home.

Eduardo and Manuel were unable to study. They finally decided to drive over to their friend's apartment. When they arrived, they found Kevin busy talking on the telephone to the authorities. It had been confirmed that his mother and father were the occupants of the Cessna. Kevin was crying openly.

He telephoned his sister, who was a student at the University of Pennsylvania and as gently as he could, gave her the news of the tragedy. Stephen, as he had done a short time before for himself, called the airlines and made arrangements for Kevin to fly to Pennsylvania on the first flight leaving in the morning. The four young men sat in stunned silence and wondered why such ill fortune had struck each of the roommates.

Early the next morning, Stephen drove Kevin to National Airport for the flight home to Pennsylvania. He then returned to the medical school and went immediately to the Dean's office. Once in the office of the Dean, Stephen gave the secretary a note that requested ten days leave for Kevin. Stephen was too pained to concentrate on the lectures, so he returned to the apartment late that morning and fell into an exhausted sleep.

Kevin returned one week later from the burial of his parents. He had met with his father's attorneys. After all the debts were paid off by selling the house, there would be little left. The end of his plans for medical school loomed near. His sister would finish this semester at the University of Pennsylvania, but then she too would have to make other plans. The deadline for application for financial aid had passed. There would be no financial help for the fall semester. The relatives of Kevin and his sister could not afford to finance the education of the two young people.

He explained this all to Eduardo as they sat in a small café on Wisconsin Avenue. He was filled with emotion. "I have finished college so I should be able to get a job in a laboratory this summer. I can work until Katherine finishes college and then she can help me."

He knew that this option sounded empty. His sister Katherine was just completing her second semester. She would have three more years of school in order to finish her undergraduate degree. He was resigned to this tragic interruption of his studies.

Eduardo knew that Kevin did not know of his arrangement with Stephen. Stephen had been sworn to absolute secrecy under threat of having the entire pact voided if he discussed the arrangement with any other person. He was not quite sure of the manner in which he would make a similar offer to Kevin. He was not quite sure that he should. Glancing around the crowded café, he quickly paid the check.

"I feel like some fresh air Kevin. Why don't we go for a walk?"

The two men walked in silence. They headed south and walked until they were on a pathway that paralleled the Potomac River. They found a bench that was unused and sat. The trees lining the Potomac were showing the first signs of budding. There was still a hint of chill in the air. Eduardo opened the conversation.

"Kevin, you know that I value your friendship. What I am about to say is between us and must never be shared with anyone else."

Kevin nodded.

"I am going to make you an offer of a gift. There are no strings attached in anyway. I am sure that were our fortunes to be reversed, that you would do the same for me. You know that I am an orphan. My father left me a sizable estate when he died. I would like to share some of the estate with you."

Kevin looked at Eduardo. The look in Kevin's eye was one of bewilderment. "But…But, you couldn't possibly have an estate large enough to fit my needs. It will take at least one hundred thousand dollars for both my sister and I to finish our studies. Don't you understand that my father had no insurance? It was difficult for him to get a policy because he flew all over in that God damned little airplane. I can understand him taking the risk, but my mother went everywhere that he went. She must have really loved him, I guess."

"I am sure that she loved your father. They are together now in heaven. And you Kevin, Katherine, and I are stuck in this place with all of the problems. I can assure you Kevin, that money is not one of your problems. I have money for both of us."

"But how can you have that much money? It isn't possible. You are an orphan. The nuns raised you. How is this all possible?" Kevin stood and walked up the pathway. "What you are saying, Eduardo, is too much to believe. I'm not even sure that I understand what you are saying."

Eduardo put his hand on Kevin's shoulder. "Let us walk some more my friend."

They walked up the pathway towards the Chesapeake and Ohio Canal. Lovers, holding hands, passed the two men. An old woman walking her dog spoke as she approached the pair. The two friends hardly noticed the others on the pathway. The two men were locked in conversation. After walking a little further along the river, they turned and headed back to the campus.

The next morning, Eduardo sent a letter to Father Sanchez. Two weeks later, a letter bearing the seal of Father Sanchez's order and containing the numbers of Kevin's Cayman Island account, arrived in Eduardo's mailbox. No date was ever set for repayment. Eduardo need only to ask for help if he needed it. Kevin made a heart-felt promise.

Chapter Eighteen

Manuel received a letter from the Law School some weeks later. He had been admitted to Georgetown University School of Law. He had applied to several other schools, but did not really want to leave Eduardo or Washington. Eduardo and Manuel celebrated at a small Spanish restaurant that night. Each of the friends settled down to the task of passing final examinations. These examinations would begin in four weeks.

Eduardo spent a great deal of time at Kevin and Stephen's apartment. They studied long into the nights. The demeanor of each was in no way changed. Kevin and Stephen were each unaware of the role of benefactor that Eduardo was playing for the other roommate. The examination period passed and all four students passed their tests.

The Augustino family invited Eduardo to attend Manuel's graduation. After graduation, Eduardo spent three weeks with the Augustino family, enjoying New York. Eduardo then returned to Washington for his medical clerkship.

The second year of medical school was harder than the previous year. Students formed into larger groups, in order to study and share data. Two other students joined the three friends. James Mercer was married and his wife was due to deliver in late November. He had lost his parents, during the summer. They had been involved in a fiery automobile accident. He had two younger brothers and a sister. The younger siblings had moved in with James and his wife. Margo, James's wife, worked as a surgical nurse. Although, the family had received a small insurance settlement following the death of the parents, they were having financial troubles. Margo's salary was barely keeping them afloat.

The last member of the group was Catherine Brinks. She wanted to specialize in Pediatrics. Her father lived in the San Francisco Bay area. He was a ship fitter who had raised Catherine by himself. Her mother had abandoned the two when Catherine was eight years old. Her father never remarried. She was very aggressive; Eduardo grew to like her aggressiveness. The two were able to share ideas with the group and as they worked together, the personality of each seldom caused conflicts. Catherine was outspoken on all issues relating to children and appeared well read in pediatrics. She shared this knowledge with the other group members.

The group would consume gallons of hot coffee while reading over lecture notes and looking at slides. Eduardo took Catherine out for dinner on several occasions. He would have considered a deeper relationship, but Catherine was quick to explain to him that her focus was only school. She knew of her father's struggles and wanted to finish school and go into practice as soon as she could. She confided to Eduardo, that her father had recently taken an extra job in order to help pay the high costs of her education. She did not think that it would be fair to her father, if she spent time dating rather than studying. Eduardo understood and they rarely went out together after that conversation. He saw her only in class and at the study group.

The group was hard at work one evening in late October when the telephone rang. Margo, who had continued to work despite her impending delivery, had gone into premature labor. Her membranes had ruptured while she had been at work. She had been taken from the operating room, where she worked, to the delivery suite. James hurriedly excused himself from the group and rushed out of the apartment. The hospital was located just a few blocks from the apartment. He ran up the cobblestone streets of Georgetown, into the cold fall night.

James did not attend class the next day; Margo had made very little progress with her labor. She was having problems and the sonogram had revealed the presence of twins. Her course was further complicated by the fact that her blood pressure was elevated as was her temperature. The obstetricians decided that she needed an immediate Cesarean section after watching her for twelve hours. She was taken to the surgical suite where the procedure was performed. She had twin boys who were delivered almost six weeks prematurely.

Several days passed before her doctors diagnosed an infection in the lining of her uterus. The use of antibiotics failed to halt the infection. Reluctantly, the obstetricians were forced to perform a hysterectomy. She spent another ten days in the hospital and lay quite near death on several occasions.

The twin boys, meanwhile, lay in the neonatal intensive care unit, their tiny bodies hooked up to numerous life-giving venous and arterial lines. Ventilators assisted their respiration.

James was sick with concern and worry. The other group members did their best to comfort him. He studied little for the next two weeks. It was almost Christmas before the twins were released from the hospital. Her obstetrician had told Margo that it would be at least six months before she would be able to return to work. James was depressed further by this news. Margo had been the financial lifeline of the family. James talked at length to the other members of the study group. They were his confidants as well as study group members. He would most likely not be able to continue his studies next term. He would have to go to work until Margo was able to work. Fortunately, Margo's insurance from work would cover eighty percent of the hospital bills. The bills, for the care of the twins and for Margo's hospital care, might well total over sixty thousand dollars. And then there was the specter of supporting his younger siblings.

The young student looked forward to a bleak Christmas. Thanksgiving had passed. Winter was fast arriving. A light snow dusted the cobblestone streets. Eduardo had called James and asked him to meet him He had something that he wanted to discuss with James. They met, near Wisconsin Avenue, and with heads bowed against the winter wind walked towards the medical school. They entered the warmth of the corridors of the building. Eduardo sought out an empty room and locked the door after they had entered. He did not want to be disturbed while they talked.

Eduardo began the conversation. James sat quietly as Eduardo talked. "James, as your friend, I have been aware of the tremendous problems that you have been enduring over these past several months. They have affected your grades, your personality, and your happiness. It has been painful for me to watch you. You have held up well. With the approach of final examinations, I am concerned."

James was angry He stood up. "I don't need you to lecture me on how tough this fucking world is Eduardo. I don't need your lecture."

Eduardo held up his hand. "Hear me out my friend. I am not here to lecture you. I am only here to help. I am only here as a friend. I know that were things reversed, you would be doing the talking while I listened. As you know, I am an orphan raised by the church. My father, before he died, left me well off. I have an offer to make to you this night. I have more funds in my country than I could ever use. I am willing to share a small portion of these funds with you. Believe me, the amounts will in no way alter my wealth. I can make arrangements to solve all of your financial problems. I need only to contact the Priest who is my guardian."

James again stood up He paced the room. His footsteps echoed from the empty walls.

"What are we talking about here? Do you mean to say that you have enough money somewhere to pay for my schooling and to help me pay all these bills? Is that what you are saying, Eduardo? I don't believe you. It couldn't be true."

Eduardo pointed to the seat beside him. "James, let us talk an amount. Let's say two hundred thousand dollars. I can give you that amount and have the money available to you by Christmas."

James stared at his friend in disbelief. "But...But. How would I repay you? How could I ever give you your money back?"

"There would be no need for repayment. If, however, in the future you wished to return the sum, then we could consider it an interest free loan.

You could repay it under your terms. We know that you will be making money when you finish your studies. At sometime in the future we could discuss repayment. Who knows? I might need a favor from you someday. I am sure that you would just as readily assist me if I had an hour of need."

James looked at Eduardo. "You could be sure of that. I would do anything that you asked, assuming of course that it was legal." He added, "And all this is legal, isn't it Eduardo?"

"Yes. Yes. The money is legally mine and is untainted."

"I will have to talk to Margo about this. Can I give you an answer in the morning?"

"We will talk again after class tomorrow."

The two young men left the room and walked back out into the snow. The storm had gathered in intensity and a cold wind blew from the Potomac.

Two weeks later, Eduardo received a package from the church. It contained the numbers of an account, in the name of James Mercer. The details were the same as the previous packets that Eduardo had received. Shortly before the Christmas break, Eduardo handed the packet to James and wished him a happy holiday. James cried as he clutched the packet. He hugged Eduardo and then hurried down the snow covered street, looking back twice as he walked.

Chapter Nineteen

The spring semester was half way over when tragedy befell another member of the study group. The father of Catherine Brinks suffered a massive heart attack and died three hours later. Catherine took a week's emergency leave and flew to the West Coast. She returned, shaken and confused. Her father had only one small insurance policy and a small pension. He had used all his meager earnings to send her to undergraduate school. The added burden of helping his daughter through medical school had taken a toll. Despite being warned by his physician, he had actually taken a second job, working a total of sixteen hours a day. He knew of his daughter's love for medicine and he had looked proudly towards her graduation from medical school. He knew that she would have only one more year of schooling left and he was determined to help her finish. The effort had cost him dearly.

Catherine was consumed with guilt. She felt that her quest for her medical degree had cost her father his life. Eduardo invited her out one spring evening after she had been back in school for three weeks. They walked through the crowded Georgetown streets. She held his arm tightly as he guided her along the narrow sidewalks.

They walked towards Pennsylvania Avenue. The White House soon appeared. As they slowly walked along the fence separating the onlookers from the well-manicured lawns, Eduardo spoke. "Catherine, you are all alone now. What are your plans?"

She looked at him. "My father's death has left me almost penniless from a standpoint of schooling. I talked to the Dean but he said that all of the financial aid money had been allocated for the coming year. He suggested that I drop out of school for a year and work to save the money.

He would have no trouble getting me readmitted in a year or so. I could finish at that time."

She turned towards Eduardo. She was crying. "I'm so close Eduardo. I'm so close. It is so unfair. I don't know what I am going to do. I'll finish this semester and then look for a job. The Children's Hospital is always looking for students to draw blood and to do lab work. But the jobs are low paying. The hospital knows that students will work for low wages. It's just so unfair, Eduardo. It's just so unfair."

They continued walking. Eduardo began as he had on three other occasions.

"Catherine, you know that I am an orphan as you are now. The nuns raised me in my country. When my father died, he let me well off. I would like to propose a plan. You know that I care for you deeply, but this has nothing to do with the depth of my feelings for you. Nor should you look upon my plan as an attempt to change your feelings towards me. This is strictly a matter of finances. You have no one to help you. No family. The Jesuits will not help. It seems that no one understands your plight. I have a fortune in my country and I would like to make you a gift. It will take thirty-five, let us say forty thousand dollars for you to complete your education. I would like to give you that amount. Remember that this is not to be viewed in any way other than what it is. It is a gift to a friend. Despite my feelings for you, I know that medicine is your life and that it will always be so. I have understood that since we had our third date. You must take this money and finish medical school. Your father would wish it and so do I."

Catherine cried unashamedly as they walked. Passersby looked at the young couple.

"But how will I ever repay you?"

"You will remain my friend forever. Someday, I may need your help and when I ask, I am sure that you will help me."

They continued walking.

Two weeks later, a packet arrived in Eduardo's mailbox. On the outside of the packet was the seal of Father Sanchez's church. In the packet were instructions and the numbers to an account in a Cayman Islands Bank. The account was in the name of Catherine Brinks.

The students studied hard as the spring rains soaked the Washington streets. Eduardo noted little change in Catherine's demeanor. The other members of the study group were unaware of her pact with Eduardo. She, in turn, was unaware of their individual pacts with Eduardo. Examinations passed and the members headed their separate ways for the summer.

Eduardo had chosen a clinical clerkship at D.C. General Hospital. This sprawling complex was chronically under-staffed and the students liked doing their clerkships at the facility. Because of the shortage of staff members, students were able to perform many of the procedures normally performed by interns or residents. The students worked long hours, but they saw much and learned much.

Eduardo was just returning to the townhouse one hot summer evening when he heard the telephone ringing. He hurried inside the house and picked up the telephone. There was a great deal of static on the line but he could just make out the wizened voice of Father Sanchez.

"Eduardo, you must return at once. There has been a tragedy. I can not tell you the details on the telephone. You must make immediate reservations to return to the Dominican Republic. When you have your flight numbers, call me. I will make arrangements to meet you at the airport. Come at once."

The connection was broken before Eduardo could question the old man.

As Eduardo was calling the airlines, Manuel entered the townhouse. He immediately walked towards the television set. Turning it on, he rapidly switched the channels. A news reporter was giving the night's news. "We have just received word that a high ranking official has been slain in the tiny country of New Savannah."

Eduardo felt his heart sink. He clutched the telephone in one hand and wiped a sweating brow with the other. Ten minutes later, he had finishing booking passage to the Dominican Republic via Miami. The flight would leave at six o'clock the next morning. He spent the rest of the night staring transfixed at the television set, hoping to hear news about the disaster in New Savannah. He saw little. He packed several suitcases and left a hurriedly hand-written note. Manuel promised to take the note to the teachers at D.C. General the next morning. It said that he had been called home due to a family emergency and would contact the faculty when he returned. He was unable to contact the other members of the study group. They were off doing their summer clerkships.

Early on a humid summer morning, Manuel drove his friend to Dulles Airport. Neither one was sure if he would ever see his friend again. They embraced in the passenger area when Eduardo's flight was called. Manuel waved as the jetliner taxied out onto the runway of the giant airport. There were tears in his eyes as he waved.

Eduardo slept little during the flight to Miami. He had a two-hour stopover at the large airport complex. He watched sadly, as passengers who were unaware of his plight rushed to and fro. Many were on their way to board large cruise ships that were tied up in the harbor. Once aboard, they would spend a glorious seven days sailing to distant points in the Caribbean. Eduardo was also headed for the Caribbean, but his task was to prove much more difficult.

While he was pacing the waiting area, he happened to past a newsstand selling the latest edition of the Miami Herald. Large headlines caught his eye. He grabbed the paper and hurriedly handed the fat Haitian woman a dollar bill. He hurried off before she could hand him his change. The banner across the front page read,

"Minister of Transportation Slain in New Savannah.

Today, authorities in the capital Doloresville announced that Fernando Amando Sierramonte, along with two members of his staff, was gunned down early Friday morning on a crowded Doloresville street. The two assassins escaped on motorcycles. Capital police gave chase and in a twenty-minute shootout that followed, shot the assassins to death. Authorities declined to comment further but stated that the assassinations may have been the work of right wing religious groups or drug cartel members. It had been rumored for years that Sierramonte had strong drug ties. Funeral arrangements had not been finalized by press time."

Eduardo crushed the paper. His face was filled with fury. They had killed his father. They would pay. He hurled the paper into a nearby wastebasket and paced the waiting area until it was time to board his flight. He sat almost at attention during the flight. He refused a small tray offered to him by the flight attendant. After several hours, the airplane banked slowly to the right and Eduardo watched the lush mountains of the Dominican Republic race by. He felt the thump as the landing gear was lowered. Ten minutes later, the airplane taxied to a stop and Eduardo pushed his way towards the exit door.

Father Sanchez met him at the entrance to the terminal. He quickly ushered Eduardo towards a side door and five minutes later they were seated in the old Chevrolet. It was then that Father Sanchez embraced him and started the engine of the old machine.

"Eduardo, much has happened in the last several days. We do not have all the details, but we do know this much. Your father has been having some very great problems with the men from Columbia. They want to make New Savannah another Columbia. As long as your father was alive, there was very little bloodshed on the island. Officials were bribed, not murdered. Those who did not want to have anything to do with the marketing of drugs were respected for their opinion. The church was not vocal. It used the money given it by drug cartel members to carry out its religious work. The work was done both on and off the island. Your father had been concerned about his safety for several months. He wrote me several letters and sent me two large packets. I do not know the contents of the packets. They are for your eyes only. The stranglehold that the United States had placed on New Savannah was a cause of great concern to your father. He had met quietly with several high-ranking officials from the United States a few weeks ago. At great risk to himself, he had gone to Aruba for a secret meeting. I do not know any of the details. I only know that he trusted me enough to tell me that he was going. Several days later, he called me. He was concerned about his safety. He advised me that he was in great danger. Should something happen to him, you would also be in great danger because you are the oldest son. He outlined arrangements that I was to make in case your return was needed."

The two men were silent for many minutes as the old car moved up the winding mountain road.

At last Eduardo spoke. "What am I to do now? How are the rest of my family members? Are they in great danger?"

The old priest turned. "It is not the practice of the Colombians to harm family members. They are quite safe, I am sure. It is your safety that concerns me. A small plane will take you to Aruba in the morning. The airport in New Savannah will be watched. From Aruba you will go by boat to Port Ricardo. From there, you will be driven to your home. Most of your movement will be made at night. You will be reasonably safe until word reaches the people who killed your father. From that moment on, you will be targeted."

Eduardo nodded and felt suddenly very tired. Sometime later, he awoke as Father Sanchez pulled into the small churchyard.

"I felt it better that I let you rest my son. We are here now. I will have the nuns fix us something to eat. You must then sleep. When you awaken, we have much to talk about."

After a late afternoon meal, Eduardo showered and was soon asleep. The old priest awakened him at nine in the evening. The two men talked into the night and dawn was approaching when Father Sanchez started the sputtering engine of the old car. They rode in silence. Father Sanchez had had a more active role in Eduardo's father's dealings than Eduardo might ever have guessed. He had been a confidant of immense proportion. He had taken nothing for himself. Any money given to him, for his efforts, went directly into the coffers of the church.

The two men embraced near a hangar at the airport in Santo Domingo. The hanger doors opened revealing a small corporate jet. Eduardo shook Father Sanchez's hand and promised to keep him abreast of the events in New Savannah. The jet wasted little time in clearing Dominican airspace. It turned Southeast and sometime later circled Reina Beatrix International Airport on the Island of Aruba. The plane landed and taxied to a seldom-used portion of the airport. The pilots shut down the engines and waited until a large black car approached and came to a halt near the door of the airplane. Eduardo was soon seated in the rear of the automobile, which quickly left the airport.

They drove for a short while passing through several towns which lined the narrow road. The neat, pastel colored houses that lined the streets looked as if they had been transplanted from the Netherlands. They soon arrived at the town of Saint Nicolaas. There, Eduardo quickly boarded an ocean-going yacht, which started its massive engines and was soon on its way out of the harbor. After negotiating its way through the harbor, the helmsman pointed the nose of the craft to the Northwest. Eduardo was on the final leg of his trip home.

Part Three

Chapter Twenty

Detective Alphonso Smith and his team continued hard at work on the investigation of Doctor James Mercer's slaying. Leads were non-existent. His team included Homicide detectives Malcolm Sledge and Elza Major. The three men had gathered in Smith's office to discuss the investigation. Smith was the first to speak.

"Elza, did you come up with anything further on that car?"

"No, Al. Three different people living in Mercer's neighborhood all remember a blue foreign car parked near the doctor's house on the morning of the murder. There was one person in the car, and he seemed to be waiting for someone or something."

"How did they happen to notice the car?"

"Oh, the usual. One man walks his dog every morning and he noticed the car was parked about one hundred yards from the doctor's house. The car was there when the man left. Twenty minutes later, when he had finished walking his dog, the car was still there."

"Any time on the car?"

"The man usually walks his dog between quarter to six and six fifteen."

"What time did the doctor leave his house?"

"As best as his wife could recall, it was probably a little after six fifteen."

Smith tapped his pencil on the desk.

"Well, the time would fit. Anybody else see this car?"

Elza flipped through his notes and then nodded. "One old lady who lives on the same block says that she saw the car parked in front of her house when she went out on the porch to get her morning paper. She didn't get a good look at the man sitting in the front seat, but he seemed to be staring in the direction of Mercer's house. We checked with the newspaper boy for the area. He usually drops off the old lady's paper at 6 o'clock. The third guy was a deliveryman. He noted the car about six o'clock, too. He was dropping off a stack of newspapers for the paperboy. He is a regular in the area. He knows most of the cars that park there regularly. This one was not a neighborhood car. He said it was a Subaru wagon, probably mid 80's. He knew the make because he used to own one."

"Did he notice anything else?"

"Yeah. He said that the car had blue out-of-state plates."

Smith tapped the desk again.

"Hell, that could mean about thirteen states, but it's worth a check."

Detective Sledge spoke for the first time. "Of the States on the East Coast, Pennsylvania and New Jersey are the only ones with blue plates."

Smith smiled. "Malcolm, how do you know all that shit?"

Malcolm laughed, "It's just part of my job, Al. It's really no big deal."

Smith laughed. "And what's the color of auto tags in California?"

Malcolm chuckled. "Well, that's a little different. Some of the older cars have black tags. Some have blue."

He was about to continue when Smith held up his hand. "OK, OK. You've made your point. I guess working in traffic all those years is paying off after all."

The three men laughed and continued their meeting. Malcolm then placed a thick folder on the desk.

"I talked to the Doctor's wife and family. He has twin boys. They are in college in Vermont. They're devastated by the death of their father. They were real close to their father. They weren't able to add anything. I took it very easy with them. They've already had enough trauma."

Smith nodded. "I talked with the Medical Examiner. Whoever did the killing, meant to kill the doctor. He had at least sixteen stab wounds, any one of which could have been fatal. He was dead before he hit the ground. At first, the doctor doing the autopsy thought there might have been two assailants, but after closer examination, the Forensic boys concluded it was one individual. Whoever did it, was pissed. Forensics told me that the direction of the wounds indicated the Doctor was attacked from behind."

"You mean someone ran up while he was jogging?"

"Yes. That means the perpetrator must have been in pretty good shape. The Doctor was quite a runner. He was even in several half-marathons."

Smith nodded and wrote furiously on a small pat. Malcolm sipped a lukewarm cup of coffee as they continued.

"You know, I don't think this is an ordinary robbery or random homicide. I think that Mercer knew the perpetrator and that somehow he had pissed the guy off."

"I'm starting to agree. But everyone we've talked to says Mercer was well liked. He had plenty of friends. He was an all around guy. He was into community involvement. Volunteered all over the place."

Smith tapped his pen on the notebook. "Let's see what we have so far:

One—multiple stab wounds.

Two—strange car in area.

Three—Perpetrator was probably in good shape.

Four—no weapon.

Five—doesn't fit a robbery motive.

You two have anything else?"

"Not right now."

Smith spoke, "I'm going over to Georgetown to talk to the Dean. There may be something in the Doctor's background that will help us."

Major nodded.

"Let's meet back here on Monday."

The other two men rose and left the cluttered office.

Smith tapped his pencil on the desk. His mind was rapidly summarizing the comments and findings of the other two detectives. He glanced at his watch. He was due to meet with the Dean of Georgetown Medical School early that afternoon. He finished his paper work and headed towards Georgetown.

He was met at the campus gate by a uniformed guard who held up his hands. Smith showed the guard his gold Metropolitan Police badge and his hastily given directions to the Dean's office. The guard placed a green guest-parking pass on the car's left dashboard. Smith thanked him and drove slowly towards the Medical School.

Ten minutes later, he was ushered in to the Dean's book-lined office. The Dean, a tall balding man, stood and walked to the front of his desk.

He greeted Smith warmly. "Come in…come in, Detective Smith. Glad to meet you." He pointed to a well-upholstered chair. "How may I help you?"

Smith pulled his notebook out of a small briefcase he carried. "I'm not sure that you can, Doctor Avery. I'm heading the investigation into the death of Dr. James Mercer. Our records indicated that he was a Georgetown graduate and I am looking for a little background information."

A look of sorrow crossed the Dean's face. "Yes, yes. It's too bad about Dr. Mercer. He was one of our rising stars. He did his post-graduate training as well here at the Center and I knew him pretty well. He was an asset to our community. He operated at practically all the hospitals in the area. He was much sought after."

"Can you think of anyone who would have wanted to harm him?"

"Not a soul. Not a soul."

"Did he have any problems while he was here?"

"Not that I can think of. Of course, his parent's died during his junior year. They were in an automobile accident. James took care of his younger brothers and sister after his parents died. He worked very hard. He was practically at the top of his class when he finished." The Dean looked about the richly furnished office. "Nothing unusual that I can think of."

"Any other problems that you can think of?"

"None whatsoever."

"Well, Doctor Avery, I won't tie you up any longer." Smith rose from the chair and extended his hand towards the Dean. In his hand was a Metropolitan Police card, with Smith's direct line added in pencil. "It's been nice talking to you, Doctor. If you should think of anything that might help us find who did this, please give me a ring. My home number is on the back of my card. I'm on call twenty-four hours a day."

The Dean escorted him to the office door and the pair shook hands. "I'll call you if I think of anything, Detective Smith."

Smith rode slowly towards the neighborhood where Mercer had lived. The Southwest area of Washington had changed greatly since Smith was a young boy growing up in the same area. Back then, there had been large housing projects dotting the area. The population, mostly black, would sit out on the small lawns in front of the buildings during hot summer nights. They would pass time talking and playing checkers or dominoes. They would talk until the tiny un-airconditioned apartments had cooled down enough for them to get a night's sleep. One by one, they would disappear back into the crowded confines of the buildings. The old apartments were all gone now. The term used was 'relocation.' Smith's family had been relocated as well. They had been moved to a new project in Southeast, called Stoddard Terrace. The new project sat on a hill overlooking the D.C. Coliseum. Nearby was a field of unused ground, which would one day be the home of RFK Stadium.

Alphonso Smith had escaped. His football talent had won him a scholarship to Morgan State, a historically Black college in Baltimore. He had received his degree four years later and joined the Army. After serving a tour in Vietnam, he joined the D.C. Police Force and rose rapidly through the ranks. He was respected by people on both sides of the law. He often met his old friends while in the course of investigating cases. Some were even suspects. He still played poker every Friday night with some of his old friends, who had also escaped the projects.

Alphonso Smith was at home in the streets of Washington, D.C. He knew how to ferret out information. This case, however, was causing him to draw blanks. There were few clues. He knew that the answer was out there somewhere. The question was, where? One thought bothered him. What had an old Subaru with out of state license plates been doing parked in the neighborhood that early spring morning? Find the Subaru and its owner and he would have part of the answer to this crime. He drove on, his mind locked on the identity of the person driving the Subaru. But why had someone stalked the doctor? The Subaru might hold the answer.

Meanwhile, on the opposite coast, detectives were hard at work on the murder of Dr. Stephen Mossler. Detectives Eugene Robinson and Ed White had been following several leads in the investigation but were unsuccessful in finding real clues. They knew that the length of time that passed often determined whether or not a case was solved. The majority of cases were solved within days or weeks. They had been working on this case for almost eight weeks now. Eugene had considered asking for additional detectives to be assigned to the case, but the overworked department was already stretched to its limit.

The two had not really found any additional information about the Doctor and his friend and lover, Jonathan. Jonathan was not considered a suspect any longer. The two detectives had considered him a suspect at first, but background checks and the man's complete collapse after the murder had all but convinced the two of the man's innocence.

The detectives had reviewed all of the materials recovered by the crime scene team. There were no unusual findings. They had questioned the manager of the complex and were told that the automatic gate apparatus had been undergoing repairs for two weeks prior to the doctor's death. The mechanism of the gate had deteriorated from the salt air. The gate had been sticking, mostly in the open position. When stuck in the up or open mode, persons other than those who parked their cars in the parking area could gain access by simply walking inside. The manager was quite concerned about this fact. He was fearful of litigation if it were later proven that the killer had simply walked in through a non-functioning gate.

Detectives Robinson and White were re-interviewing a member of the Forensics team late one Friday afternoon. They had made several lists of objects found in and about the car driven by Doctor Mossler. Dorothy Wright was a forensic technician who was nearing retirement. She had made quite a name for herself in the department by virtue of her meticulous research techniques. She had made slides of the various bits of evidence. The two detectives and Mrs. Wright sat hunched about a slide projector.

Almost an hour had passed and the review was nearing its end when she clicked on a slide.

Mrs. Wright spoke. "We cleaned that whole garage and excluded obvious things. You know, condom packages, chewing gum wrappers. Things that are to be expected in that setting." She pushed the button on the projector's control column and a new image flashed on the screen.

"I don't know why this intrigued me. It's a business card. It was stuck on the wheel of a car parked five spaces from the Doctor's car. It had evidently fallen out of someone's purse or pocket. There was a small oil puddle that it must have fallen into. The oil completely obliterated any fingerprints. The dark areas are tread marks made by the car when it ran over the card. I put it on a slide because the address on the card was not a local address. The letters are smudged. Here, I'll give you a close up."

She clicked a button and the image enlarged. The detectives read the card, taking notes as they read.

Eugene Miller, Sgt. U.S. Army Retired
Specializing in Self Defense Weapons
1238 Jacobs Road
Mitchellville, Maryland20027
Telephone (301) 888-3022
FAX (301) 888-3021

Mrs. Wright continued. "I kept the card even though it didn't have any prints on it. I just thought it odd that an out of state business card would show up stuck to the tire of a car on the night of a murder. Certainly, if you are going to throw away a business card, you don't carry it three thousand miles and then toss it away in a garage. It may not be anything, but you never know. You just never know. It may have dropped out of the perp's pocket. From the condition of the card, it didn't look like it had been carried in a wallet."

Detective Robinson leaned forward. "How do you know that?"

Mrs. Wright picked up a laser pointer. "If a card is carried in a wallet and assuming the individual has a credit card or any object with numbers embossed on it, certain things happen. You'll develop the faint imprint of the credit card. We can pick up the imprint under a microscope or by laser enhancement. The second thing is that certain stains from leather or dye from money carried in the wallet will show up. We tested this card. There were none. As I've said before, the card may have been there for weeks, but I doubt it. People tend to pick up business cards that they see laying around. The typical person will look and then, just as quickly, throw the card back on the ground. I looked at the oil slick, also. It didn't have that many tire tracks through it, so it was probably no more than a couple of days old. This would mean that the card was probably dropped within several days of the murder, if not on the day of the murder."

Both detectives nodded towards one another. They knew now why Mrs. Wright had gotten her reputation of "Witty Wright". She was brilliant when it came to piecing bits of evidence together. The detectives gathered up their notes and thanked Mrs. Wright.

"We have a couple of telephone calls to make. We'll get back to you as soon as we contact this Sergeant Miller. Maybe he was visiting and dropped one of his cards. You never know in this business. You never know."

It took the two detectives almost a week to contact Sgt. Miller. He was out on the road working several sports conventions. It was almost 11:30 p.m. Eastern time, when Detective Robinson was able to make contact.

"Hello. This is Sergeant Miller. How may I help you?"

"Hello, Sergeant Miller. This is Detective Eugene Robinson of the Los Angeles Police Department. Sorry to bother you at this time of the night, but I know that you have been a busy man."

A sleep filled voice on the other end of the line answered. "No problem at all. What can I do for you."

"We were wondering if you had been on the West Coast, say in the last three months?"

"No, I don't work the West Coast. I stick to the East Coast. I drive up and down the East Coast. There's usually a show every one or two weeks. I usually sleep over at one of my old Army buddies. Sometimes, I even shack up at one of the Army bases. You know how we NCO's are. We look out for one another even after we get out of the service."

"So, you haven't been out this way in quite a while."

"Well, the closest I came to the West Coast was about eighteen months ago. I have a brother in Denver. Spent some time with him and his family. Never did get down to the Los Angeles area. Can you tell me what this is all about Detective Robinson?"

"Yes, Sergeant. We found one of your business cards near a murder scene. We think that someone who visited one of the shows you participated in probably picked up one of your cards and carried it with him when he came back to California. We found the card in a parking garage. Someone probably dropped it in the normal course of his day."

"I give out about two thousand cards a year. You know how it goes. 'I don't want to buy anything now, Sergeant, but let me have one of your cards.' It works both ways. Two months after a show, some guy will call and order a two hundred-dollar knife he saw on my table. Some days you win. Some days you lose."

"Well, I'm sorry I woke you up Sergeant Miller. I'll let you know how things turn out."

"No problem at all, Detective Robinson. I'm just sorry I can't be of more help."

Detective Robinson hung up the telephone and looked at the reproduction of the business card. He slid the exhibit inside a manila envelope. He and White would check out the Sergeant's story, but he knew in his gut that this was another dead-end. Another dead-end in what was becoming a series of dead-ends. L.A.P.D would have to keep looking. He was sure that they would develop a lead. They always had in the past.

The investigation into the murder of Dr. Kevin Pointer in Seattle continued. Detective Leron Baker and Edward Garcia were spending long hours conducting the investigation. They were anxiously awaiting the results of the fingerprints on the shell casings. Leron had called the FBI Laboratory in Washington on two occasions. He was told politely that the technicians were still working on the set of prints, which had been submitted. The two detectives decided to visit the home of the slain doctor in an attempt to pick up any previously overlooked clues. They were under intense pressure, both from the department and from the doctor's colleagues. Everyone wanted the case solved. The slaying of physicians was a rare event in Seattle.

They entered the Waterview Towers and went directly to the manager's office. The manager accompanied them up to the deceased physician's condominium. The manager opened the door of the unit and stood aside as the two detectives entered. Detective Garcia thanked the manager and closed the door. The apartment had been virtually untouched since the day the doctor was murdered. His sister had been given the apartment under the terms of his will. She was waiting for the attorneys to contact her. She then planned to sell her late brother's home.

Detectives Garcia and Baker stood in front of the large living-room window and admired the view. Sailboats dotted the waters of Puget Sound even though it was mid-week. The two men removed their jackets and began to systematically search the house. This was their third trip to the premises and they wanted to make sure that they had not overlooked some small clue. Each man took a room and made a thorough search of that area. When he finished, the second man entered and searched the same room for a second time. Thoroughness was the key to success in homicide investigations.

They had worked about three hours when Leron Baker called to Detective Garcia. He rejoined his partner, who was standing in the small library lined with medical books and journals. The doctor also kept his computer on a large modern desk. The computer screen stood dark and empty. It was a newer model. Garcia noted that Leron Baker was holding a list, which had been neatly folded and placed under the mouse pad of the computer.

"I found this list. I was nosing around the computer. Strange place to put a list. I think we need to get one of the hackers out here and have them open up the good Doctor's computer files."

The two men continued their search. As was their pattern, Detective Garcia searched the library after Baker had finished. He had been searching for almost ten minutes when something caught his eye. It was Doctor Mercer's college yearbook. He took the book from the shelf and began to thumb through its pages. He was half way through the yearbook when he encountered a tightly folded page of paper. There were a series of numbers written on a bank's letterhead. The letterhead read

National Bank of the Cayman Islands

Georgetown Branch

Georgetown, Grand Cayman

There were several lines of numbers and below the printed numbers was a handwritten date. March 1, 1973.

120-06-59-206-18-301

80-1608-59-207-19-302

In clearly legible handwriting was an amount—$150,000 US.

Garcia tapped the paper with his finger. He called to his partner. "It looks like we know where the good doctor had the money that he needed for his education stashed. The question is where did he get the money from in the first place? And why was it in a numbered account in the Cayman Islands?"

Detective Baker smiled. "I wonder how much he has left in the account? In 1973, he was a freshman in medical school. Now where does a freshman in medical school come up with that kind of money? I think we're in over our heads here, Eddie. We need to turn this whole mess over to the Feds. Of course, with the way they're dragging their ass on the prints, we might as well keep plodding away. These foreign accounts typically need a password of some sort. We'll see what our computer boys come up with when they get into the computer files. Maybe he kept the account password in the computer."

Detective Garcia nodded. "That would be the first break that we have had in this case. Let's hope so."

Detective Baker placed the letter in a small clear plastic evidence bag and Garcia continued his search of the library. They left about forty-five minutes later, carrying the small evidence bag.

Arriving back at the police headquarters, the two detectives went immediately to the Computer Crimes Special Unit. They met with Doug Curry, a bespeckled middle-aged man, known for his genius with computers. They outlined their problems and made arrangements for him to accompany them the next day to the slain doctor's condominium.

Early the next morning, the three men arrived at the Waterview Towers. Doug carried a small bag containing his portable PC and multiple diskettes. The trio did not want to actually move the computer, but instead make copies of all of the software and files the doctor's computer contained. They were looking particularly for access codes, which would allow them to unlock the computer's secrets. At this, there was no one better than Doug Curry. The detectives left Doug alone in the library. They resumed their search of the premises.

The detectives left three hours later, returning to the condo laden with large deli sandwiches, sodas, and coffee. Doug Curry met the men at the door of the apartment. He wore a broad smile as he opened the door.

"I think we're in luck, folks! I'm into the hard drive and I think I have the password you have been looking for."

"You can't be that good, Doug! You can't be that good." Detective Garcia playfully punched Doug's arm.

"Let's eat and you can tell me what you've found."

They talked as they ate the large sandwiches and the other detective continued his search of the premises. Crumbs littered Doug's tie as he gestured toward a large note pad.

"The doctor made the same mistake that a lot of folks make when they are composing passwords and access codes. They tend to stick with things they know: addresses, nicknames, ages, birth dates, pet's or kid's names. That kind of thing. If it's something they are very familiar with, they will use it. In this case, his access code was simple. It's the birth dates of his kids."

He then wrote out several numbers on the pad. "I read his file last night after you guys approached me. You know. I sort of got to know him. It helps if you have an idea of how a person thinks. That way, you can often figure out how he might develop his access codes. There is also the element of luck. Today, my friend, we had a little luck. As close as I can figure out, he had one access code for the account. Another for a second account, not in the Caymans, and a third code for an account in Seattle. It will be hard to access the data on the Cayman account, but we know that it is there. A simple way would be to try to set up a wire transfer, say from the Doctor's Cayman account to a known account here, using one of the three code words."

Garcia laughed. "We could always have the money wired to my account."

Both men laughed and continued eating their sandwiches.

"Medical students don't have off-shore bank accounts unless they mean for the funds to be hidden. Of course, the person who deposited the money may not have wanted the money in a U.S. bank. Deposit that much money and the government gets nosey."

"Yeah. They want to know how you made one hundred and fifty thousand dollars and you just finished undergraduate school."

"Of course, there may not be any link at all between the account and the murder. We just don't know at this point. We just don't know. We will have to keep looking."

The men finished their lunch and headed back to police headquarters.

The Oakland police continued their investigation of the murder of Doctor Catherine Brinks. They had been told that the complete DNA analysis of the samples might take as long as six weeks to complete. The forensic laboratory in Washington assured callers that the samples were being given top priority. The Oakland Police Department would be notified as soon as the results were available.

The team continued to canvas the area. They returned several times to the actual scene of the crime and revisited several of the neighborhood homes. They were talking to one of Dr. Brinks' neighbors one morning when they noticed a car laden with suitcases parked across the street. Detective Porter looked at his notes. There was a notation by the house number. "Family away on vacation."

The family that was now busy unloading suitcases had been on an extended vacation. He finished his interview and walked slowly towards the family's station wagon. They were still busy unloading suitcases from the luggage carrier atop the car. He approached the father.

"Good morning, sir. Did you have a nice vacation?"

The man, obviously fatigued from the drive, spoke. "Yes, but never again! Next time I go on vacation, I'm catching an airplane or renting a motor home. I am sick of motels! Sick of motels, I tell you!" He laughed, but grew suddenly serious as Detective Porter showed him his Oakland Police Department badge.

"Did someone break in while we were gone? Did something happen to the house?" The man asked with a worried expression on his face.

Detective Porter shook his head. "I'm afraid it's a little more serious that that. One of your neighbors was murdered."

The man sat a duffle bag on the driveway and stepped forward. "Oh my God! Who was it?"

Detective Porter watched the man's face as he answered his question. "It was Doctor Catherine Brinks. She lives in the house up..."

The man interrupted him. "We know where Catherine lives. She is one of our friends. My wife used to take her to the gardening shows. Dr. Brinks was always very busy, but she loved to garden. When did this happen."

Detective Porter read the date to the man.

"Why, that's the day before we left for vacation. What time of day did it happen?"

"Our forensics experts think she died between eight o'clock and midnight."

"Hmm. That would be the night before we left."

"We have been canvassing the neighborhood. I guess no one questioned you because you and your family had left on vacation."

"That's right. We left early in the morning. I like to get a head start when we are going on a trip. That way you are not tied up in commuter traffic in every little town. Of course, the kids don't like it. They are usually asleep in the back of the car anyway. So I always leave early for trips."

"I was wondering, Mr....I didn't get you name, sir."

"George Roberts."

"I was wondering, Mr. Roberts, if you might have noticed anything strange the night before you left for your vacation. I wouldn't think so. You were probably busy packing."

"You know, officer, now that you mention it, I did notice one thing. In fact, I told my wife about it and wrote it down on a piece of paper."

"Wrote it down on a piece of paper?"

"Yes, yes. I was loading the bags. I always load the bags the night before. My wife packs the stuff, but I load the bags. I find that I can save an hour if I'm all loaded and the car is gassed up the night before. Well, I'm getting a little off the track, here. Anyway, I was loading the bags that night and I noticed a blue Subaru wagon driving slowly up and down Saroni. I didn't think much of it at first. People often get lost up in these hills. Some of the houses are set back and not all of the houses have prominent house numbers. What normally happens is that after looking for a while, the lost drivers will usually pull off to the side and ask directions from the first person they see. The driver of that car didn't stop. I was pretty sure that he saw me. Even though it is pretty dark up here, our house is near one of the few streetlights in the area. As I was saying, I'm loading bags and I see this car pass up and down. It must have rolled by at least four or five times. On one of its passes I got a look at the license number. Well, not all of the number, but I got the state and first three letters. The state was easy because there was a big keystone in the center of the license plate. That could only be Pennsylvania. You know, 'The Keystone State'. I saw the first three letters clearly, but the fog was beginning to roll in so I never got a good look at the last three numbers. They are in the glove compartment, if you would like to look."

"Yes, I'd appreciate that Mr. Roberts." Porter responded. His years of experience had taught him that with a talkative person like Mr. Roberts, you often got more information by just letting him ramble than by asking pointed questions.

The man opened the glove compartment of his car. A large bundle of well used road maps accompanied by napkins and drinking straws fell onto the floor of the car. He looked up apologetically.

"Vacation, you know. Stuff just collects while you're riding. Ah...Here it is."

He handed a slip of paper to the detective. Written on the paper were the letters "PA TLC".

"The letters were easy to remember. TLC–Tender Loving Care."

The two men talked for a while and finally Detective Porter thanked the man. He assured him that the Department would keep in touch. Once inside the unmarked police car, he picked up the radio handset and asked the operator to be patched through to Chief Dobson's office. They discussed this latest clue as Detective Porter descended the steeply angled road that lead from the Oakland Hills.

They finally had gotten another clue. Porter was somewhat frustrated by the fact that the paper which he held had only three letters written on it. The fact that Mr. Roberts had been alert enough to write down the letters might help the Oakland Police Department solve the case of Doctor Brinks' murder in the long run. The detectives would continue to sift through the evidence as they attempted to solve the case.

Chapter Twenty-one

Samuel drove West on the Pennsylvania Turnpike. The sun shown brilliantly on the countryside. It was Spring. The sunlight fell on the rear of the blue station wagon. Its rays lit the reflective paint of the car's license plate. The letters seemed to glow. TLC 663. Samuel was in no hurry. He drove through Pennsylvania and on into Ohio. He pulled off at a rest stop in Ohio and dozed for several hours. He woke up and remembered that he had not taken his pills. He went into the bathroom of the rest area and splashed cold water over his face. Cupping his hands, he took three of the pills from the new bottle of medication Dr. Eaglin had prescribed for him.

After swallowing the pills and drying his face, he looked in the mirror. There was a light growth of hair over his face. He realized that he had not shaved for three days. His eyes peeped out at him from the mirror. They were reddened from sleeping and from driving. He looked older. Samuel realized that he was hungry. At the next stop, he pulled off the Turnpike. He filled the car up with gas and had a large cheeseburger, fries, and a cup of coffee. He walked slowly back to the car. Cars whizzed by on each side of the service area. A spring chill was beginning to come, brought on by the sun falling from the western sky.

Samuel drove on into the night. From time to time he would adjust the knobs of the radio. He listened to the news, but as the towns and cities passed by, the radio station would fade. He talked for hours with Stacey and Claudette. Mrs. Donatto often joined the conversations. Samuel was totally involved with these conversations with the dead. The miles passed. He left the country's urbanized middle section and was soon driving through Iowa and Nebraska. His features were gaunt. A thickening black beard covered his face. He had not showered or washed for several days. He ate little. The front seat of the car was littered with candy wrappers. Empty soda cans rolled around on the floor of the car. He would occasionally pull into a rest stop and doze fitfully. He would use the bathroom, swallow several pills, and begin again. He stopped for gas as the gauge approached empty. The engine of the tiny Subaru purred as the landscape passed.

Samuel had been driving and dozing for three days. His wrinkled clothing hung from his body. Fellow travelers looked at him cautiously as he walked through the rest areas. Miles swept past the windows of the car. Signs welcoming travelers to places such as Cheyenne, Rawlings, Fort Bridger, and Ogden appeared and fell behind as Samuel headed west. Samuel now talked constantly with Stacey and Claudette. The radio was left unplayed. He was going to see the three doctors. He was going to see if they knew why Stacey was sick. He was going to see the doctors. He was going to see when they would let Stacey out of the hospital. He knew that the doctors would know. He knew that they would know.

The sun was climbing in the eastern sky when Samuel found himself in Wendover, Nevada. He had driven through the night. He was tired. He saw a sign advertising a Motel 8. He left the freeway and pulled into the parking lot. Although it was still early in the morning, heat shimmered off the salt flats that surrounded the area. The early morning sky was cloudless. He paid the attendant for two days' stay. The attendant looked at the crumpled twenty-dollar bills handed to him by the red-eyed traveler. The traveler's clothes were as crumpled as the money that he placed on the counter. A stench drifted from his body. His reddened eyes peered out from sunken sockets.

Samuel unloaded his bags from the car and walked towards his room. He entered the tiny room. As he looked around, he was suddenly reminded of his room in the Leesburg Psychiatric and Neurological Center. The furniture reminded him of the hospital. The disinfectant's scent and stale cigarette smoke lingered in the air. Samuel did not unpack his suitcase. He showered and fell naked across the bed.

Thirty-six hours passed before he awoke. He was dizzy and his throat was filled with the taste of vomit. He realized that he had been sick. He was probably taking too much medicine. He would have to stop taking the medicine. The medicine was making him sick. Dr. Eaglin must have given him the wrong medicine this time. He was sure of it. Why else would he be sick? He wanted to throw the bottles into the wastebasket in the bathroom, but decided against it. He would keep his pills, but he would only take them if he felt better.

He showered and put on clean clothing. He was suddenly hungry. He ate a large hamburger at a small restaurant near the motel. The waitress watched him warily. Samuel did not notice the furtive glances of the other diners. He paid for his hamburger and walked unsteadily out into the hot desert air.

Samuel continued west. He was in the West now. Snow-capped mountains stood in the distance. The harsh desert landscape, which was just emerging from the winter's grasp, passed by the windshield. He began to see signs by the side of the road. "RENO 112 MILES", "RENO 40 MILES". "WELCOME TO RENO, THE BIGGEST LITTLE TOWN IN THE WEST".

Night had fallen. He saw the sidewalks lined with crowds of people. The mass of people walked quickly from casino to casino. It was Friday night. Cars honked their horns at his small blue car as he drove slowly through the downtown area. Neon lights flashed. He decided that he would spend the night here. He found a motel. Its neon sign proclaiming "Vacancy".

He pulled into the crowded parking lot, paid in advance and was soon settling into another small room. He had not taken his medicine in several days. He unwrapped a plastic cup that was sitting on the sink and turned on the water in the well-used sink. He swallowed three pills and washed the bitter medicine down with a glass of heavily chlorinated water. He took a long hot shower. The warm water seemed to soothe his cramped muscles. His headache, which had been pounding when he arrived, relented.

He quickly dressed and strolled out among the gamblers. He entered a large casino. A din greeted him. The sounds of coins striking the sides of the metal machines mixed with the ringing of bells. Shouts filled the air as gamblers proclaimed their luck. Samuel was overcome by the activity. He jostled several patrons as he ran towards the exit. Sweat ran down his face and he gasped for air. He walked unsteadily back to his motel. He lay down on the bed fully clothed.

It was morning when he awoke. A cleaning lady was knocking on the door. It was eleven o'clock. Would he be vacating the room? Samuel staggered to the sink and turned on the cold water. He splashed the frigid liquid on his face. Drops ran down the yellowing mirror. He held on to the sink tightly. He was dizzy. The medicine had made him sick again. He would have to stop taking those pills.

He repacked his small suitcase and was soon driving slowly through the streets of Reno. The throngs of gamblers who had been present the night before were gone. The neon lights had lost their glow. Bits of paper blew across the street. Cigarette butts lined the sidewalks.

He saw a sign that read "Highway 80 West.". He turned onto the on-ramp. He was soon surrounded by mountains. The flanks of the mountains seemed to throw themselves at the roads. A roaring river ran beside the road. Railroad tracks, which shared the river's course, led further into the mountains. Samuel continued west. He drove for almost an hour and then pulled into a rest area. From the glove compartment, he took out a map. He gazed intently at the map. He would soon reach a turn-off that would take him south towards Lake Tahoe. From there, he would find Highway 50. This would take him to Placerville and the Mother Lode Country. He would finally see the places he had read about while he was alone at Mrs. Donatto's house. He would finally see the West.

Samuel drove slowly. He stopped for lunch at a restaurant that overlooked Lake Tahoe. He walked around the edge of the lake.

Weekend boaters roared about the waters of the deep blue lake. Weekend visitors, many with campers in tow, drove slowly along the many roadways lining the area. Above the lake, Samuel could see the snow-capped mountains. Many of the mountaintops would remain cloaked in snow for most of the year.

It was late afternoon when Samuel started his trip down the mountains. Placerville was less than one hundred miles away. He would have to find a place to stay. He would not stay long. He still had to see the doctors. The doctors had taken care of Stacey. Would they be able to help his little girl? Would they be able to help Stacey?

Samuel found the small town of Placerville. Placerville was built on the sloping sides of ravines. It was interspersed with tiny, narrow streets that made their way up the sides of the ravines. The small houses seemed to cling to the sides of the steep hills. In keeping with its old West heritage, it had proudly kept the name "Old Hangtown" as its nickname. People strutted about the narrow streets. The men, as well as some of the women, wore western attire. Small shops offered western gear and yet another shop sold gold panning equipment. There was a friendly air about the town. Samuel found a small hotel and paid for three nights' lodging. He would not be staying long this time, but would perhaps come back after he saw the doctors.

Samuel spent the next three days riding around the area. He saw the riverbed where gold had been discovered in 1848. He visited the river's edges and watched men panning for gold. He spoke to several men who were crouched near the cold roaring river shaking large metal pans in a search for the elusive gold nuggets. Samuel considered buying equipment so that he could join the search, but he knew that he had a greater search to complete. He had to find the doctors for Stacey. He felt renewed after spending three days in the town.

He studied several maps until he felt that he had the route to the doctors memorized. He would go to Los Angeles first. He would see Dr. Mossler. It was noon as he filled the Subaru with gas and headed farther west. He followed the signs that pointed to Los Angeles and was soon driving south through the verdant Central Valley of California.

He had not taken his medication for three days. He drove for several hours until he saw a large gas station. He bought a bottle of soda and swallowed three pills along with the cold liquid. He talked with his daughter Stacey as he drove. He drove for almost seven hours until he realized that he was in the city of Los Angeles. He drove for another hour and found that he was in a city called Santa Monica. He slowly circled through the area, until he saw a parking space near a beach. He parked the Subaru and slept soundly. He woke the next morning as the rays of the rising sun were reflecting off the blue waters of the Pacific Ocean.

Samuel was hungry and his body ached from sleeping in the front seat of the car. He left the car and walked towards the beach. It was early morning. Joggers ran at the water's edge. Gulls circled overhead intent on finding their first meal of the morning. Samuel walked towards a long pier that jutted out into the ocean water. There was a small shop at the entrance to the pier. Samuel bought a cup of coffee and a bag filled with warm donuts. He found a bench on the pier and ate his breakfast. He watched the fishermen as they pursued their early morning hobby. A breeze drifted in from the ocean bringing with it the smell of salt and the presence of a slight chill. Samuel looked around him. To the east, he could see high-rise buildings. To the north, the beach continued as an unbroken golden strand. Out on the waters he could see fishing boats returning with their night's catch. Samuel stood up and stretched his tired muscles. He was a little tired but he knew that he had much to do today.

Samuel approached an old man who was busily attaching squirming bait to a fishhook. Samuel waited until the old man had cast the baited hook far out into the gently undulating water. He then asked the man for directions to the Marina Del Rey area. The old man did not look up, but instead, watched the dark line that disappeared below the water's surface some thirty yards away.

"That's easy young fellow. You just follow the coast highway south. It's about a half an hour from here. When you get to Venice, you are getting close. It's the next town after Venice. You can tell when you're getting close to Venice. You'll see all the weirdoes running all over the place. Have to be careful though. They'll run you over with those bikes and those god damned roller skates."

Samuel thanked the old fisherman and walked slowly back to the car. He drove slowly south and after a half-hour, he entered an area of wide streets and high rise buildings interspersed with shops and restaurants. He parked the car in an all day parking lot and began to walk towards the marina area. There were hundreds of pleasure boats of all sizes and colors. The area was near an inlet. Samuel found a bench overlooking the inlet. He watched the pleasure boats as they made their way through the crowded waters of the inlet.

In his coat pocket he found a crumpled piece of notebook paper. He held the paper up in the early morning sun. Dr. Mossler's home address was at the head of a list that contained the names of Stacey's doctors. He watched the boats for several hours. He then walked towards the street address that was on the list. He found the street with little difficulty. He walked around the building several times. He noted that there was a tenant call box on the outside of the door. He cautiously approached the door. He read the names on the call-box list. "Stephen Mossler, M.D. 1118". He quickly jotted the apartment number on the sheet of paper and walked back towards the Marina.

He looked around him as he walked. The gate to the parking structure seemed not to be working. It seemed stuck in the open position. He would come back later that night.

Samuel watched the boats sail through the inlet for hours. He bought a hamburger and a large soda later that afternoon and swallowed four pills along with the soda. He sat as the sun disappeared below the edge of the western horizon. Night came and with it a chilling breeze. Fog began to roll in off the water. Samuel returned to the Subaru and took a long stiletto from a towel, which had been rolled up on the back seat. It was evening and he watched as couples strolled by and as diners hurried towards their dinner dates.

He noticed that he was a little unsteady as he walked.

The condominium loomed in front of him. The parking gate was open. He read the numbers on the floor of the garage. He found number 1118. There was no car parked in the space. He flattened himself against the darkened wall near the parking space. He would wait. He waited quietly in the darkened space. In the dark, he became more dizzy. The taste of hamburger rose in his throat. He was nauseated. After waiting for what seemed an eternity, he saw a new shiny car head slowly towards parking space 1118. He crouched. The lights of the car sent a bright beam towards his hiding place. He crouched even lower. A dimness clouded his vision. He descended into blackness.

Sometime later, he aroused himself. The stiletto was grasped firmly in his hand. There was blood on the blade and his hand was bleeding. He hurried towards the still open gate. As he took his hand from his pocket, he dislodged a tiny business card from among the pocket's contents. The card fluttered to the floor of the garage and landed in a small puddle of oil. The uplifted face of the card proclaimed, "Eugene Miller, Sgt. U.S. Army Retired"

Samuel walked quickly towards the inlet. He hurled the stiletto with the bloody blade and handle into the darkened waters of the inlet. He was suddenly very tired. He found the car in the parking lot and was engulfed in darkness. He awakened after a short while and drove out onto the crowded streets. He saw a crowd lining the front entrance to the condominium. The lights of a large ambulance and several police vehicles cut a swath through the rapidly enveloping fog. Samuel turned at the next intersection and drove rapidly out of the Marina area. He drove until he saw a highway sign that said 405 North. He entered the lanes of fast moving traffic and drove North though the night.

Chapter Twenty-two

Samuel drove north for the next several days. He did not bother to take his medicine. He did not bathe. He ate very little. He would only eat when he was forced to stop by the need to put gas in the Subaru. He drove north through Northern California and was soon entering Oregon. He was oblivious to the beautiful landscapes that passed by the windows of the speeding car.

The cut on his hand throbbed and was soon discharging a yellow puss. Samuel pulled off of the highway and entered a small drugstore. He had not bathed in days and a scent of perspiration accompanied by the smell of decay from his injured hand surrounded him. Shoppers watched him as he selected the needed items from the shelves of the small store. Several women spoke to each other in hushed tones as he passed them in the aisles. The druggist hastily bagged the items that Samuel had placed on the counter. He offered Samuel his change, but Samuel was already on his way out of the store. An unwashed scent pervaded the area he had just left.

Samuel drove north. He talked constantly with Stacey and with Claudette. He would occasionally pull into a wayside truck stop and sleep for hours on end. Finally, awakened by the engine noises of the giant tractor trailer units, he would scare awake and continue driving. He neared Eugene, Oregon and saw a sign pointing towards Florence. He turned west and was driving through Florence several hours later. He drove along the beaches and finally pulled off in a town called Waldport. The area was beautiful and Samuel found that the crashing surf helped him to feel better. His hand was healing slowly. Gone was the purulent drainage. The swelling had almost gone.

Samuel was very tired that evening when he saw a small dirt road that lead up into the bluffs. The bluffs had a commanding view of the ocean and the surrounding area. He would be able to detect visitors coming up the dusty road when they were several miles off. Samuel found a small cabin that was unused and smashed the lock on the front door. Entering, he found several small rooms with a well-stocked pantry. Although he still had money left, he decided that he would rest for a while in the cabin.

The cabin was located in a National Forest. Samuel stayed in the cabin for almost three weeks. No one came up the dirt road that joined the cabin to the busy highway. Samuel washed his clothing in a nearby stream and dined heartily on the provisions that the cabin owner had left in the pantry.

Samuel had several concerns. He was running low on his medication and he did not know how he would get his medication refilled. He was also concerned about his hand. Although improving on a daily basis, he continued to have pain in his hand when he drove. He thought about his problem and decided that perhaps he should find a doctor when he arrived in the next town. He realized how much he had missed Stacey and Claudette and how much he needed to see the next doctor. He stayed in the cabin for several more weeks. He had now spent over a month in the cabin and the supplies were almost gone.

He left early the next morning and continued his trip north. In the next small town he found a clinic. He registered and was seen by a young doctor who was newly hired by the clinic staff. Although hesitant at first, she refilled Samuel's medications as written by Dr. Eaglin. She also gave Samuel a prescription for antibiotics for the infection in his hand.

Samuel continued his trip North. He was soon entering the state of Washington and he knew that it would not take him much longer to reach Dr. Pointer. It took Samuel almost two weeks to get to Seattle. The Subaru developed a problem with its cooling system and he was forced to wait in a small town until the dealer ordered the part. Samuel stayed in a small hotel and spent the time reading hunting magazines.

One morning he called the dealer, who informed him that the car was ready. Samuel paid the cashier in cash and was soon on his way north again. At last he entered the suburbs of Seattle. He was nearing the place where Dr. Pointer lived. He would find Dr. Pointer.

Although the young female doctor had given him a fresh supply of medication, he soon returned to his pattern of missing medication for several days at a time. On the days when he took the medication, he would gobble down a handful of the pills. His psychosis deepened. He narrowly missed having several accidents on the crowded highways. He ate sporadically. He clutched the well-worn list of addresses in his coat pocket.

He circled the city of Seattle and finally found the town of Waterview. It took him a short while to find the address on the slip of paper. He parked the car and watched the entrance to the building. He had taken the pills early that morning and was again suffering from dizziness and nausea.

He had been sitting in front of the apartment for several hours when he saw a car drive up. He thought that he recognized the driver. The man was somewhat older than Samuel had remembered him, but Samuel was sure that the man was Dr. Kevin Pointer. The car entered through a sliding gate and Samuel was unable to follow. The apartments sat on a high hill and Samuel did not want to risk being seen if he attempted to climb the hill. He would wait until the doctor left and then he would follow him. He reached under the front seat and felt the small automatic pistol that he had placed there when he left Mrs. Donatto's house. He cradled the pistol in his hand and inserted the shells into the gun's magazine. His hand was still sore and he had some difficulty loading the weapon. He finally managed to squeeze all of the bullets into the magazine of the gun. He waited for the doctor to leave the apartment.

Samuel was awakened sometime later by the glare of an automobile's headlights coming through the sliding gate. It was the car driven by the doctor. Samuel started his car and followed at a distance. The car entered the on ramp of Highway Five and headed north. Samuel was careful not to be seen by the car that he was following. The car's turn indicator flashed. Samuel followed closely as the car left the freeway and headed towards a town called Edmonds. A little farther up the road the car made a right turn and drove though a gate marked "Marina."

Samuel circled the area several times and then drove slowly into the dirt road. A fog was drifting in from Puget Sound. Samuel turned the car lights off and drove cautiously down the darkened road. He parked the car near a fence and stepped out onto the gravel. The fog had thickened, but he could make out the shape of the doctor's car, which was parked beside one of the slips. The doctor was intently unpacking boxes from his car and loading them on to the sailboat. The fog only served to heighten Samuel's balance disturbance. He knew that he should not have eaten all of the pills that day, but he also knew that he had missed several days' medication.

Samuel sat back in the car. He would wait until the doctor had finished packing the boxes on the boat. He awoke after a short while and, clutching the automatic pistol at his side, he silently approached the boat. He felt dizzy as he walked and he was very unsteady. He read the name on the transom of the boat, "The Spirit." He felt a surge of nausea arising from his stomach. The darkness increased. The letters were blurred. He mounted the cockpit of the boat and held on to the boom as he approached the hatch. The boat swayed and he felt his dizziness increase. He was overcome with darkness.

When Samuel awoke, he was seated in the Subaru. His clothing was drenched with sweat. He had somehow lost the small automatic pistol. He started the car and drove slowly down the dirt road towards the highway. His temples pounded and he could taste vomit in his throat. He lowered the windows of the car in an attempt to get more air. He was gasping as he saw the sign beckoning him to Highway Five South.

Samuel drove slowly along the darkened interstate highway. He finally saw a sign beckoning towards a rest area. He parked the car and was soon fast asleep.

He woke the next morning. The sun was shining brightly into the east-facing window of the car. Samuel climbed stiffly out of the car and headed towards the bathrooms. He washed his face in the small sink and returned out into the warming Washington sunlight. He drove down the crowded road for several hours. He realized that he had not eaten for almost a day. He pulled into a gas station and after paying for his gas, he walked over to a small fast food restaurant. He left clutching a bag of food. He sat in the car and ate ravenously.

He reached under the front seat and removed an old revolver from a paper bag. He had also placed a hunting knife in the bag. He loaded the gun and placed the bag under the seat. He reentered the highway and headed south. He had one more doctor to see.

Samuel was in no hurry to get to the San Francisco Bay Area. He took his time. The doctor would be there when he arrived. He glanced frequently at her handwritten name on the piece of notebook paper that he carried. He took almost a week to reach the bay area. He had been out of medication for six days. His long black beard now covered his face. Red rimmed eyes glared out at him from the mirrors in the restrooms that he used. He talked constantly to Stacey and Claudette. He carried on rambling conversations with the two unseen passengers. He was a madman.

After driving south for almost a week, he saw the signs that beckoned him towards San Francisco and Oakland. It was late in the evening when he saw the signs indicating that San Francisco was only thirty miles away. He drove into the darkness. The swirling fog that covered the highway from time to time slowed his speed.

He was nearing Oakland when he saw a neon sign fronting a rundown motel. Samuel turned off the freeway and was soon parked in a nearly deserted parking lot of the peeling building. He paid for three night's stay and soon entered the small room. Roaches scurried up the walls when he turned on the lights. There was the constant sound of water running from the broken toilet. He could hear the moans of lovers as prostitutes serviced clients in the adjoining rooms. The walls were paper-thin. He showered under a faucet, which would only give him cold water. The towels on the rusting rack had a smell of sourness and the corners of the cold tile floor were covered with mildew. Samuel was tired. He slept beneath the moth eaten blankets and did not awaken until early the next evening.

He dressed and drove around the area until he found a restaurant that served an assortment of Mexican food as well as dishes that he was familiar with. He ate a plate of chicken with mashed potatoes. He washed the greasy meal down with several cups of hot coffee and headed out into the evening chill. Fog was drifting in from the bay and the air was filled with billowing clouds of fog interspersed with areas of bright moonlight.

He stopped at a nearby gas station and asked for directions to Saroni Drive. In broken English, the attendant pointed Samuel in the direction of the Montclair section of Oakland. Samuel was soon driving up the winding road called Saroni Drive. Fog swirled among the Eucalyptus trees that lined the road. He could smell Eucalyptus and pine trees as he drove. There was condensation on his windows that made it difficult for him to make out the house numbers. From time to time, he glanced at the small tattered piece of notebook paper that he clenched tightly in his hand.

He thought that he saw the house number and he circled the block. He passed the house again. He noticed that there was a man who seemed quite busy packing suitcases into a small car. The man was still there when Samuel drove by the house for the third time. Samuel circled the block again. He parked in a darkened area above the house and walked slowly down the path towards the house. He held the knife in his gloved right hand. He had put on an old pair of gloves when he left the motel. His injured right hand had begun to throb in the cold night air and the warmth of the gloves made the pain leave his hand.

Samuel was short of breath from the exertion of climbing down the narrow pathway. He approached the house silently but was forced to hide in the bushes when the lights of another vehicle drove up the darkened street. The car passed and Samuel continued his cautious approach. Large drops of water splattered his clothing as he walked. Further down the hill, he could just make out the shadow of the man who was still packing another suitcase into the already overloaded vehicle.

There was a car parked in the front of the house that Samuel was approaching. He crept silently up the stairs of the porch. His gloved hand twisted the doorknob. The door was unlocked. He slid inside the darkened house. He clutched the knife firmly. He left the house running and reclimbed the hillside path. He started the engine of the car and drove quickly down the winding road. He was dizzy and it took all of his concentration to avoid running off the twisting road. Near the bottom of the road, he rolled the window of the car down. He flung the knife into a ravine that was capped by a large guardrail. The knife struck the top of the rail and sailed into the depths of the ravine. Samuel drove until he had rejoined the main road. He drove back to the hotel and collapsed across the bed in the roach infested room.

He awoke early the next morning. He packed his small suitcase and drove down towards a large body of water. He saw a sign signaling a turn to Jack London Square. He meandered slowly through the waterfront streets that were normally lined with tourists. The shops were not yet opened for the day. He parked the Subaru near the water's edge. He was exhausted despite having slept through the night. He shook the pill bottles in his coat pocket. There was no more medication. He had gobbled the last of the pills days before. Tears flowed down his cheeks as he sat at the water's edge. He missed Stacey. He missed Claudette.

Part Four

Chapter Twenty-three

On board the ocean going yacht were four men who Eduardo had never met. There was also a crew of five men, all of whom appeared heavily armed. Eduardo was introduced to the four men as the boat cleared the harbor. Marcellino Lucero was a middle-aged man who seemed to be the leader of the group. Miguel Aponte was the quietest member of the group. He seemed to be especially close to the members of the crew of the boat. They would approach him from time to time as the boat crested the waves of the sparkling ocean. He would nod his head and the crewmember would head off towards the direction of the wheelhouse. Madera Delacruz was the smallest member of the group. His facial features bespoke a strong Indian heritage. Marcos Serrrano was the second in command of the group. He spoke heavily accented English and was apparently not a native of New Savannah.

The five men had gathered in the salon of the boat and they began to discuss the death of Eduardo's father with the young man.

Marcellino was the first to speak. "We are sorry to have to meet with you under these circumstances, Senor Sierramonte, but your father has told us much about you and we almost feel as if we know you. Your father's death was a great shock to us and we are all saddened by his murder. We were his friends and business associates and he trusted us. We are here to offer you our friendship and the guidance that you will need during the next several months."

Miguel spoke, "We are also here to offer you our protection. We feel that the government is partly responsible for the death of your father. They did not guard him properly. You and your family will be guarded around the clock. My men will protect you and your family members at all costs. You will be safe."

Madera Delacruz spoke next. "I was your father's accountant. I helped him run his financial affairs. I will bring you up to date on the financial affairs of your family and will offer you advice in your financial and other dealings."

Eduardo waited until each man had finished and then began to question each member of the group.

"Why was my father killed? Who was responsible for his death? Will they be caught and punished for his murder? How are the rest of my family members? Where are they?"

Marcellino was the first to reply.

"We have a very good idea who the murderers were. Their identity was sealed forever when they were slain in the shootout that followed the deed. We think that even the murder of the actual slayers was part of the plot. The police seemed to know the exact escape route that the murderers would take. We believe strongly that their murder was part of the over-all scheme."

Miguel added. "We have reason to believe that there is a right wing group of men who have strong ties to the government and to the church who are directing the whole project. Their end is to see New Savannah rid of those persons who they believe have ties to the drug cartel. They will do anything to achieve their ends, including murder and kidnapping of family members."

"It is not a good country that you are returning to Eduardo. Things have changed since you left." It was Madera Delacruz who spoke. He was filled with anger as he spoke. "The United States has placed the country in a stranglehold. Our products both from honest work and from coca are being boycotted by the United States and those who are stupid enough to listen to her government."

He handed Eduardo a pile of papers.

"Read these and you will understand what we are up against."

The first was dated January 1975. It read.

"New Savannah—Travel Ban

Violence by narcotic traffickers, guerilla, paramilitary groups and other criminal elements continue to affect all parts of the country of New Savannah. Foreign nationals of several countries have been victims of recent threats, kidnapping and murder. This is to reemphasize the continued ban on all travel to and from the country of New Savannah. Since it is the U.S. policy not to pay ransom or to make concessions to terrorists, the ability to assist kidnapped citizens is limited. Kidnapping of foreign nationals has occurred in all regions of New Savannah."

Another flier noted that the continued policy of freezing all assets, which were owned by citizens of New Savannah, in the United States, would be continued indefinitely.

Still another flier stated that any company found to be doing business with the Island country would be banned from selling its products in the United States.

Eduardo read the notices and frowned. "The United States has no right to do this to our country."

Marcellino spoke. "You will see the effect that this is having on our country. We have millions of dollars to spend but have difficulty spending it. We are just able to bring in enough medicine and foodstuffs from our neighbors to the south to survive. Things are bad and getting worse."

"Of course, certain countries such as Cuba defy the ban outright but they are limited in their exports and have to feed their own people first."

"There is a growing number of people who think that if we get rid of the drug cartel, everything will return to normal. The question is what will we export then. Our bauxite is almost all gone. Sugar prices are at an all time low. Everything we grow now is consumed at home. Our once proud fleets of merchant ships have been all but sold off. It was impossible to find spare parts for the fleet. They sit and rust in Port Ricardo. Automobile spare parts are difficult to come by and the condition of our buses is deplorable. We have had several bus accidents in the past year due to the non-availability of spare parts such as brake linings."

"Do the Colombians not help us?"

"Columbia is much like New Savannah. They have plenty of money but no sellers."

"And who are the leaders of these right wing organizations?"

"There are several judges and several church members, including the bishop of New Savannah. Within the government, there are several senators who made their money years ago and then, after investing their ill-gotten gains in legitimate businesses, began to scream loudly about the drug cartel. They are hypocrites in the most extreme form. They are sworn enemies of those such as your father who have drug cartel connections."

Eduardo sat back in the chair. The rocking of the powerful boat was almost hypnotic. His eyes fluttered.

Marcellino spoke. "You are tired. You should rest now. We will wake you when we are nearing the harbor. We will talk again after you have reached home."

Eduardo was awakened by the change in the sound of the engines of the boat. He looked off to the right side of the craft and could make out the outline of the high mountain range. He was home at last. It was over nine years since he had left. He longed to see his family again. It took the crew another hour to navigate through the reef and they were soon tying up the boat at the dock in Port Ricardo. Eduardo walked towards the bridge and spoke to the helmsman.

"Why did we not go into Doloresville or into Port Allison?"

The helmsman swung the silver wheel as he neared the dock.

"It is not safe for you to land at either of those places Senor Sierramonte. They are watched day and night and they are indefensible should there be any fighting."

Eduardo was stunned. "Are things really that bad here?"

"Yes, my young friend, I am afraid that they are."

Eduardo was escorted to a large Mercedes station wagon. His luggage was placed in the back of the car. Two other vehicles took up positions in the front and in back of the large car. The windows were thickened and heavily tinted. It was impossible to see inside the car from outside. The three car convoy made its way along the south side of the island through Port Allison and eventually up the incline to the home that Eduardo had left over nine years before.

He looked around the estate as several men unloaded his baggage. He walked slowly towards the heavy wooden doors of the home he had left so long ago. The doors opened and his mother ran into his waiting arms. She shook with sobs as she kissed her son on both cheeks. Eduardo cried as they embraced. They were joined by the twins Katrina and Miguel, and then by Trinidad and Semalina. They stood in the courtyard, tears falling into the dry pavement. Eduardo was home at last.

They entered the large living room and as they talked, Eduardo understood how much he had missed his family. They would be protected now. He was home.

They continued talking for hours. A servant who announced that supper was ready finally interrupted them. They filed into the large dining room. Several servants, who Eduardo recognized as long term members of the household, approached him. He embraced them all and then sat down with his family. The questions continued into the night.

Eduardo was struck by the changes in the appearance of the members of his family. His mother's hair was graying. Both Miguel and Trinidad had grown into tall young men. Miguel was twenty years old and Trinidad would be eighteen on his next birthday. Semalina was sixteen and had grown into a beautiful young woman. Katrina was the picture of her mother when her mother was young. Eduardo noted a sense of maturity far beyond his years in Miguel. Miguel had been close to his late father and he had adopted an air of confidence.

The women said their good-nights and went off to their bedrooms. The three men talked until the dawn was breaking over the distant horizon. They had much to say and Eduardo listened to all that they said.

Two days later, the four men who had accompanied Eduardo home paid the family a visit. They walked into the library and were soon joined by Trinidad and Miguel. The group had brought several briefcases laden with documents. Madera Delacruz stood in front of a large blackboard and detailed the holdings of the Sierramonte family. They had large amounts of money in banks of both Switzerland and the Cayman Islands. They owned many businesses in New Savannah. They still owned the shipping business, although the ships were titled in Panama. This allowed the ships to enter American ports although they were subject to search and seizure by the U.S. Coast Guard if thought to be carrying drugs. They had various holdings in Lebanon and in several Arab countries. They did not trust the Arab countries. Things were politically unstable in the Arab world. They had been slowly moving their liquid assets out of the Arab countries and into such places as the Cayman Islands.

They had arranged a tour of the Island for Eduardo. He would see, first hand, the effects of the embargo. They left the sprawling ranch house and spent the whole afternoon driving about the island. The once bright hospital was sand-blown. Eduardo talked to several of his friends who had finished medical schools in an off shore school in Grenada. They talked about the lack of instruments and medications. The Cubans brought some medications when they came to visit but they actually had little to spare. Members of the New Savannah community who made clandestine trips to their neighbor to the north purchased most of the medications in Mexico. The Mexican officials were under intense pressure from the United States to end any form of commerce with New Savannah. This included the purchases of even small amounts of medication by travelers carrying New Savannah passports.

He visited the bauxite mines that were running at thirty percent of their capacity. He talked to factory workers who told him that they had large inventories of finished products but nowhere to ship the products. They also were concerned about the lack of ships that would be available to ship the products. He visited the Baja airport, although the men guarding him would not let him leave the car. There was only one airplane sitting on the runway. It bore a large Cuban flag on its tail section.

He was dejected when the large Mercedes returned to the front gate of the ranch house. He invited the men into the house and they were soon involved in a discussion concerning the government of the country. How could they overcome the lethargy that was so evident in the places that they had visited? Should the government be changed?

Marcos Serrrano, who had been quiet during most of the conversations spoke. "I think that many of our problems are due to government officials who want to blame all of their problems on the drug cartel. It is time to take action against these officials. If the government cannot be changed, then the officials will have to be changed."

"But the elections were held last year and the Unified Party won by a large margin."

It was Miguel who spoke with a voice far beyond his years. "The church is actually controlling the people. The fathers tell the people who to vote for and the election is decided."

Eduardo spoke. "And who are these church leaders?"

Marcellino answered. "Perhaps the most vocal of the leaders is a young priest who was recently assigned here. He has only been here for a little over two years, but he incites the voters."

Eduardo looked around the room. "And who is this man?"

"He is Father Mario Deguzman. He is a native of the Dominican Republic. He has inflamed the public with his anti-cartel rhetoric. He needs to be removed from this earth."

Eduardo felt a chill run through his body. Could this possibly be his high school friend? "Describe this man to me."

"He is a tall man who wears glasses and is a fiery speaker. He walks with a slight limp, which he says, came from a soccer injury. He is about your age, Eduardo. He should be killed."

Eduardo looked at the speaker. "I think I know this man. We were friends at Puerto Plata. He was like a brother to me. Perhaps I shall have to go and talk to him."

Miguel Aponte spoke up. "It is not safe for you to visit this man. We have reason to believe that he is deeply involved with the rightists. He is a dangerous man. You should hold him at arm's length. He is often seen in the company of right wing sympathizers. He is dangerous, Senor. He is dangerous. The time will soon come when he will have to be dealt with. Mark my word, the day will soon come. He cannot have it both ways. He is either a man of the cloth or he puts the cloth over our closed eyes."

Marcos Serrrano spoke next. "We have reason to believe that he was involved in the slaying of your father. We have sources within the right wing and they say that Father Deguzman was involved in the planning. At this very moment, we are awaiting information that will definitely implicate your friend. In the meantime, I would avoid him at all costs. Once he knows for certain that you are back in New Savannah, he may take steps to harm you. Stay away from him, Senor, at least until we can confirm our suspicions."

"I will take your advice, Senor Serrrano. In the meanwhile, what am I to do now that I have returned home?"

"We have a group of men who wish to meet with you. They need a leader who can help them to solve the problems that have overtaken our government. They want to meet with you by the end of this week. We will meet with you again in the morning and over the next several days. You will be knowledgeable in all of our problems by the day of the group meeting."

The men entered the dining room and ate a large meal that had been prepared by the servants. Father Deguzman's name was not mentioned any further.

Various men briefed Eduardo over the next several days. He insisted that Miguel attend the briefings. He emphasized that Miguel was the heir apparent should Eduardo himself meet an untimely end. The two brothers listened attentively as the intricacies of the various businesses were explained to them. They were also shown tables of organization, which showed both cartel leaders and legitimate business structures.

Friday approached and the two brothers awaited the cars which would transport them to the meeting site. The transportation arrived and was actually an old truck. The leaders figured that the old trucks would attract far less attention than a convoy of newer cars. They were right. The truck arrived safely at a ranch that was located high up in the mountains. It had taken them three hours to arrive at the ranch. In the truck sat three men who had been sent by Miguel Aponte. The men were heavily armed and spoke little during the trip.

There were approximately thirty men gathered at the mountain ranch. Eduardo knew several of the men. They had been business associates of his father. There were several men who he recognized as cabinet members of the ruling government. There were a good number present who he had never seen before. The men seemed familiar with each other. Marcellino introduced Eduardo and Miguel to the various members of the group. They all expressed sorrow concerning the death of Eduardo's father.

Several more men arrived and the meeting was about to begin. The men were ushered into a larger room. The room contained a large oaken table. The men arranged themselves around the table. Eduardo noted that many of the men carried briefcases. He also noticed that three armed men stood guard at the sides of the room.

Marcelino rose to his feet and called the meeting to order. He introduced Eduardo and Miguel to the seated audience. Eduardo noted that Madera Delacruz was seated near the head of the table, as was Marcos Serrano. Marcellino spoke for only a short while. He then introduced Juan Medina who Eduardo knew to be a business associate of his late father. Senor Medina spoke at length about the hard times that were affecting the country. He also talked about possible solutions to the current situation. He was followed in turn by several men who gave their options aimed towards solving the problems faced by the country. There followed a long period of discussion among many of the members of the group. Options ranged from overthrow of the current government to the abolition of the drug trade. Each suggestion seemed to have its number of backers. Those in favor of overthrow of the government cited the current government's inability to get the United States to soften its economic embargo of the country. Others argued that the embargo would never be relaxed as long as coca was the main cash crop.

The arguments continued. It was clear to Eduardo that the men were divided most deeply on the issue of what to do with the current government. The men seemed to know that there were men in office who had made their fortunes off the drug trade. After making their fortunes and sending the money safely overseas, they had turned their backs on those who had worked with them. It became apparent to Eduardo that most of the men in the room still had strong ties to the drug cartel. He listened as each man spoke.

The group took a one-hour break and many met in the courtyard and spoke while smoking large cigars. Eduardo was approached by one of the older members of the group. He was Senor Simon Garrison Deluis. He traced his lineage back to one of the first settlers of the island. He had been a member of one of the wealthiest families even before the drug trade.

"It is good to see you here my son." He placed an arm around Eduardo's shoulder. "We have a very bad situation here. We may be facing a civil war before too long. There are many in the country who want the drugs removed at any cost. They do not offer any alternatives. They are not even sure that the United States will change its embargo if the drug trade is gone. It is a matter of sovereignty. What we do in our own land should be our business. We did not create the demand for coca. We merely allowed those who sold coca to use our airstrips. That we could have gotten so involved is understandable. We are too much involved to back out now. We shall just have to find new trading partners who will sell us the much needed products."

Eduardo nodded in agreement. "I am just returning to my home. I am not sure that I understand all the intricacies of the problem. I do know that the murder of people like my father is wrong. The killing must be stopped. I think that both sides of the drug problem need to sit down and discuss the options. The life of our country is threatened."

"But you must take an active role, Eduardo. You have spent years among the Americans. You know how they think."

"There is a big difference between the American people and the American government. The Government does not always echo the thoughts of the American people. I am sure that the people are unaware that our hospitals do not have medicine or that our buses do not have needed parts."

"You must help us understand the Americans better. You must help us to have a government that understands our needs. You must help us fight the right wing and the Jesuits."

Eduardo nodded his head and waited as the old man walked off into the crowd.

During the course of the recess, several older men approached Eduardo. The men had all been associates of his father. They voiced opinions similar to those spoken by Senor Deluis. They must meet with the opposition. It would be almost two years before members of either side sat down to discuss their differences.

The meeting adjourned long after night had fallen. The two young men climbed into the back of the truck and arrived home safely sometime after two o'clock in the morning. Eduardo slept soundly as he dreamed of Washington, D.C. and its quiet restaurants. He awoke the next morning and spent the rest of the day discussing the problems that were inflaming the country.

He spent the rest of the weekend riding over the slopes on a new horse that had been given him by Trinidad, his youngest brother. Trinidad had been left out of the meetings and as they rode the rolling hills together, Eduardo did his best to fill the young man in on the details of the meetings.

Trinidad had been only nine years old when Eduardo left for the Dominican Republic. Eduardo had grown very fond of the young man during the first weeks at home. He wondered what fate held in store for his brother. Was it too early to discuss sending him to Father Sanchez at Puerto Plata? Or was it too late? If the danger increased, both Trinidad and Semalina might have to be spirited off the island to safety. Eduardo was sure that the next several months would be critical in the development of New Savannah. His father's death had been only one of a series of events that would bring about great changes.

Chapter Twenty-four

Eduardo spent much of his first year at home learning the intricacies of his father's many and varied business dealings. He learned that his father had at least five foreign companies operating in such scattered cities as Brussels, London, Madrid, Panama City, and on Tortola in the British Virgin Islands. Income from these enterprises was deposited in accounts in Switzerland or in the Cayman Islands. The companies were all run by trusted managers who reported to him via mail and by direct wire service that was routed through South America.

These businesses were not connected by any direct paper trail and their ownership was masked through the use of dummy corporate names and organizations. He felt confident that his family would remain well funded in the foreseeable future. He did not worry about the legitimate businesses. It was the drug operations, which concerned him greatly. He considered ways to divest his family of the drug related incomes but there appeared little likelihood of this happening. The four Ms, as he had begun to call them, were at his side as he waded through the mass of documents and corporate flow sheets.

Marcellino was quick to offer advice while Madera tended to look at the bottom line on all transactions. His counsel was always financial in nature and he did not appear to be bothered by the social consequences of various dealings. Miguel Aponte appeared to be the most ruthless of the four men and urged violence as the solution to many of the problems. Marcos Serrano, while second in command, added balance to the group. He evaluated both sides of the opinions offered by the other men and usually took a course that was midway between the extremes.

The larger group of men met on a monthly basis and discussed the directions that New Savannah was taking. There was repeated concern about Father Mario Deguzman and about the effect that he was having on the population as a whole. Near the end of the first year, there was an event that served to polarize the two forces even further.

A large jetliner that was carrying a great deal of coca destined for a transshipment point in the Bahamas was attacked at the Baja Airport. A group of twenty men, heavily armed and wearing camouflage clothing, shot its way into the air terminal. The group killed the guards around the airplane and then blew up the airplane and its cargo. In the melee, stray bullets killed several German tourists. As a result of the death of the tourists, Germany barred its citizens from visiting new Savannah.

Reprisals were quickly carried out. Five days later, a car carrying the deputy judge of the Customs Court was ambushed and its passengers slain. It had been rumored that the judge had strong ties to right wing sympathizers. Tensions were at an all time high on the Island. There were sporadic acts of violence by both sides over the next six months. Members of the large group, which Eduardo had nicknamed "Los Jeffes," wanted to meet with leaders of the right wingers. It took several months before a meeting could be arranged. Eduardo was chosen to meet with Father Deguzman to work out the details of a meeting. This meeting would involve the principal leaders from both sides. They would attempt to arrive at a course of action that would not only defuse the present situation, but would provide a plan for the future.

Eduardo looked forward to the meeting with his friend. They had not seen each other since Mario had graduated from the high school in Puerto Plata. They had taken different paths. These paths now placed them in opposite camps. Eduardo wondered if his one-time friend would be open to compromise.

Three heavily armed men escorted Eduardo as he approached the site of the meeting. The meeting was held in the town of Joansville. Eduardo noted that Mario had brought three armed men with him. The two old friends embraced and walked into the living room of an old adobe building that stood on the edge of town. Eduardo had been warned of the dangers that attending the meeting held, but had decided to meet with the activist priest. If there was anyone on the island who could reason with the fiery priest, it was Eduardo.

The two men faced each other across a well-used desk. Eduardo noted that Mario had grown thin during the past ten years. He wore the collar of a Catholic priest beneath a well-worn black shirt. He wore horn-rimmed glasses and smoked a small cigar. Father Deguzman offered a glass of wine to Eduardo. He poured from a silver container that stood near the corner of the desk.

He held his glass toward Eduardo and spoke. "To our friendship and to our days together in Puerto Plata."

The two men touched glasses and each swallowed the sweet liquid.

Eduardo opened the conversation. "How is your family in Samana, Mario? I hope that all goes well with them."

Mario's face clouded. "Things have not gone well for them. My father was jailed soon after I left for Italy. He passed away some four years later. The rest of my family lives in Florida now. I hear from them infrequently. Their mail has to go to the Dominican Republic. A Church courier to New Savannah then routes it. It can take months for word to reach me. My only contact with the Dominican Republic is through Father Sanchez. He bids you well. Incidentally, he is getting up in years, but still is lively and still drives the old Chevrolet."

Eduardo laughed. "I saw him about two years ago and was amazed at his stamina. He is an extraordinary man. He means a lot to me."

"And what of you, my friend? You have been home for several years now. Your movements are always well guarded, but you have been kept abreast of the events of the island. What do you think is the future of this land?"

"Mario, I grow saddened by what is happening to my country. The people are suffering through no fault of their own. I am saddened by the violence that is almost constant. I am not privy to all of the reasons for the violence, but I know that the anti-drug forces are intent on gaining the upper hand. I see little hope for the future at this point. Were drugs to be gone tomorrow, it would take ten or twenty years to rebuild our commerce and infrastructure. I think that in the meantime, we will continue down this path. I think that there are members on both sides of the drug question that have respected views. These men are making the determinations which affect us all."

"I, too, share your sadness Eduardo. I was sent to new Savannah because the church thought that I would be too much of a risk if they returned me to my home in the Dominican Republic. The leaders thought that I had been tainted by the politics of my father. Although I thought that the church was wrong at the time, I have come to accept their logic. I entered a country that was basically cut off from the rest of the world. The only other comparable land being Cuba. In the case of Cuba, there were ideological reasons. The United States could not tolerate Communism near its doorstep. The New Savannah situation is of another nature. It is fed by greed. The profits from the drug trade leave the country or go into the hands of a few wealthy families. In the majority of these cases, these are members of the original families who came here in the last century. Unfortunately, your family has been the recipient of much of this great wealth that has accumulated from the drug trade."

"Is that why my father was killed?"

Father Mario nodded. "There are groups on this island who want to see the end of the drug trade as well as the end of the drug traders. They are prepared to act through the courts or though the bullet. At this point there is little concern for which method is used. The drug involvement must end. As a church leader, I must speak out against the drug traffic and the drug traffickers. I have no choice. I am doing the work of God as I see it. I am ashamed when I visit the hospitals. While many, including yourself, live in luxury, the average person cannot get needed medications. The Catholic Church has sent emissaries to talk to the President of the United States. He is adamant. The current restrictions on New Savannah will not be lifted until the country divests itself of the drugs. I have little say in the matter. There are men both within and outside of the government who are providing the direction."

Eduardo poured a glass of wine for each of them. He drank slowly and then spoke. "And how will this be accomplished, my friend? Surely the killings must be stopped. What is the direction that the country must take to curb the violence?"

"As you are aware, there is an election scheduled in two years. By that time, members of the group of which I am a member will put forth a slate of candidates. These men will all be men who have managed to have no part in the drug operations. Backed by a strong paramilitary force recruited from those who have strong anti-drug interests, the scourge of drugs will be swept from New Savannah. Once the house is in order, we will petition the world for reentry into the world of the law abiding. It will not be easy. There will be many deaths along the way, but New Savannah will survive and prosper. Tourists will return to our beaches. Our ships will be welcomed in foreign ports. The landings of jetliners will overwork our airports. You will see, Eduardo. You will see."

"And what will you do after all this is accomplished?"

"I will return to what I have been trained to do. I will return to praying for the souls of mankind and tending to the sick. I have no other agenda. I could, of course, return to the Dominican Republic, but I do not want to be an embarrassment to the Church. One does not know. Perhaps by the time my work is finished here, things will have reached a point in the Dominican Republic that I can return to my real home and do my work. Until that time, New Savannah is my only home and my love for the land and its people is no less than yours."

Eduardo smiled. "And what role do you see me playing?"

"You will continue to be a voice of reason while continuing to divest yourself of your drug related holdings. You might even consider running for political office. Although not a doctor, you would do well as the Minister of Health. You have learned much at Georgetown that could aid the country. When things are settled and travel bans are lifted, you could even return to the United States and complete your studies."

"In the meantime?"

"The violence will continue until the scourge of drugs and those who profit from them is eliminated. We will await the elections in two years. Unfortunately, the constitution does not allow for early elections."

"But by that time I will have been back in New Savannah for almost five years. Are things to continue as they are now?"

"The groups will make note of those individuals who are making efforts to divest themselves. They and members of their families will not be harmed. It is a different matter with the others."

"And what of yourself?"

"I have been marked for a long time. God watches over me. He will decide when it is time for me to meet him."

The two friends continued talking for several more hours. When Eduardo and Mario separated, each took with him a better understanding of the other's point of view as well as the date of a meeting to be held among the warring factions.

Several meetings were held over the next six months. Little progress was made and the violence continued. Time passed and the date of the elections neared. Eduardo had filed to run for the Minister of Health position. For his part, Father Mario seemed to be everywhere, urging the people of New Savannah to use the ballot box to remove the drug connected politicians.

Father Mario had assured Eduardo that no harm would come to him as long as he continued his attempts to divest himself of his father's drug related businesses. He continued to do this, heeding the advice of "the four M's" as he did so. He realized that each of these men was well situated financially and that they wished to see some semblance of normalcy return to the island republic.

Eduardo, for his part was seen more openly on the streets of Doloresville. He still traveled with an armed guard provided by Miguel

Aponte. He attended several social functions and while at one of these functions he met Alicia Magdalene Doubleday Cortez. She was the oldest daughter of a prominent fruit grower. She lived with her family in a large villa that overlooked the town of Kissie Bay. Her father owned hundreds of acres of surrounding farmland and he was able to export much of his fruit, not consumed in new Savannah, to neighboring South America. A hurricane had wrecked most of the trees on the north facing shores of South America and there was an increased need for fresh fruit. Alicia's father shipped constantly to cities such as Caracas. He owned several refrigerated vessels that flew Panamanian flags. The ships were home ported in Port Ricardo.

The couple began to see each other regularly. The elections were approaching and Eduardo was kept busy campaigning. He found himself being involved in two campaigns, one for political office and the other for the heart of Alicia Magdalene. He was successful in both.

The election results were announced on a humid morning in the daily paper. The party called the Nationalist Democratic Party had been victorious. Although Eduardo was not affiliated with the party, and had actually run as an independent candidate, he had scored an upset victory. He was the new Minister of Health. Friends gathered at the Sierramonte household that evening. Eduardo thanked them for their support and announced his engagement to Alicia Magdalene Doubleday Cortez. Six months later the couple was wed.

Eduardo was kept busy during the six months following the election. He was sworn in at the large Government palace fronting the Center Square in Doloresville. He attended the sessions of the cabinet and spent considerable time visiting the island's several hospitals. He was saddened by the condition of the hospitals and clinics, but felt powerless to change the conditions. Following the elections, the violence stopped. The right wingers had swept the elections. They hurriedly put forth legislation that made involvement with the drug cartel a high crime. It seemed that the country was on its way to ridding itself of the scourge of drugs.

Eduardo and Alicia were married in the spring of the next year. Eduardo had been home for almost six years. He had a new political office and a new bride. Due to the severe travel restrictions, which allowed for virtually no air travel, the couple boarded the same ocean going yacht that had borne Eduardo to the island and headed to Aruba. Customs officials who were in the employ of members of the drug cartel stamped the couple's passports and they were off for a week's stay.

While in Aruba, the couple stayed at a brand new house. Madera Delacruz, using funds from a numbered account in the Cayman Islands, had left New Savannah carrying a large amount of money. He had gone by boat to Aruba two months before the couple arrived. He had purchased, with a cash payment, a three-bedroom house that was situated on the oceanfront in the town of Savaneta.

The couple enjoyed the freedom offered by Aruba. They visited the casinos and the beaches that lined the island. Eduardo bought gifts for his family members and for "the four M's" They made love. The week passed rapidly. The couple reluctantly boarded the large vessel that awaited them in the harbor and headed northwest towards their isolated and troubled homeland.

Nine and a half months later, their first child was born. The child was named Maria, after Eduardo's mother. Three other children would join the first child. The last child born, and the first boy born to the couple, was named Eduardo, Jr. He was the first son and was adored by his three sisters as well as by his parents. The couple had been married almost four years by the time that he was born.

The new family lived in a sprawling house that Eduardo had constructed on land that had been owned by his father. The house was located less than half a mile from the Sierramonte's ranch house. Visits by family members occurred daily. It was a time of happiness for Eduardo, but also a time of increased activity.

He saw Father Deguzman on many occasions. The priest warned him that there were groups on the island who were still not satisfied with the rate of curtailment of drug activities. A new election would be held the coming year and the new government was certain to enact more and stricter drug reforms. The United States, for its part, was unrelenting in its efforts to force the island to comply. Father Mario Deguzman remained a vocal advocate of drug reform.

The elections were held in the fall of 1985. Once again, Eduardo was victorious. Although he had done little to improve the health of the people of New Savannah, his presence was needed in the government chambers. The Nationalist Democratic Party swept the remainder of the cabinet positions. The ruling party, with its anti-drug stance, began to tighten the anti-drug legislation. The situation again grew tense.

"Los Jeffes" held meeting after meeting. They were beginning to get pressure from the large Colombian cartels. New Savannah was needed as a transshipment point. Indian farmers who lived in the high and inaccessible mountain areas were often caught in drug raids. The newly formed paramilitary task force, organized and funded by the members of the new government, carried out these drug raids.

Father Mario Deguzman was often seen entering and leaving the offices of high government officials. He continued his harangue against drugs. There were scattered armed clashes as the remaining cartel members began to strike back. They realized that there was nothing that they could do to appease the government leaders.

Meetings of the "Los Jeffes" group became more strained. Influential members of the group openly advocated overthrow of the government. Cooler heads urged restraint. Father Mario Deguzman's name was spoken often at these meetings. There were few that doubted that he was actually controlling the actions of the ruling party. The tropical spring changed into a hot tropical summer. With the heat came an increase in the tone of the dangerous rhetoric.

In August an event occurred that stunned the nation. The vice president was gunned down while on his way to a cabinet meeting. Also wounded in the incident was the Minister of Finance. The police responded quickly arresting thirty men. Included in the arrests was Marcos Serrano. The men languished in the fetid cells at the government's prison in Port Allison. They were all charged with conspiracy, murder, and attempted murder. Lawyers on the island were denied permission to see the suspects. Members of the jailed men's families were allowed brief visits once a week.

"Los Jeffes" members held a series of meetings. Miguel Aponte left the island and returned several weeks later having completed a deal that would bring arms into the island. Father Deguzman continued to be a main item of the heated discussions. While off the island, Miguel Aponte had arranged for a party of one hundred armed men to be landed on the deserted north coast of the island some four weeks later. The men would be transported by trucks high into the central mountains. There they would await the signal that the overthrow was to begin.

The police and the paramilitary government teams continued their raids on the homes of men who they believed were still involved in the drug trade. Eduardo was untouched. He believed that the reason for this was Mario's belief in Eduardo's sincere and concerted efforts to withdraw from the cartel.

Eduardo's restraint dissolved the day that Alicia ran crying into his office. Her father had been arrested and one of his cargo ships had been blown up in the harbor. Her father had been accused of using his container ships to transport drugs. Eduardo knew that this was not true. Alicia's father was strongly against the drug trade. He had even been somewhat hesitant to give his daughter's hand in marriage to Eduardo. He knew of Eduardo's late father's involvement with the drug cartel. He was certain that Eduardo had retained these connections. His daughter's pleas had finally convinced him. He allowed the marriage to go forth.

"Los Jeffes" held another meeting. There were several votes taken. The tone of the meeting was one of anger. Father Deguzman would have to be executed. After the din had died down. Eduardo stood.

"As you know, my friendship with Father Deguzman is a long one. He made a promise to me when I first talked to him on this island. He would see that my family was kept in relative safety. They would not be touched. At this very hour, my father-in law, the grandfather of my children, and the father of my wife, sits in a stinking government jail. We have only been allowed to see him for twenty minutes since his arrest. When we saw him, it was obvious that he had been tortured. We must gain his freedom and that of our many friends who languish with him. I will attend to Father Mario Deguzman. I will carry out your orders. He has betrayed both my family and me. For that he will die!"

The meeting adjourned. Within the week, emissaries were sent to the outspoken priest. He agreed to meet with Eduardo to work out terms of a cease-fire. Little did the young priest know that his assassination would be the signal for armed revolt on the island. He did not know that Eduardo carried, tucked beneath his coat, an automatic pistol given to him days before by Miguel Aponte.

The two men shook hands. As usual, Eduardo had not been searched before entering the room where the meeting was to be held.

Father Deguzman was first to speak. "Once again my friend, we meet to settle the differences of those around us. My concern grows for our country."

Eduardo poured a glass of cold water from a condensation-rimmed pitcher and settled back in his chair. The young priest spoke for almost twenty minutes. Yes, there were many people in jail. Yes, Eduardo's father-in law was among them. Yes, there had been torture of some of the prisoners. No, the action of the government would not stop. The total eradication of the cancer called drugs was still a long ways off.

Eduardo waited for his friend to finish speaking. He then stood up and paced about the room. The pistol lay hidden under his folded coat in the middle of the richly upholstered chair.

"Mario, you promised me that my family would be safe."

"I have kept my word."

"But what of my wife's father?"

"He had been warned."

"But he is innocent. He has no involvement with the cartel."

"My...Our sources tell us a different story."

"And you believe these sources?

"Yes, I do and he will stay in prison until the government can prove otherwise."

Eduardo returned to the chair. He picked up the jacket as he sat down. He felt for the automatic weapon.

Father Deguzman began to pace about the room. His voice rose as he talked. "Your father-in law and his friends will receive a fair trial. In the meanwhile, he will rot in jail with the rest of the drug runners."

Father Mario Deguzman turned and his eyes grew large. Eduardo had stood up. In his hand he clutched the automatic weapon. Before the young priest could speak again, Eduardo squeezed the trigger. The young priest clutched his chest and fell to the floor. Eduardo approached the body and fired several more shots. From outside the building, Eduardo could hear the sound of automatic weapons. The shots soon stopped. The door to the meeting room was thrown open and one of Miguel Aponte's lieutenants stepped inside. He glanced around the room and then walked over to the body on the floor.

"You have done well, Eduardo. You have done well."

Eduardo looked at the man. "I will burn in Hell."

"But he betrayed you."

Eduardo spoke. "Yes, he betrayed me and for that he deserved to die."

Chapter Twenty-five

When news of the death of Father Deguzman reached the men who had been waiting in the mountains, they unleashed a savage attack on the police and other government forces. The battles raged for days. The Baja airport came under heavy attack. Most of the airplanes parked on the runways were damaged or destroyed. The police barracks was reduced to smoking ruins. Government leaders were summarily executed. Brother fought brother. It was a civil war in all its agony.

The hospitals were overwhelmed with victims. There was little that the workers at the hospitals could do. The hospitals had long ago run out of anesthetics and meaningful medicines. The few doctors on hand operated using local anesthetics. The death toll climbed. The prison was stormed and the prisoners released. The fighting was to continue for months. The remaining members of the Nationalist Democratic Party surrendered and Marcellino Lucero was sworn in as the Acting-President. A shaking judge administered his oath.

Summer passed and the subtle changes of the tropical fall caressed the Island. Word of the overthrow had reached the United States. The U.S. responded by enacting further sanctions. The restrictions read in part,

"U.S. credit card companies will not accept vouchers from New Savannah or from persons who are known to carry passports from that country.

"As there is no direct commercial air service by local carriers at present, nor economic authority to operate such service between the U.S. and New Savannah, the U.S. Federal Aviation Administration (FAA) has not assessed New Savannah's civil aviation authority for compliance with international aviation safety standards for oversight of New Savanna's air carrier operations.

"Entering New Savannah territory, territorial waters or airspace without prior authorization from the New Savannah government may result in arrest or other enforcement by New Savannah authorities for violation of New Savannah law. Any vessel or aircraft that enters the twelve mile limit off New Savannah would be inside New Savannah territorial waters or airspace and thus subject to the jurisdiction of the government of New Savannah.

"Control regulations of the U.S. Treasury Department require that persons subject to U.S. jurisdiction have a license to engage in any transactions related to travel to, from and within New Savannah. Transactions related to tourist and business travel is not licensable. This restriction includes tourist or business travel from a third country such as Mexico or Canada."

The stranglehold continued on the country of New Savannah. Thousands of miles away, another man who had been a virtual prisoner for the past ten years had his first taste of freedom. Client number 107 walked through the doors of the Leesburg Psychiatric and Neurological Center. Samuel Jones, while still a very sick man, was released and walked slowly down the hospital's winding walkway. Samuel Jones was going home. He was going to see Stacey.

The events following the coup were relatively quiet for Eduardo and his family. Alicia was overjoyed by the release of her father. Although his body still carried the scars of his imprisonment and torture, the emaciated man was soon attending to his business activities. Armed guards who patrolled the area twenty-four hours a day ringed his house.

All was going well until Eduardo, Jr. got sick. The once lively four-year-old became more and more lethargic. His body became covered with large bruises. He soon developed large swellings about his neck and under his arms. He refused to eat. Eduardo took him to the clinic at the largest hospital on the island. The physicians there examined the child and advised Eduardo that they would have a diagnosis in a few days.

When Eduardo returned a few days later, a grim faced doctor met him at the clinic entrance.

"I am afraid that the news is not good, my friend. It appears that your child has an acute form of Lymphoblastic Leukemia. His outlook is not good."

"But,...but how will you treat him?"

The doctor raised his outstretched hands in a show of desperation. "The treatment of this disorder is usually divided into three categories. We use chemotherapy for the first phase. We next irradiate the brain and the spinal areas. We next use additional chemotherapy for the maintenance phase of this disease. Unfortunately, as you are aware, we have none of these treatments available to us in New Savannah. Your son has some tumor that is growing near his trachea. He might even benefit from surgery to remove these collections of tumor. What he needs now in addition to the drugs and radiation is a team of doctors skilled in handling these diseases. We have no such specialists in this country."

Eduardo was filled with anguish.

"Can I not take him elsewhere?"

"He is too sick to travel, Eduardo. He would not survive a trip. Airplanes can not take off or land at our airport due to the sporadic fighting. He would not survive a boat trip that was longer than twenty minutes. I hate to be the one to bring you this news. In New Savannah, we can only make diagnoses at this point. We can do little to treat the sick. My heart weeps for you and your son."

Eduardo returned home and shared the bad news with his family. Eduardo, Jr. was his only son. And now the child was gravely ill. The doctor had told him that the child had only four to six months to live. Eduardo was crushed with grief. Alicia cried into the night.

Father Sanchez had made it a practice to forward Eduardo's mail from Georgetown University. Several months before, one of the packets had included a directory of Georgetown graduates. Eduardo searched through his papers and found the large new book entitled "Georgetown University

Graduates, 1950–1985." He rapidly turned the pages of the book and noted the information on each of his former friends and classmates. He then typed out a list using the small typewriter that sat on his desk.

Brinks, Dr. Catherine E; BS '72, MD '76;
r. 311 Saroni Drive, Oakland, CA 94611 (415) 666-3499
Office: Oakland Children's Hospital, Oakland, CA (415) 444-2349
Mercer, Dr. James S.; BS '72, MD '76;
r. 801 I St, S.W., Washington, DC 20001 (201) 555-2948;
Office: 3100 DuPont Circle, #10, Washington, DC 20001 (201) 555-9900
Mosslcr, Dr. Stephen L; BS '72, MD '76;
r. 4504 Marina Way #1118, Marina Del Rey, CA 90293 (213) 651-0001;
Office: 5914 La Cienaga Blvd. #248, Los Angeles, CA 90036 (213) 689-8877
Pointer, Dr. Kevin H; BS '72, MD '76;
r. 1208 Spinnaker Way, Waterview, WA 98683 (206) 445-2234;
Office: 1809 Fifth Street, Seattle, WA 98677 (206) 455-0777

The next morning, Eduardo packed a small suitcase and drove to the home of Miguel Aponte. By noon of the same day, he was aboard the ocean-going yacht heading towards Aruba. They arrived later that evening and several men met Eduardo at the dock. The men drove him to his house in Savaneta.

After a fitful night's rest, he was driven to Reina Beatrix International Airport. This was one of the few locations from which he could make a direct call to the United States. Furthermore, the anonymity of a phone call from the airport suited his need to be circumspect. He found a telephone booth and inserted the coins as instructed by the international operator. He started with James Mercer in Washington, D.C.

He got no answer at the doctor's office, but was able to reach him at home.

"Hello, James. This is an old friend of yours."

"An old friend?"

"Yes, Eduardo Sierramonte."

"Eduardo! Where have you been all these years? I've tried to contact you many times. The church in Puerto Plata had no idea where you had gone after your father died."

"I have traveled a lot. It is a long story. The story brings me to my present need. I am the father of four children. My only son has recently been diagnosed with a form of Leukemia. The doctors in my homeland think that he needs surgery to relieve an obstruction caused by the enlarged lymphatic tissue. One doctor has even recommended removal of my son's spleen. My homeland is poor. We have neither the surgeons, the medication, nor radiation to treat my son's condition. I need your help."

"I'd be happy to help you. Can your son travel?"

"No, the doctors think that he is too ill to travel. Can you come and see him in my homeland?"

"Isn't your homeland the Dominican Republic? Getting there should not be a problem."

"That is part of the story, my friend. My homeland is really New Savannah."

There was a lengthy pause at the other end of the line. The line was filled with static. After a while, Dr. Mercer answered, "Is this the same New Savannah I've been hearing about on television and in the news?"

"It is one and the same, my friend."

There was another pause. "Eduardo, Americans have been banned from traveling to New Savannah for years. The television commentators have been discussing an armed revolt in the country. Are these stories true?"

Eduardo answered, "Sadly enough, my friend, they are true. There would be a great deal of risk involved, but I have access to the forces that can guard you."

"My safety is not my primary concern. The American government would strip me of my credentials and my ability to practice medicine would be destroyed. Isn't there some other way that I can help you?"

"I'm afraid not. I need you here."

"I'm afraid I cannot take the risk, Eduardo. I cannot take the risk. I know I owe you a lot. But I also owe my family. I owe my patients here even more. I must be available to them. I cannot endanger my ability to practice medicine here in this country."

Eduardo placed the telephone slowly in its cradle and broke the connection. A tear ran down his cheek. He walked around the crowded terminal for almost an hour before placing his second call.

Due to the time difference between Aruba and the West Coast of the United States, it was still early morning on the West Coast. He called each of his former friends at their homes. He first called Stephen Mossler. After several rings, the telephone was answered by a man's sleep laden voice. The man identified himself as Jonathan. Yes, Dr. Mossler was home. He'd be there in a moment.

A new voice was heard on the other end of the line. "This is Dr. Stephen Mossler."

"Stephen, this is an old friend."

"Who is this?"

"It's Eduardo."

"Eduardo! Where are you?"

"I'm in the Caribbean."

"You mean the Dominican Republic?"

"No, I'm in my country."

"Your country? How have you been?"

"I've been fine, but that is not my concern. My concern is with my only son."

"What is wrong, Eduardo? What is wrong?"

"He has been diagnosed as having an acute form of leukemia. I need your help. My country is a poor country and does not have the necessary medications and specialists to treat him."

"Where are you living now?"

"My country is called New Savannah."

"But we always thought you were from the Dominican Republic."

"That was not necessarily so, my friend, but we can discuss that when I see you. I need your help. I need you to come to my country to save my son's life."

"I have been reading about New Savannah in the newspapers and the country seems to be in turmoil now. Quite frankly, I am concerned about my safety."

"There are safety concerns, my friend. But we have no medicine and no specialists. I am at my wit's end."

"From what I have read, I would not even be able to get a visa to go to New Savannah. I would more than likely end up losing my medical license when I returned. I have too many patients who are depending on me, Eduardo. Can't you fly your son here?"

"That is not possible. The doctors have advised me that my son will not tolerate a trip, no matter how short. He is already experiencing breathing difficulties due to the enlargement of the lymph nodes."

"Is there some way that I could send you medications?"

"The United States Government prohibits mail service to New Savannah. We rarely get mail from other countries. It could take months. My son does not have that long. Can you not help me in my hour of need?"

"I don't see any way that I can, Eduardo. I am sorry for you and I am sorry for your son."

Eduardo listened as the line went dead. He gazed at the mute telephone through tear-filled eyes. Composing himself, he placed another call.

The response was the same when he was finally able to contact Kevin Pointer. His friend could not leave Seattle for such a risky venture. His obligation was to his patients in the Seattle area. No mention was made of the financial obligation owed by Dr. Pointer to Eduardo. His last hope was Catherine Brinks.

She answered her telephone after several rings. She was as surprised to hear from Eduardo as the others had been. She talked at length about her attempts to find him during the years that had passed.

"There is a reason that I have called you after all these years. My son has an acute form of Lymphoblastic leukemia. As you are well aware, this illness causes neurological symptoms. As a pediatric neurologist, you are aware of the battle my son faces. He is entering this battle unarmed. In my homeland, we have no chemotherapeutic agents. We have no radiation machines. And we have no doctors who have any specialized training. His condition is deteriorating as we speak. I need you to come to my homeland."

"Are you still living in the Dominican Republic?"

"No, I left there years ago. My home is in New Savannah now."

A gasp was heard from the other end of the phone line.

"New Savannah! I just saw something about it on television the other day. Are conditions there as bad as they say they are?"

"They are as bad or worse."

"I've heard that there has been fighting and shelling between rival factions. Is this true?"

"Yes, Catherine. It is true."

"It is my understanding that the United States Government will take strong action against anyone traveling there. I would be stripped of my medical license when I returned home. No amount of humanitarian purpose would influence the U.S. Government. I've had friends who went to Cuba via Canada. Their only purpose was to work in Cuban hospitals for six-week periods. They all lost their medical licenses when they returned to the United States. I have too many young patients who depend on me here in Oakland. I can not sacrifice their well being for your son. Can't you bring him here?"

He related the reasons why that was an impossible option.

"I'm very sorry for you, Eduardo. But I can not help you. My heart goes out to you."

Eduardo walked slowly from the telephone booth. He had not bothered to hang up the telephone. The receiver dangled from its twisted cord. He was driven back to Savaneta and spent the night drinking the powerful Aruban rum. Early the next morning, he boarded the ocean-going vessel. He stood dejectedly at the stern of the boat as it headed back to New Savannah.

Eduardo returned from his trip to Aruba both angry and depressed. He could do little but watch as his tiny son's condition worsened over the next several months. He sent one of Miguel Aponte's men to Mexico. The man took with him a list of medications that the doctors on New Savannah hoped would stem the child's illness. The physicians in the island's run-down hospital were ill equipped to battle the illness. The child's condition worsened. He became very anemic and although given transfusions on a weekly basis, he continued his decline.

Eduardo had lost his interest in the unstable political climate that gripped the country. He seldom went near the government offices. He was withdrawn from his family. He would sit with Alicia at the child's bedside. The sight of his son's suffering tormented him. Eduardo refused to eat. He refused to shave. A heavy black beard covered his normally clean-shaven face. When the child would sleep, Eduardo and Alicia would sit on the veranda and talk. Eduardo was sure that he was being punished for killing a priest. Alicia tried to soothe her distraught husband. He did not reveal to Alicia his frantic calls to his old schoolmates. He did not talk of their response. He would deal with their failure to come to his aid later. For now, there was only Eduardo Junior. Eduardo had taken a large sofa into his son's room. Mornings usually found Eduardo slumped on the sofa, often fully clothed.

Eduardo talked on occasions to Marcellino. The older man understood Eduardo's anguish and spared him the details of the continued sporadic fighting on various parts of the island. Family friends visited the house from time to time, but their visits were kept brief. Sorrow filled the air. The Christmas holidays approached. Eduardo and the family gathered around the bed of the sick child. The child was suffering the nervous system effects of the illness. He drifted in and out of a coma. There was no need to take the child to the island's run-down hospital. It was better to care for the child at home. A nurse from the clinic slept at the house. The doctors visited daily but there was little that they could do.

Early one February morning, with Alicia and Eduardo at his bedside, the child passed away. Two days later, in a meadow behind the family's house, Eduardo Junior was buried. Eduardo was almost crazed. He wept and paced the house. His only son had been taken away. There was no help to be had in his time of need.

The next day, Eduardo sent one of Miguel Aponte's men to Aruba by boat. From there, the man was to fly to the Dominican Republic. He was to meet with Father Sanchez. Eduardo had instructions for the old priest.

The man returned two weeks later and met with Eduardo in the library of the family home. In early March, Eduardo received a message by church courier from Father Sanchez. One morning in early March, Eduardo said goodbye to Alicia and the rest of the family. He said only that he was going away on business and would be gone for several weeks. He boarded the ocean going yacht and headed for Aruba.

Chapter Twenty-six

The police investigations in the four cities continued. Each department was unaware of the other's work. There was no link between the four crimes and so they continued to be investigated separately. The FBI had not been able to match the partial fingerprint on the shell casing found on Dr. Kevin Pointer's sailboat. There was no suspect to link to the DNA evidence that had been found in the home of Dr. Catherine Brinks. Motor vehicle checks in Pennsylvania were at a dead end. The Motor Vehicle Department needed at least one more number before they could even attempt to run the license plate check on the vehicle seen driving up and down Saroni Drive on the night of the murder. In Los Angeles, the police were all but convinced that the death of Dr. Mossler was a "hate crime".

The leaves were falling from the trees in Washington on a brisk fall afternoon. Detective Alphonso Smith had been investigating the murder case of Dr. James Mercer since early spring. The investigation had made little headway. The addition of several other detectives to the strike force looking for clues had produced nothing new.

The detective was writing another report on Washington's growing list of homicides when his telephone rang. A secretary on the other end of the line said that she had a call from Dean Avery of Georgetown University. Could he take the call? Detective Smith picked up the telephone.

"Detective Smith?"

"Yes, this is Detective Smith. How are you Dean Avery?"

"Oh, I'm fine Mr. Smith. I was wondering if you would have a moment to drop by my office today? I'll be in a meeting until about five thirty, but I'm free after that time. There is something that I think might be of interest to you."

"I'll be there at five thirty sharp. I look forward to meeting with you."

Detective Smith spent the rest of the afternoon working on his papers and reports. He was puzzled by the call from the dean. He left the office at four thirty and headed cross-town to the medical school. He was caught in the peak of the rush hour. Harried government workers driving cars of every description, darted in and out of lanes. Many drove while preoccupied with thoughts of unfinished government business. Many drove faster than normal. They were in a hurry to escape the clutches of the big city with its after-dark crime problems. At some intersections, drivers defied traffic signals and sat in the middle of the intersections, trapped by their own haste and thoughtlessness.

It took the officer almost forty-five minutes to make his way across the congested city. He arrived, at last, at the medical school complex. He approached the campus gate and flashed his badge to the man who was guarding the gate.

"I'm Detective Alphonso Smith of the Metropolitan Homicide Department. I have a five-thirty meeting scheduled with the dean."

The guard smiled. "You're running with the big boys today, sir. Must be something awfully important."

"Just routine police work."

"Just put this pass on the dashboard. Do you know how to get to his office?"

"Yes, I have been here before. Thanks for your help."

With a green guest pass on the car's dashboard, he drove onto the campus. There were fewer students and workers on the campus at this time in the afternoon. The officer had little trouble finding a place to park the unmarked police vehicle. He walked into the main corridor of the building and took the elevator to the floor that housed the office of the dean. Dean Avery's secretary ushered him into the dean's office.

"Dr. Avery will be with you in a few minutes. He asked me to tell you to make yourself comfortable. I'm leaving for the day, but he will be here shortly."

Detective Smith walked around the office and read the many diplomas and certificates lining the walls of the well-appointed office. He noted that the dean had graduated from Georgetown. He had done his specialty training at Harvard. Smith was glancing at the diplomas when he heard the dean enter the office door. He heard a lock click. It was obvious that the dean did not want their conversation disturbed.

The dean walked into the room and put a large well-stuffed briefcase on the floor by his desk. He then turned and shook the detective's hand warmly.

"I do hope that I did not keep you waiting too long, Detective Smith. I was tied up in a faculty meeting. You know how meetings can go? Especially with the faculty. They seem to be a long-winded bunch. Can I offer you something to drink? Coffee? Tea? Perhaps a soft drink?"

Smith smiled. "I'll have whatever you're having, sir."

The dean reached into his desk drawer and pulled out a small bottle of whiskey. He went to a small refrigerator that stood in the corner and removed a tray of ice cubes.

"I'm off duty now, Detective Smith. Will you join me?"

Smith laughed and poured some of the amber mixture into his glass. The men sipped their drinks and began a conversation that would last well into the night.

The dean leaned back in his chair and sipped his drink. He loosened his tie and took four folders out of his desk drawer. He then began to talk. Smith wrote notes as the dean talked.

"I kept your card in the top drawer of my desk." He held up the card that the detective had given him months before. "I expected to hear from you any day. I thought that you would call to inform me that the sad death of Dr. Mercer had been solved. Time passed and you did not call. I was about to call you after several weeks had passed, but I didn't want to interfere with your work. And then a strange thing happened. During the summer I received word of the deaths of three other former students. They all seem to have died suddenly and violently. They lived in scattered parts of the United States. I learned of their deaths while attending meetings or through telephone calls. The police department from Seattle contacted me, but they really did not ask me too many questions about one of our graduates.

"I was disturbed at first. I considered the events to be unrelated until about a week ago. I then pulled the records on each of the four deceased doctors. Several things worried me. That is when I decided to give you a call. You know how these things are? I'm good at investigating medical problems, but I'm not a detective. Oh, and incidentally, I would appreciate you keeping this information strictly confidential. We don't want to cause undue concern among our graduates. Especially since all of the victims seem to have been members of the same class."

Detective Smith put his glass on a small table that sat beside his chair. He leaned towards the dean. "You say that they were all members of the same class?"

The dean continued. "Yes, they all finished medical school here in 1976. I pulled the yearbook from that year. Here are their pictures. Dr. Mercer, as you well know, lived here in the area. Kevin Pointer lived just outside of Seattle. Catherine Brinks lived in the San Francisco Bay area and Stephen Mossler practiced in Los Angeles. They all had one thing in common. Their specialties were all related to the treatment of children. They were all specialists in pediatric subspecialties or pediatric surgery.

Their records are here for your review. I can have copies made if you so desire Mr. Smith. My secretary is gone for the evening, but you could have the copies by, say, tomorrow afternoon at the latest."

"I would appreciate that, sir."

"There are some things in their records that I do not quite understand. Each one had some type of family problem during his or her tenure here at Georgetown. They all lost family members during the time that they were training to be physicians. That in itself is not unusual. Many of the students have personal or family problems while they are attending undergraduate or graduate school. I just thought it odd that these very same four would all have serious problems. Many of the problems might well have curtailed their studies, but they continued. All four of them graduated on time and all four had above average grades. After graduating, each of the four doctors became leaders in their fields and took a short while to achieve their status. I would like to say that graduating from Georgetown helped and I am sure that it did, but they were all high achievers once they finished medical school. We are talking about as short a time as ten years. That is rather unusual. It takes many of our graduates twenty to thirty years to achieve the recognition that this group had won. That is why their death seems even more tragic. They were all gifted young physicians who had the majority of their careers ahead of them."

"Are there any other features common to the group?"

"There are some similarities and some dissimilarities. They were all from different parts of the country. Three of them ended up practicing medicine on the West Coast. Poor Mercer was the only one who stayed on in the area here. Mercer was the only one who was still married. Kevin Pointer had been only recently divorced. Doctors Mossler and Brinks had never married. I have it on good authority that Dr. Mossler might have adopted a gay lifestyle, although his friends were not aware of his homosexuality. You know, it was considered, but he never confided his gender preferences to any of his classmates. They found out about his homosexuality in roundabout ways.

"I did find out that two of the men were roommates during a good portion of their school days here. I also found out after reviewing their records that all four of them did a clinical rotation together in a small town in Pennsylvania."

Detective Smith looked puzzled. "A clinical rotation?"

"Yes, in the early seventies, Georgetown was involved in sending doctors in training out to smaller hospitals. It was hoped that they would gain insight into the treatment of medical problems not treated in a large university center. You know. They would see how the real physicians, so to speak, handled day to day medical problems. The students would get a so-called reality check. They might not have access to all of the sophisticated tests and on-call specialists. They would actually have to solve complex clinical problems with a minimum of help."

Smith nodded and continued taking notes. "Is this program still ongoing?"

"Yes, it has been an absolute success. We make such a rotation mandatory beginning with the first year medical students. It is also a well-received program by the small community hospitals. We do not have enough students to fill the demand. In many instances, the students will be so impressed with a particular area that they will return to practice there after graduation. It is a very popular program."

"And you say that these four doctors spent a rotation together in Pennsylvania?"

"Yes, they went to a small community hospital called Oakmill General. It is located in the Pocono Mountain area. It is about three or four hours from here. They stayed there for three months. That is the usual length of time that one of these rotations lasts."

"Did anything unusual happen while they were there?"

"I am unaware of any unusual occurrences. If something occurred, it was not indicated in their records."

"Was there anything that would have occurred involving them while they were here in Washington?"

"Absolutely nothing that we can ascertain from their records. As I mentioned before, they all had family trauma while they were attending school here. There was no hint of scandal. As far as I know, they had little or no connection after finishing their residencies. They never practiced together. I have heard of no mention of business dealings. No, nothing at all."

"It seems as though I may have to take a trip to the Poconos. After I return, I will contact each of the other departments working on the cases. We will pick their collective brains and see if there is something or someone that resulted in harm coming to these four doctors."

The two men continued examining the records of the slain physicians. Detective Smith made arrangements to pick up copies of the records.

They would be ready the next day. Dean Avery filled in all of the gaps pertaining to the careers of the four. They had lived and practiced in separate areas of the country for over ten years. They visited Georgetown infrequently. They had last been together at the tenth anniversary reunion. Each had been a speaker at the reunion, so the dean was reasonably sure that they saw one another during that time. Each had been a donor to the university scholarship fund. Dean Avery produced a list of donors for Detective Smith to read. Each of the four doctors had given well over ten thousand dollars during each of the postgraduate years. The dean also had other assorted information, which he read to the detective.

The two men continued to search the records. The clock in the bell tower, high above the campus, had just finished striking twelve. Both men were tired. Over six hours had passed when the meeting ended. Detective Smith would call the school as soon as he returned from Oakmill.

The next day, Detective Smith called the chief of police in Oakmill. The Washington detective would be arriving in Oakmill later that afternoon. He would like to meet with the chief before starting the investigation. Chief Brown said that he would be awaiting Smith's arrival and was ready to help in any way possible. Detective Smith packed an overnight bag and was soon driving up Interstate 95 towards Philadelphia and beyond.

Late that afternoon, Smith arrived in Oakmill. He registered at the Holiday Inn. After dropping his bag in the room he drove to the police department Headquarters. He spent a long time briefing the police chief on the full purpose of the visit. The two men continued their conversation over dinner at a crowded restaurant. Detective Smith would be happy to have the Chief of Police accompany him to Oakmill General Hospital. He would need to talk to the administrator, who might provide him with information relating to the doctor's stay at the hospital.

Detective Smith was tired from the long drive North. He left the operator a request for a 7 A.M. wake up call and slept fitfully through the night. After breakfast the next morning, he met Chief Brown at headquarters. The two men drove through the leaf-lined streets towards Oakmill General Hospital. Chief Brown pointed out features of the town as he drove. The chief had headed the town's ten-man police force for about five years. He had formerly worked in Philadelphia but had grown tired of the crime ridden streets. Oakmill offered police work but at a reduced volume. He had taken the job with some hesitation, but was happy with his choice. He pulled into the parking lot of the hospital and the two men walked towards the hospital's main entrance. Gray squirrels darted across their path. People who passed the two officers spoke to the chief as they passed.

Chief Brown had called ahead and the hospital administrator was waiting for them when they arrived. They met in his office for a short while. Detective Smith outlined his concerns and the details of information that he was seeking. The administrator offered no real information. He had only been at the hospital for five years. He would have the two policemen talk with Mrs. Valerie Washington. She had been in the records department of the hospital for over twenty years. If anyone had any information concerning the four physicians, Mrs. Washington would be that person.

The administrator led them to a nearby elevator. He pushed the button marked 'basement'. They emerged and walked up a long, darkened corridor. Mrs. Washington met them at the door of a large office marked, "Medical Records Department. Authorized Personnel Only."

"Come in, gentlemen. Do come right in."

Introductions were made and the four of them sat at a large table. Piles of medical records and sheets of loose-leaf paper cluttered the top of the table. Mrs. Washington moved a pile of documents aside and picked nervously at an unseen spot on her dress.

"Now, how may I help you?"

Detective Smith pulled out a notebook and began to question the woman. "Mrs. Washington. I'm with the Washington Metropolitan Police Department. We are investigating the murder of a Dr. James Mercer. He rotated through your hospital back in the 1970s. It was in the summer of 1976 to be exact. Dr. Mercer was part of a group of Georgetown University students who were doing a so-called clinical rotation at your hospital. I was wondering if you might recall anything about Dr. Mercer or any of the resident doctors who were here at Oakmill during that time?"

Mrs. Washington looked at the three men. "Of course, that was along time ago. Now let me see."

A look of question covered her face, and then a smile appeared. "Oh yes, I do remember now. Dr. Brooks?"

"One of the students in the group was Catherine Brinks." Smith interrupted.

"Yes, yes. I remember now. Dr. Brinks was the first female medical doctor that we had ever had here at the hospital. I remember now. That was the first year that we had had doctors from Georgetown University. I remember that the staff was divided about the need to bring outside doctors into our tiny hospital A lot of the staff members were against bringing in the new doctors. They didn't want those new doctors experimenting on our townsfolk. It caused quite a stir. And then, to top things of, they sent a woman doctor. Things were really in an uproar, but the group worked out all right. Dr. Brinks was very smart and I remember that a number of staff members would seek her out for medical opinions. We really wanted Dr. Brinks to stay with us, but she said that she had to return to Georgetown to finish her training. She even said that she might consider returning after she finished her training."

Detective Smith spoke. "Mrs. Washington, did anything unusual happen while the group was here?"

The woman looked at the detective. "Now let me think. Anything unusual?"

She paused. "Oh yes, there was one thing that happened. It was very sad. It wasn't due to the fault of any of those young doctors. Yes, one thing did happen."

She looked at the Oakmill Chief of Police. "Maurice, I don't think that you had even moved up here then. No, I'm sure that you weren't here. There was a death here at the hospital. There was a child named Stacey Jones. Poor thing. Old Dr. Harry Waterman, God rest his soul, was her attending physician. He was a stubborn man. He wouldn't listen to what those young doctors were telling him. I forget the details. If you gentlemen will excuse me for a moment, I will pull her chart."

She returned after a few minutes carrying a yellowed medical record. She sat down and began to thumb through the record. The three men watched.

"Yes. Yes. Here it is. Patient's name was Stacey Jones. Her parents were Samuel and Claudette Jones. Claudette worked at a computer company and Samuel worked here at the hospital. He was a nurse."

She continued flipping though the child's medical record. "The admitting diagnosis was viral illness. Of course, after the poor child died and the autopsy was completed, that was all changed. The final diagnosis. Yes, here it is; Ruptured spleen. Perforation, large bowel. Peritonitis secondary to perforated large bowel. I remember it all quite clearly now. Of course, the death of the child was bad enough, but what happened later was really sad."

She continued. The men moved closer to the table.

"The father, Samuel, had a mental breakdown. He was admitted to Leesburg Psychiatric and Neurological Center and stayed there for ten years. While he was in the hospital, his wife committed suicide. After he got out of the hospital he went to live with his mother-in law. She died shortly after he was released. The poor man. He really had it rough. Daughter gone. Wife gone. Mother-in-law gone. Mind gone. The poor, poor man."

"Do you know when he was released from the hospital?"

"No. I couldn't be sure. It was over a year ago, I think. The hospital discharged all of the patients. The place went belly up. I do know one person here in town who might know. That would be the family attorney."

She looked at the police-chief.

"Maurice, I'm sure you know Darren Murph. His office is over at Sixth and Main. I'm sure that he could answer your questions. Why don't you take Mrs. Smith over to talk to him? I'm sure that he could fill in some of the blanks. I had heard that the young man moved out west after Mrs. Donatto passed."

The group stood up. Detective Smith thanked Mrs. Washington for seeing him and began to gather up his notes.

"I can run by Attorney Murph's office if you would like, Detective Smith. Or we could get a bite to eat first."

"If it is alright with you, Chief Brown, I would like to catch up with the lawyer first. I am too excited to eat right now."

"Suit yourself. We'll be there in ten minutes."

They returned to the police car and drove towards Main Street. The police officer picked up the microphone in the vehicle and spoke as he drove.

"This is Chief Brown. I'll be at Darren Murph's office at Sixth and Main if anyone is looking for me. I should be back at headquarters in about an hour."

The two men talked as they rode. "Do you think that this fellow Samuel Jones had anything to do with the killings? It looks like the doctors were involved in the death of his kid even though old Doc Waterman was calling the shots. Sounds like this guy Jones might be a dangerous person. I mean. To stay in the nut house for ten years. He must have been one sick cookie."

Smith nodded.

"He might have been out for revenge. You never can tell. It sure sounds like he had a motive. This is the strongest lead that we have had so far. We'll just have to see how it all turns out."

"You may even have to call in the Feds."

"I'll talk to the members of the other departments who have jurisdiction. They may be further along than we are. I'll see if they want to bring in the Feds. It sure sounds like that is what will happen."

The police car pulled to the curb in front of a small office building. Attorney Murph was in the office. He seldom left his office, preferring to let the younger lawyers handle cases that involved court appearances or traveling about the area. He confined his practice to managing items of probate and to property issues.

The old man rose stiffly from his chair as the two men entered the office.

"Good afternoon. I'm Attorney Darren Murph. It's good to see you again, Chief Brown. I understand you drove all the way up here from Washington, Detective Smith. The drive should be beautiful this time of the year. The Autumn foliage is spectacular this time of the year. Did you enjoy the scenery?"

"Yes sir, it was beautiful. It made the trip go by that much faster."

The old man sat back down in his chair.

"Now, how can I help the two of you?"

Smith took his notepad out of the folder and folded back a new sheet of paper. "We understand that you handled an estate about a year or so ago. We are doing some background checks on people involved with the estate. We are wondering if you might be able to fill us in on the Donatto estate?"

The old man's eyes lightened. "Oh, you mean Audrey Donatto. Tragic situation from beginning to end. First her granddaughter died. Then her son-in-law was sent to the mental institution. Then Claudette, Mrs. Donatto's daughter, killed herself. The old lady waited for years, until the son-in law was released. She wasn't alive for six months after his release before she died."

"We are particularly interested in the whereabouts of the son-in law."

"I could not really tell you that. I think that they buried him somewhere in the San Francisco Bay Area."

Detective Smith stiffened. "You said buried?"

The old man nodded. "Yes, the poor man committed suicide."

"When did this happen?"

"Oh, a couple of months ago. They found a letter with my letterhead on his body. With my letterhead, they were able to call me and I filled them in on all the details of Sam's life. They concluded that he had enough reason to want to take his life. Yes, that was in late July or early August. I'll have the secretary get the file."

The old man pushed a tiny button on his desk and spoke a few words into the box. His voice rattled as he spoke. A few minutes later, a young secretary entered carrying a thick folder. Papers escaped the confines of the folder and fluttered to the floor.

"As you can see, I did all of Mrs. Donatto's paperwork for years. Secretary thinks that I should scan most of these documents and put them into a computer, but I have been holding off. I have worked this way for years. I probably wouldn't even be able to turn on the computer when I needed something."

The secretary laughed and picked several pieces of paper from the floor.

"Here's what you want to see. There are no surviving family members, so I'm not violating confidentiality laws. One of the police officers on the West Coast even sent me a newspaper article detailing Samuel's death. The date is in the article, Detective Smith. I'll get this photocopied and you can take the copy with you. I had not heard from Sam since he left to go out west. I had sold Mrs. Donatto's house and put the proceeds into a special account. Here, look, I even got the registration on the old Subaru that Samuel drove out west." He held out a motor vehicle form. The paper trembled as the old man held it. The paper seemed to magnify the old man's tremor. "See. The car was all registered."

Smith jotted down the numbers on his pad. "Commonwealth of Pennsylvania. TLC 663."

The three men talked for a short while longer. Detective Smith waited while Attorney Murph's secretary copied some of the documents. While he waited, Detective Smith rechecked his notes. From time to time, he asked the old attorney questions. As the old man responded, Smith could be seen underlining areas in his notebook.

The secretary returned carrying the newly copied documents. Included in these documents, was a photocopy of a page from the Oakland Tribune detailing the story concerning the finding of Samuel's body in the Oakland Estuary off Jack London Square. It had been determined later that the cause of death was an apparent self-inflicted gunshot wound. Detective Smith thanked the old man for his assistance.

Police officers Smith and Brown rode back to the Oakmill police station, discussing the case as they rode.

"I don't know what this does for your investigation, Detective Smith."

"I guess it all depends on what the homicide detectives in the other three cities have to say. I'll call you as soon as I get some answers."

The two men shook hands as they stood in the police station parking lot. Detective Smith began the long ride back to Washington.

Chapter Twenty-seven

Detective Smith worked late into the night, organizing the information he had received from both Mrs. Washington and Attorney Murph. He met with detectives Elza Major and Malcolm Sledge. The three men discussed the case, which was growing more intriguing with the presence of the new information.

"We need to pull the telephone records on Dr. Mercer. Have the telephone company give you records from both his office and home for a twelve-month period prior to the doctor's death. It will be interesting to see if he communicated with any of the other three doctors during that time. Can you handle that for me, Elza?"

"Yes, I'll get right on that, Al."

"And Malcolm, I want to set up a conference call for later this afternoon. We'll make it about one o'clock our time. There is a three-hour time difference between D.C. and the West Coast. Call the Homicide Departments in Los Angeles, Seattle, and Oakland and have the detectives who are working on the cases ready to talk with us. Give them an overview of what we have and we'll see what they have. The three of us will handle the call in the conference room. Make sure that it's available for our use at one o'clock."

"I'll get busy."

"Oh, yes. One other thing, Elza. See what it will take to get a copy of the doctor's bank records. After we finish with the conference call, we'll probably have to call in the FBI."

The three men started working, each knew that this would be a very busy morning. Hopefully, the morning would be as productive as the visit to Oakmill had been.

The morning passed rapidly. Well before the scheduled call, the three men had gathered in the conference room. At the agreed upon hour, the telephone began to ring and shortly after, the conference call had started. Detective Smith introduced his staff to the listeners on the other end of the line. The detectives from the other cities introduced their staff.

Detective Smith read a statement he had prepared. He could hear the surprised tones of the men who responded.

Detective Jones from the Oakland police department gave a synopsis of the death of Dr. Brinks.

"We have information from a neighbor that a car with out of state tags was seen driving around the area the night of the murder. We got the first three letters on the plate, but that was all."

Detective Smith joined the conversation. "Were the first three letters TLC?"

A startled voice answered. "You bet your ass they were!"

"The car is a blue Subaru, license number Pennsylvania TLC 663. It is registered to a Samuel Jones. He is reported to have committed suicide in Oakland on or about the thirtieth of July."

"I'll be damned. That was the day after the doctor was murdered. We will talk to our people at the automobile yard and see what they come up with. They may have towed the car into the lot thinking that the car was abandoned. We never hooked the car up with the suspect. The perp's car may have been sitting under our noses all this time. We also have some DNA evidence. I'll talk to our boys in Forensics and see if that will do us any good."

Leron Baker and Edward Garcia of the Seattle Police department were the next officers to give their report. They gave a background check on Dr. Pointer. They described the numbered bank account that had been found in the doctor's home. They suggested that the members of the other jurisdictions check for the presence of numbered accounts. They then talked about the fingerprints that had been found on the shell casings.

"The FBI has been looking for a match. Nothing has turned up yet. It would sure help us if you sent us a set of the suicide's prints."

Martin Jones answered. "I'm sure that they took his prints. They probably drew blood for toxicology. I hope that they didn't throw the samples out."

Smith told of the efforts to get the victims' telephone records.

"As soon as we have the records, we will fax you a copy."

Merlin Dobson replied. "It sounds like it is time to bring the Feds into this mess. Don't you guys agree?"

"Let's work on this for a couple of more days. We should talk again, say on Friday. At that time, we can decide to follow it jointly."

The conference ended in the late afternoon. The three Washington D.C. policemen sat in the chief detective's office discussing the information that had been shared by the departments.

"Who do you think would want to kill four doctors? The biggest question is why? They must have really pissed somebody off. It's certainly a Murder One case when we catch the joker."

"He's probably that poor bastard that they found floating in the bay with a self inflected gunshot wound."

Elza Major laughed. "We may be spending all of this time and the murderer is already dead. The poor guy sure had the motive. His car was seen in the area of one of the killings. All we need is a match on the prints and for the DNA materials to match and we have him. In a way, you feel…kinda feel sorry for the poor bastard."

"Oh course, if he was mentally deranged, he'd beat the charges anyway."

"Well, we'll have to wait until Friday. What do you guys think about bringing in the Feds?"

"There are a lot of angles to this thing. It's an automatic federal case if he went out West to do the hits. I don't think that we have any choice."

"We'll see what the other detectives think. I agree with you. It's a federal case."

The remainder of the week passed too slowly for the three detectives. At the agreed upon time on Friday, the men huddled around the conference room desk.

Detective Dobson of the Oakland P.D. was speaking. "Gentlemen, we got a little bit lucky. The lab guys had saved the samples. The FBI will have an answer for us in ten days. The suicide had been in the military. We sent to Saint Louis for his prints. Forensics had taken a set of post mortem prints. We are sending those prints up to you guys in Seattle. I sure hope they match the ones that were on the shell casing. If this works out, we can at least tie him to two of the cases. Of course, that won't do much for you guys in D.C."

"Were you able to get the telephone records from both home and office telephones?"

Each of the members of the four departments said that this had been done.

"If you send them to Washington, we can get them organized and researched. Since the Washington aspect of the case seems to be going the slowest, we can help by doing the comparisons of the lists."

"That sounds like a good idea."

"Now, what about the Feds?"

"I'm in favor of waiting until we have the cases packaged a little more. The Feds are already helping us with the prints and the DNA. You know how these cases can get bogged down once the Feds come in. I think that we can wait."

The other officers agreed. They would keep working on the case until the solution was closer at hand. They would then turn all the evidence that had been developed over to the FBI.

Nine days had passed. The detectives were due to have the conference call the next day. The three Washington, D.C. homicide detectives had spent the better part of the nine days examining the boxes containing the reams of telephone records from each of the doctors' home and office telephones.

It was Elza Major who first made an interesting finding. In the fall of the prior year, within a space of two hours, each of the doctors had received a long distance call. The call had been an over-seas call. In checking with the Telephone Company, Elza had determined that the calls originated from the island of Aruba.

Alphonso Smith had visited the home of Doctor Mercer's widow. She was still very distraught. Smith explained to her that they were following several leads into her husband's murder. Was she aware or had she ever been aware that her husband had any overseas bank accounts? They sat in the living room. He noticed that Mrs. Mercer grew suddenly tense.

"He's dead now, so I guess it doesn't matter anymore." She sighed and continued. "Yes, he did have an overseas account. When he was in medical school, we ran into some financial difficulty. Three months before I delivered the twins, James's parents were killed in an automobile accident. James had everything on him. We became responsible for his younger brothers and sister. I had a complicated delivery and needed surgery before I left the hospital. Things had been hard enough for us before his parents died. But with their passing, I was almost the sole support of the family. When I wasn't able to go back to work, we were crushed. We spent many a night crying and looking for solutions. One evening, James came home and told me that he had found a solution to our problems. One of the students that he studied with was evidently very wealthy. He had offered to finance the rest of James's schooling. I was against it at first, but I knew how badly James wanted to become a doctor. We agreed and he talked to the student. Shortly after that, James told me that money had been placed in a bank. He never told me where the bank was. And he never told me the amount of money that was involved. It made all the difference in our lives. And so I did not ask any more questions. James told me that there was a letter in the family bible. Whenever we moved, we always knew where the bible was. The letter is still in the bible. It fell out one night when I was reading it after James's death. To this day, I have not opened the letter."

Smith sat back. "Might I be able to see the letter?"

"Oh, yes. No problem. It will only take a minute to get it." She left the living room and went upstairs.

She returned a short time later carrying a yellowed envelope. Neatly written in the upper corner of the envelope were two words. "Bank Account".

She handed the letter to the detective.

"May I open this?"

"Yes. Yes. It can't hurt James now."

She handed Smith a small letter opener that she had picked up from a nearby table. He opened the envelope and unfolded the letter inside. The letterhead read:

National Bank of the Cayman Islands

Georgetown Branch

Georgetown, Grand Cayman

There were several lines of numbers:

330-20-08-879-29-004

80-1608-59-207-19-302

Handwritten was an amount. $100,000 US

Smith jotted down the information that the yellowed paper revealed. He neatly refolded the letter and looked at Mrs. Mercer, who was sobbing.

"Mrs. Mercer, would it be all right with you if I took this letter with me for a while. I would like to make some copies. I'll have one of my officers return it to you later this afternoon. You'll be at home, won't you?"

"Yes, yes. I'll be at home. Do you think that this letter will help you find the madman that killed James?"

"We're getting closer, ma'am. We're getting closer. This letter may help."

Smith stood up and walked towards the door. "My officers should be back here in an hour or so. I'll call you as soon as we are closer to solving your husband's murder."

She thanked him and slowly closed the door behind him.

Meanwhile, in Los Angeles, Detectives Eugene Robinson and Ed White went back to Marina Del Rey to question Jonathan, Doctor Mossler's roommate. The young man was still grief-stricken despite the fact that the murder had occurred over four months ago. The detectives told him that they were looking for additional documents that might shed more light on the death of his roommate and lover. Jonathan produced several boxes of papers from the doctor's library. The detectives searched through these boxes and found little of interest. He then brought out a large gray metal box.

"I don't know if this will help you. The lawyer's have all of Stephen's other papers."

"Well, while we're here we can take a look anyway, if you don't mind." Robinson answered.

They sorted the papers, each detective taking half of the contents of the metal box. They had been sorting the papers for a short while when Detective Robinson held up an envelope. Written in the corner of the envelope were the words "Rainy Day".

Robinson looked at his partner and then at Jonathan. "Would it be all right with you, sir, if we opened this envelope?"

Jonathan nodded his approval.

The detectives opened the envelope. Inside was a letter with the following letterhead:

National Bank of the Cayman Islands

Georgetown Branch

Georgetown, Grand Cayman

There were several lines of numbers:

250-20-08-557-89-773

80-1608-59-207-19-302

Handwritten was an amount. $150,000 US

Detective Robinson saw a small copier in the doctor's study. "Would it be OK if we made a copy of this?"

"Yes, go ahead." Jonathan answered.

The detectives made a copy and returned the original to Jonathan. They thanked him and returned to police headquarters.

Oakland police made a thorough search of the effects of Dr. Catherine Brinks. They searched her house and the effects from her office. They found nothing that indicated the existence of a foreign account. They contacted her lawyer to see if she had any knowledge of an overseas bank account.

"Catherine was a very independent person, Detective Porter. Although we had an attorney client relationship, we were also good friends. I handled her legal and financial planning affairs. She never mentioned any off-shore accounts. We were friends, and I'm sure she would have told me about anything as important as an off-shore account."

Unknown to the two, in a safe deposit box at a downtown Wells Fargo Bank, was the document that they were seeking. Dr. Brinks had taken the secret of its existence to the grave.

Friday came and with it the conference call between the detectives. Elza Major detailed the facts surrounding the calls from an unknown person from Aruba. The fact that the timing of the calls was close suggested that the calls had been made sequentially. The Washington detectives had contacted telephone officials in Aruba. They were informed that the calls were placed from a telephone in the airport. There was no way to identify the caller.

Detectives from Los Angeles reported their findings relating to the fact that Doctor Stephen Mossler had also maintained an account in the Caymans. Detective Smith from the Washington, D.C. police filled the listening officers in on the details of his visit with Doctor Mercer's widow. Oakland detectives related their unsuccessful attempts to find similar evidence in Doctor Brink's personal effects and documents.

Seattle detectives were disheartened. The fingerprints on the shell casings did not match those of Samuel Jones. The FBI Forensic

Laboratory in Washington, D.C. had informed Oakland police that the DNA samples taken from Doctor Brinks' house did not match those taken from Samuel Jones.

At this point, there was no way to link Samuel Jones to the murders that had occurred in either Seattle or Oakland. Still unexplained was the presence of his car in the Oakland foothills on the night that Doctor Brinks was murdered. The detectives agreed that they would continue following leads in the case, although they admitted that their primary lead had dead-ended. As the men spoke, the disappointment could be heard in their voices.

Detective Smith spent a restless weekend. He was unable to sleep. The cases weighed heavily on his mind. Early Monday morning, he called Dean Avery at Georgetown University Medical School.

The Dean agreed to meet with him at 11:00 a.m. Detective Smith left his office at 10:15 and drove to the campus. The guard at the gate recognized him.

"Don't tell me. You're going to see the Dean again."

"You guessed it."

"Here's your visitor pass. You're getting to be a regular around here now."

Detective Smith thanked the guard and drove on to the campus. A little before eleven o'clock, he entered the Dean's office. The two men shook hands and Detective Smith brought the Dean up to date on the progress of the cases.

"I really couldn't sleep all this weekend. I've given these cases a lot of thought. To be honest with you, Doctor Avery, I think that a classmate of the victim's may be the murderer. It's just a hunch. Don't ask me why, but I think that their murders relate to an unknown benefactor that each one of them had during their medical school years. We have evidence that at least three of them had offshore bank accounts. Approximately six months before they were murdered, they all received calls from an unknown person in Aruba."

He then told the Dean about Samuel Jones and the medical disaster that had occurred while the four doctors were training at Oakmill General Hospital.

The Dean was surprised. "No word of this incident reached our offices here."

"From what I've been able to find, the death of the child was not their fault. The attending doctor made the wrong diagnosis and then would not listen to advice given to him by these four students. They were totally innocent. With the deceased child's father having a diagnosis of a severe mental health problem, he looked like a perfect suspect. All the evidence has done so far is to rule him out as a suspect, although we still can not explain the fact that his car was seen in Doctor Brinks' neighborhood on the night of her murder. I don't know. Maybe he was stalking her, with the idea that he would harm her. The fingerprints found by the Seattle Police Department and the DNA evidence found by the Oakland Police Department seem to point to another person as the actual murderer. My problem is to find either a set of fingerprints or to capture a suspect so that we can do DNA comparisons. Frankly, Doctor Avery, I don't see that happening."

Dean Avery rocked back in his chair. He tapped his forehead lightly with a pen.

"There may be a way, Detective Smith. There may just be a way."

Smith was puzzled. "And what might that be, sir?"

The Dean explained. "Since 1970, we have had an ongoing research program here at the Medical School. I'll give you a quick run down. All incoming freshman medical students have blood samples drawn. These blood samples are frozen and stored in our research department. In order to authenticate the samples, fingerprints are taken from each student. The premise of the research project is that long after these students graduate and pass away, we will be able to analyze the samples and determine if any markers for subsequent disease processes were present when they were students. In other words, Detective Smith we are looking for markers.

Does the fact that you have a certain protein present in your blood as a young student indicate that at advanced age you will suffer from heart disease? Might there be a marker for certain types of cancers? Since most of the follow-up will come from autopsy, it is necessary to have fingerprints. We will use the fingerprints to authenticate the fact that the samples match the deceased."

Detective Smith stood up and paced the office. "Are you telling me, sir, that you have fingerprints and blood samples on all of your medical students?"

"That is exactly right. Of course, we would not want to thaw all of the samples. My suggestion, and keep in mind that I'm not a detective, is that you try to match the fingerprints first. Then if you find a match, we can have that sample thawed."

The Dean made several calls to the large research institute that was part of the Georgetown University complex. Detective Smith walked across the campus to the research building and left carrying a booklet in which were the fingerprint cards of each member of the medical school class of 1976. He drove hurriedly to his office and was soon busy making arrangements to have the cards transferred to the FBI fingerprint laboratory, which was located within walking distance of the Washington Metropolitan Police Department. He next called the Seattle police department to share his find with them. He then waited.

Six days later, he had his answer.

Part Five

Chapter Twenty-eight

Eduardo arrived in Aruba after a three-hour voyage on the motor vessel. He was met at the dock by several of Miguel Aponte's men. They transferred the two small bags that Eduardo was carrying into a large black sedan. The car left immediately for the airport. There was an hour's wait for the scheduled flight. The three men chatted in the passenger lounge. Eduardo did not tell the men of his ultimate destination.

Eduardo boarded an American Airlines jet and after several hours, the airplane was circling the airport at Santo Domingo. Father Sanchez met Eduardo at the waiting area. The two men embraced as other passengers hurried off to the baggage claim area.

"You are looking well, my son. I have performed all the tasks as you directed me."

"Will you ever age, Father Sanchez? It is as if time stands still for you."

The two men laughed.

"Your flight will not leave until tomorrow morning. You will stay with me at the rectory."

"I would be delighted to see the school again and we have much to discuss."

The two men retrieved Eduardo's luggage and walked outside of the crowded terminal. Although it was early spring, the humidity hung to the air like a giant blanket. Eduardo was accustomed to the heat but Santo Domingo seemed much more humid than New Savannah. They soon found Father Sanchez's old Chevrolet in the airport parking lot. The car's engine immediately roared to life despite its age. It was much like its owner.

The two men talked as the car negotiated the twisting roads leading to Puerto Plata. Groups of school children wearing brightly colored uniforms walked along the open roads. The passage of the old car was at times slowed by men driving heavily burdened donkeys. Eduardo could not help noticing the gaiety in the faces of the people they passed on the road. The looks on the faces of the people they passed were so much different from those of the people they would have passed in New Savannah.

Off in the distance, Eduardo could see the tops of the mountains that he had come to know so well during his high school days. The car continued up the mountain roads. They finally entered Puerto Plata. The town had not changed. Old men sat in the town's center square talking and playing dominoes. There were several cruise ships tied up at the docks. Tourists carrying newly purchased straw bags and wearing straw hats made their way wearily back to the ships. Small children chased after the groups of tourists. The children were attempting to sell last minute gifts to the tourists who were about to sail away. Occasionally, one of the members of a group of tourists would stop. The tourist would hold out money towards the eagerly outstretched sea of brown hands. A wooden statue or some other item of value would appear and rapidly change from the brown hand to the white hand. The tourists would continue their walk to the dock. A small street vendor would hold the coins aloft, a smile on his sun-tanned face.

Eduardo knew, all too well, that this scene was seldom repeated in New Savannah. Those tourists who happened to visit the island were usually the owners of small sailboats. The sailors would land, quickly reprovision their craft, and sail off towards safer islands. The visitors seldom ventured far from the docks of Doloresville or Port Allison.

Father Sanchez parked the old Chevrolet next to the rectory. Eduardo unloaded the bags and the two men walked into the dark interior of the rectory. On the campus of the school, they had passed several groups of students playing soccer. Eduardo hoped for those simpler times. He knew that was not to be.

"You must be tired from your trip, Eduardo. Shower and then sleep. I will wake you when dinner is ready. We will eat and talk about what has occurred in your young life. You will need to go to sleep early tonight. You have much to do tomorrow."

"I will take your advice, Father. I will dine with you when you call me."

Eduardo quickly showered and was soon fast asleep. The cool rooms of the rectory were in marked contrast to the air about the campus. He awakened sometime later. It was the hands of the old priest gently tapping on Eduardo's shoulder. "It is time to eat Eduardo. All is ready."

The nuns had prepared a simple dinner for the two men. The old priest and Eduardo talked as they ate. Eduardo remembered how good the times had been when he was a student and the venerable old man was much younger. He reminisced about the soccer team and the trips taken by the team. Eduardo remembered well, the trips that the team had taken. The team had visited many of the distant points on the island. The team returned from these visits flushed with the victories that the team had won. It was while talking about the soccer team that Mario's name was first mentioned. Eduardo had noted that the old man had not mentioned Mario's name during the long drive from the airport.

"The passing of Father Mario Deguzman was sad. How did he come to meet his death, Eduardo? You must tell me."

"Mario had done much for New Savannah. He was an active voice for the church. I did all that I could do to protect him. He was doing God's work. There are extreme elements on both the left and on the right in New Savannah. I shielded Mario."

Eduardo continued the lie. "One night, Mario was with a group of men who were headed into Joansville. They were waylaid and taken captive. Their bodies were found several days later. Mario's body was among them. I felt so helpless. He was like a brother to me. I felt that I had failed my friend. The police never caught the murderer of Mario. I was crushed. I still carry a sadness in my heart."

"And what of your own son, Eduardo Junior?"

"His death was a blow to all of my family. The doctors could not help him. Our hospitals could not help him. As in Mario's case, I could not help him. I failed them both." A tear welled in Eduardo's eye.

Father Sanchez reached a trembling arm across the table and grasped Eduardo's hand. He could not help but notice the perspiration that clung to the younger man's hand.

"Let us say a prayer for both their souls my son. I know that you will see them again."

The two men continued their meal, which had grown cold as they talked.

"I will not ask you the purpose of your trip to Washington. I can only caution you that the trip will be somewhat dangerous. I have taken the liberty of obtaining a new set of documents for you. You will be traveling as Father Paul De Tomas. We took the liberty of having credit cards and an international driver's license made out in the name of Father Paul De Tomas. The pictures, while not exactly in your likeness, will stand up to official scrutiny. You understand, of course that the Church is unaware of the existence of Father Paul De Tomas. If for some reason you should be detained, the Church will not be able to verify your existence. You will be at the mercy of the United States Authorities. I will not lecture you on the futility of vengeance. I only pray that the reason for your trip is not fired by vengeance."

"Vengeance is not my purpose, Father." Eduardo lied again.

"Well, it is late and we must rise early. Sleep well my son. I will pray for you."

Eduardo rose and hugged the withered priest tightly.

"I thank you for your efforts and counsel."

The next morning dawned all to soon. Eduardo and Father Sanchez drank cups of strong Dominican coffee and munched on hard toast. They spoke little. Father Sanchez waited as Eduardo placed the bags in the car. They were soon on their way to the airport. Eduardo would fly to Miami, change planes and fly into Washington National Airport. Father Sanchez had reserved a room for Eduardo under the name of Father Paul De

Tomas. The hotel was located in Southwest Washington D.C. The priest was unaware that the hotel was less than a mile from the home of Dr. James Mercer. Eduardo dozed during the Miami leg of the flight. His documents would receive their first test when he cleared customs at the Miami airport. The rotund customs inspector glanced at the documents hurriedly and stamped them.

"Welcome to Miami, Father De Tomas. I hope that you enjoy your stay."

"Thank you, my son." Eduardo answered and walked slowly through the gate and onto the next terminal. In less than three hours, the jet was circling Washington D.C.

Eduardo took a taxi from the airport to the new hotel that sat on the banks of the Potomac River. He checked into his room and changed his clothes. He returned to the lobby of the hotel and asked the bellman for directions to the nearest sporting goods store. He opened the door of a cab that was parked in front of the hotel. Using the directions that the bellman had given him, he rode the taxi to a large sporting goods store located in downtown Washington. He paid the driver and entered the store. Twenty minutes later, he returned to the curb. He carried a large bag. In the bag were a newly purchased black sweatsuit and a large stiletto. The stiletto was designed for self-defense. The clerk had been somewhat surprised when the bearded man had bought the first knife shown to him.

Eduardo stood at the curb of the crowded street and was soon able to attract the attention of a cruising taxicab. He gave the driver directions to the hotel. Shortly thereafter, he was resting in the hotel room. Dr. Mercer's home address rested on a nearby nightstand. He called the rental car agency and reserved a car for the next four days. He told the reservation clerk that he would be dropping the car off at Washington National Airport.

The next morning, Eduardo picked up the car from the rental agency and spent the rest of the day riding around the Southwest Washington area. He passed Dr. Mercer's home on three occasions, always noting details such as parallel streets. He jotted down notes as he passed. He was careful not to attract attention to either himself or the rental car. After darkness had fallen, he walked from the hotel to the corner on which the Mercer house stood. He did not change his steps as he walked by the well-lit house. He knew that he would visit the house next morning.

He awoke early the next morning. He drove the short distance to the Mercer neighborhood and parked about one hundred yards from the house. He looked at this watch. It was almost six thirty. He had been parked for just a short while when he saw a figure emerge from the house. The face looked older and the man had graying hair. It was his one-time friend. Eduardo felt the taste of bile in his throat. He watched as the man started up a car that was parked in front of the house. Eduardo followed the car of his one-time friend. The man who had refused to help Eduardo Junior. The man drove to East Potomac Park and parked his car.

Eduardo drove slowly by the car. In his rear view mirror, he could see that the man was exercising. Eduardo stopped near the end of the park in an area that was called Hayne's Point. Ten minutes later, James Mercer jogged slowly by the car. He was completely oblivious to the danger that lurked nearby.

The next day he repeated the procedure. He took care to arrive slightly earlier than the day before. He followed the Mercer car and was happy to note that the doctor repeated the same time schedule. Eduardo returned to the hotel. On the next day he would strike.

He awoke early on the morning of his planned attack. He changed into the black sweatsuit and donned a newly purchased pair of jogging shoes. He placed the stiletto in the waistband of the sweat pants and pulled the bulky sweatshirt down over the stiletto. He then drove to the Mercer home to wait. He was unaware that another car carrying a driver with the same purpose had parked in the neighborhood five minutes earlier. The car was a blue Subaru.

Shortly before six thirty, James Mercer emerged from his house. He started his car and drove along the route that was now familiar to Eduardo. Eduardo noticed that a blue Subaru followed closely behind the doctor's car. Eduardo followed the two cars. He noticed that the Subaru's driver glanced furtively at James Mercer when Mercer parked his car. The Subaru drove a little further up the road and parked. Eduardo parked some distance behind the blue car.

From time to time, Eduardo looked into the rear view mirror. He could see James Mercer approaching. When his former friend was twenty-five yards in front of Eduardo's car, Eduardo quickly opened the door of the rented car. He clutched the stiletto tightly in his right hand. He ran down the jogging path after the doctor. He was soon just several yards from the doctor. The doctor, hearing the footsteps of an approaching jogger, moved slightly to the right of the path.

Eduardo clutched the stiletto.

He called softly, "James. James. You would not come to me, so I came to you."

Mercer turned his head towards the voice. For a fleeting moment, there was a look of both recognition and horror. Eduardo plunged the glistening blade into the doctor's back. He continued striking him even as he fell to the ground. Eduardo stood up immediately and threw the knife into the deep dark waters of the nearby Potomac River.

For an instant, he caught the flash of movement out of the corner of his eye. A man was approaching Eduardo. The man's gait was unsteady and he appeared disoriented. In his hand, he held a long knife. The man came closer. Eduardo grabbed the man's hand and the man lost his grip on the knife. The knife sailed into the nearby waters. Eduardo ran back to the rental car. As he passed the Subaru, he noted that the other man staggered towards the Subaru and was awkwardly trying to enter the vehicle.

Eduardo drove slowly back to the hotel. He returned quickly to his room. He was careful to use the stairway. He did not want to be seen in the elevator. He showered while still wearing his clothes. The blood that had soaked the arm of the sweatshirt ran red into the drain. He placed the 'Do Not Disturb' sign outside of the door and slept the rest of the day, totally exhausted.

The next morning, he awoke early and drove to the airport. He returned the rental car and took the shuttle to the terminal. In the terminal, he sought out the nearest men's room. Fortunately, it was unoccupied. He placed a small bag containing the shoes and sweatsuit in a nearby trash receptacle. On the way to the passenger waiting area, he purchased a copy of the Washington Post. An hour later, he was on an American Airlines jet heading back to Miami. As the jet roared through the skies, Eduardo unfolded the newspaper that he had held under his arm. The headline read, "Prominent Washington Physician Murdered While Jogging." Eduardo closed the paper and dozed.

He awoke as the plane was circling Miami. Below him lay the beautiful beaches and hotels of Florida's largest city. He was again struck by the differences between New Savannah and other countries.

He relaxed as the jet rolled to a stop at the side of the arrival gate. He stood as the passengers slowly made their way out through the front exit. He was in no hurry. His flight to Aruba did not leave for another hour.

He slept during the flight to Aruba. He was tired. The last days had been stressful, but he was satisfied. He knew that although his revenge was incomplete, the other former friends would soon join James Mercer.

He made reservations while he was at the airport in Aruba. He would go via Mexico City to Los Angeles. He was even able to book a hotel and rental car using the name 'Father Paul De Tomas'. He left the large air terminal in the company of two of Miguel Aponte's men. He was soon aboard the large yacht heading back on the final leg of his trip. When he finally reached the dock at Port Allison, he looked at his watch. It had taken less than thirty-six hours, from the time that he left Washington, to reach the island. In less than thirty-six hours, he was back in New Savannah, back in a different world. The changes were even more marked than he had realized even though he had been gone for only a little over a week.

He was secretly glad to be home, but he knew that he would soon be leaving. He had made the reservations for the flight that left Aruba in two weeks. He knew that the section of the journey that involved the use of the ocean-going vessel was the most uncertain part of the trip. Storms while at sea could force the vessel to lose precious time. He added two more days to the time that he was due to leave Reina Beatrix Airport. He would have less then twelve days to spend with his family.

He spent the next ten days resting and comforting Alicia who was still morning the death of Eduardo Junior. The sparkle had gone out of her eyes. She was often tearful. They visited the grave of the tiny child every day.

He met with Marcellino on several occasions. Marcellino had formed a new cabinet using moderate thinking former politicians and men who were openly sympathetic to the drug cartel and its operation. The junta was hard at work enacting compromise measures aimed at restoring peace in New Savannah.

Right wing sympathizers were arrested in large numbers and held at detention centers. It was known that large numbers of right wing sympathizers had fled to the Aggie Mountains. Among those fleeing to avoid detention were many former members of the National Police Force. They were believed to be re-arming themselves for future attacks on the capital.

While Eduardo was at home, one of the bands of resistance fighters struck the airport at Doloresville. They had somehow purchased mortars. They had pock marked the runways and hit several hangers with their errant mortar rounds. Five airplanes were hit and burned, leaving twisted metal shells. The greatest damage had involved the fuel storage tanks located on the West End of the airfield. One of the tanks had been struck and exploded. The adjoining tanks caught fire during the attack. Great plumes of smoke drifted over the Doloresville area for several days after the attack.

Although thirteen of the raiders were killed and several captured, the bulk of the attacking force had been able to escape. Using darkened roads running along the north edge of the island, they had escaped their pursuers.

Miguel Aponte had sent his heavily armed men chasing the raiders. The raiders drove into the mountain flanks. It was decided not to follow them into the mountains. The mountain roads offered many sites that were ideal for ambush. It was better to catch the raiders in the open.

Due to the degree of sophistication of the attacks and the weaponry possessed by the attackers, it was thought by many that the attackers had been assisted by the C.I.A. It was known that the C.I.A. had in-country operatives. There were many who wondered if the United State's covert operations units might not have been involved. Rumors swept the island.

Miguel Aponte met on a daily basis with his lieutenants. They were determined to wipe out the members of the resistance forces. Miguel had promised Marcellino that the raiders would soon be brought to bay.

Miguel was sent to Columbia by boat. He returned after four days with a commitment of aid from the leaders of the Colombian drug cartel. An additional one hundred-man force would soon be arriving from Bogota. They would all be heavily armed. They were skilled jungle, as well as mountain, fighters.

Eduardo was undecided about his trip. He considered delaying the trip. His hate propelled him. After talking with Marcellino, Eduardo decided to follow his previously arranged schedule. During his short time at home, Eduardo formulated the rest of his plan for revenge. He would track down Stephen Mossler as his first victim on the West Coast. He would return home and wait four to six weeks. He would then fly to Seattle, find Kevin Pointer and then go to the San Francisco Bay area where Catherine Brinks lived. After he visited her, he would leave from the San Francisco Airport and fly to Mexico City. After reaching Mexico City, he would be safe. He would then return home via Aruba. Once home, he would then dedicate all of his energies to helping the Junta survive. His plans were set.

He boarded the boat early one morning and the crew headed southeast towards Aruba. The weather was clear and the voyage took less time than Eduardo had anticipated. He spent the next day waiting at his house in Savaneta. He reminisced about how different times had been when he and

Alicia were last here together. They had been newly-weds then. They were happy. Now they were both sad. Their unhappiness caused in part by the unwillingness of his former friends to help Eduardo Jr.

He left the house and rode to the airport with one of Miguel Aponte's men. Eduardo instructed the man to meet him at the airport in five days. The boat should be fueled and ready for an immediate departure when Eduardo returned.

Eduardo was soon settled aboard the Aero Mexicana jet. Tourists laughed and talked excitedly about their just ended vacation. A carefree spirit filled the cabin. Eduardo looked down at the azure sea far below the airplane and thought. He would have his revenge. He would have his revenge at all costs. Then he could rest.

The giant jet landed after descending through the smog-laden air of Mexico City. A young customs inspector glanced at Eduardo's documents. He studied Eduardo's face. He hurriedly stamped Eduardo's passport.

"I see that you are going on to Los Angeles. I have two brothers in Los Angeles. They are both active in the church there."

Eduardo answered with a smile. "Perhaps, I shall see them my son. What are their names?"

"Junipero and Octavio Perez, Father. Perhaps you will see them."

"I will give them your regards, should I see them."

"Gracias, Father. Your flight leaves from gate seven in one hour. Enjoy your trip."

"Gracias Officer Perez. Gracias."

Eduardo walked slowly towards the gate. He spent the time watching the travelers who swarmed the airport walkways. There were travelers from many nations. He heard many different languages being spoken. The airport seemed to be alive. There was a sense of gaiety. Eduardo felt the depths of his own sadness. He missed Eduardo Junior. This trip was for his child.

Eduardo's flight was announced and he boarded the airplane. He noted that there were several nuns on the airplane. Fortunately, they were seated in another area of the cabin. Eduardo slept for the majority of the flight. He woke up as the jet was lowering its wheels and descending over Los Angeles. The freeways and buildings spread out below the wing of the airplane for miles. The city was even larger than Miami.

He was cleared through the customs area in less than fifteen minutes. He looked directly into the inspector's eyes as the harried officer asked a few simple questions. With his stamped passport in hand, he walked towards the baggage area. From there, he went to the car rental stand. His papers were in order. His car was ready. He was given a map of the Los Angeles area and was soon on his way to the hotel.

After checking into the hotel, he unpacked and slept for several hours. He showered and dressed and went to the parking area. He left the hotel area and drove until he found a large mall. It took him a short while to find a sporting goods store. He left carrying a large bag containing a glistening hunting knife and a sweatsuit. He was ready for his next victim.

It took him several days to track the movements of Stephen Mossler. He found the condominium that the doctor lived in without any difficulty. The Georgetown Graduate Directory was correct to the smallest detail. He went on foot to the area and strolled up to the front door of the complex. He looked at the names on the call box. He found the name that he was looking for. "Stephen Mossler, M.D. Apt. 1118." He walked casually towards the entrance to the parking garage. He noted that the gate was broken. It seemed caught in the open position. He would watch the apartment. The doctor would come in at some time.

Eduardo waited for two more days. The doctor did not return during the hours that Eduardo waited. Eduardo considered driving to the hospital-parking garage. He decided against this because he knew that hospital areas were usually well patrolled. His years at Georgetown had taught him this. Not wanting to attract attention, Eduardo decided that the next night he would actually enter the parking structure and would wait in the shadows. Eduardo had been in Los Angeles for four days and he knew that his time was running out. His flight would leave early the next afternoon.

He entered the garage from a foggy Marina Del Rey street. The fog had begun to roll in earlier in the evening. He walked towards the center of the garage. He pretended to be removing car keys from his pocket. He followed the numbers that were printed on the floor of the garage. He saw the space that he was seeking. 1118. He thought that he saw a figure move from the shadows off to his left. He heard voices and decided that the shadow belonged to a couple that was entering a small car parked several rows from space number 1118.

He blended with the shadows, which are so much a feature of parking garages. A cold oil-filled breeze drifted through the area. He had been waiting for almost two hours when his patience was rewarded. He saw a car pull into the darkened area. The car lights cut through the darkness of the garage. Eduardo backed further into the darkness. In his hand he held the knife. He saw a face illuminated by the interior car light as the driver opened the door. It was Stephen. Eduardo approached quickly.

He called softly. "Stephen. Stephen. It's your old friend."

The startled driver turned and gasped. The knife's blade moved through the darkened air. Stephen did not even sense the presence of the lethal blade until it entered his body. Eduardo leaned closer to the stricken man. The wounded man's eyes opened. He seemed to be trying to mouth the word "sorry." The gasp was the last sound that left his lips. Eduardo plunged the knife into his chest again. The stricken doctor clutched his chest. Eduardo struck again and again. His former friend fell to the floor.

Eduardo walked slowly from the garage. No cars entered the structure while he was walking. He had parked his car by an inlet. He walked to the inlet. His knees shook as he walked. As the waves lapped at the sea walls, Eduardo hurled the knife into the dark waters. He wiped the signs of carnage from his bloodied hands. He started the car and drove back to the hotel.

After showering, Eduardo slept until the next morning. He packed his suitcase, checked out of the hotel and was soon headed towards the airport. He returned the car and was seated in the rental car shuttle bus.

He looked across the aisle at a fellow rider. The man was reading a section of the Los Angeles Times. The front page faced Eduardo. Across the top of the page in large letters was a bright headline. "L.A. Doctor Slain In Marina Del Rey Garage"

Eduardo walked about the terminal until his flight was called. He landed in Mexico City and was soon on a flight to Aruba. The same man who had driven him to the airport met him.

"Did you have a good trip, Eduardo?"

"Yes, Ernesto, my trip was fruitful. I am glad to be heading home."

He boarded the ocean-going vessel later that afternoon and twelve hours later, stood on the bow of the vessel as the mountains of New Savannah loomed on the horizon. Eduardo returned from the long trip feeling elated, but tired. He had settled half of his debts.

It would be several months before he left the islands again. He spent the time meeting with Marcellino and Miguel on a regular basis. The raiders had been quiet for almost a month. The presence of the well-armed Colombian reinforcements was an intimidating factor. The Junta met on a monthly basis and addressed the problems of governing the island. They knew that the present condition of New Savannah was growing more intolerable every day.

It was shortly after the spring planting season and newly planted vegetables sent their sprouts through the rich earth. At higher elevations, the coca plants were almost ready to be harvested. The crops often grew side by side.

Eduardo spent the time with his family. Large men drove the other children to the private school that they attended. The automatic weapons concealed under their jackets increased the men's girth.

The sanctions placed on the country by the Americans were unchanged. Alicia's father had purchased several more container ships. The ships made many voyages, bringing in badly needed staples from South American countries who still continued to trade with New Savannah.

Eduardo had planned his next trip to the United States in great detail. He would go by boat to Aruba and then fly to Mexico City. From Mexico City, he would fly to San Francisco. Changing planes, he would then make the short flight to Seattle. He would find Kevin Pointer, exact his revenge, and then return to the San Francisco area. He would deal with Catherine last. She, who he had loved. She, who would not help his son.

The weeks passed quickly. The hot tropical sun baked the island's lush tropical foliage. Islanders visited the beach almost daily in an attempt to escape the heat. The pace of life slowed. The afternoon siestas became longer. The resistance groups remained quiet, the tropical heat bringing about a malaise. They would attack later, when it was cooler. When it was easier to carry the ammunition and mortar rounds. When it easier to climb down from their mountain encampments.

The hurricane season had started with the month of June. Eduardo watched the seas off to the East of the island. It was from the East that the storms came. He did not want to delay his final trip. He told Alicia that he would be gone for six to eight weeks. He assured her that this would be the last time that he would be separated from her and the children. He notified Miguel Aponte. The message was simple. Have the ocean going yacht ready for departure the next day.

Bright sunshine bounced off the crests of the tropical sea the next morning. Eduardo boarded the vessel and the graceful boat headed towards Aruba once again. Some weeks before, Eduardo had instructed one of Miguel's men. The man, who was going to Aruba, was told of Eduardo's choices for reservations. As Eduardo stopped on the dock in Aruba, the man approached him with a large brown envelope. All was ready for Eduardo's last trip.

The Aero Mexicana flight left early the next morning. Eduardo encountered no difficulties in clearing Mexican customs. After a short delay, he flew on to San Francisco. A seemingly disinterested customs officer quickly cleared him through customs. His flight to Seattle left forty-five minutes later.

Eduardo picked up a small foreign car from the rental unit at Seattle-Tacoma International Airport. His hotel was located eight miles from the airport. He found the hotel after circling the area several times. Checking in as Father Paul De Tomas, he was soon settled in his room.

From the lobby in the hotel, he called Miguel's cousin. The man agreed to pick up Eduardo later that day. Eduardo stood in front of the hotel at the appointed time. He turned when he heard a driver call his name.

"Senor Sierramonte! Senor Sierramonte! It is I, Senor Espinola."

Eduardo opened the door of the large sedan. He got into the car and the driver drove off into the traffic.

"Miguel sends you his blessings. He asked me to contact you as soon as I arrived."

"I am pleased that you arrived safely, Senor Sierramonte. Your flight went well?"

"Yes. No problems. I do, however, have one problem. I am in need of a weapon. A handgun will do. I will, of course, need ammunition. The gun should be untraceable, of course."

"That is not a problem, Senor. I can deliver such a weapon to your hotel tomorrow. Is there anything else that I can provide for you?"

"A nice meal would be in order."

"I know just such a place, Senor. The cook is from Guatemala and the food is delicious."

"I would like that."

They drove across Seattle towards the outskirts. Eduardo looked at the skyscrapers as they passed. In the background, he could see the snow-capped summit of Mount Rainier. They finally pulled into the parking lot of a small restaurant. The parking lot was crowded with many cars. Alfredo Espinola found a parking space and the men entered the small building. Salsa music blared from speakers that hung from the walls. There were thirty tables scattered about the central room. A bar ran the entire length of an adjoining room. Most of the patrons were speaking Spanish. The owner approached the two men.

"Good evening, Senor Espinola. It is good to see you again. I will have a table ready for you in several minutes."

Alfredo introduced Eduardo to the owner. "This is Father Paul De Tomas. He is visiting our city for several days. He comes from far away. I have told him that your food is the best in Seattle."

The owner laughed. "I will do my best to please you and your guest, Senor Espinola. I hope that you enjoy your meal."

The two men were soon seated at a table in a small section of the restaurant. The room was separated from the main dining area by a large oaken door. The door served to mute the blaring Salsa music. They were soon served heaping platters of chicken and pork, and bowls of spicy vegetables.

They ate slowly and talked for some hours. Alfredo was from Guatemala. Miguel had sent him from Colombia to oversee activities related to the cartel's interests in the Seattle area. He had not been back to Colombia in over four years. His family had joined him two years ago in a Seattle suburb. He missed Guatemala, but had made his home here in the Pacific Northwest. He worked hard protecting the interests of the cartel and was kept ever vigilant. He was in constant fear of being found out by DEA agents or by the police. He had been able to purchase several legitimate enterprises. Miguel had promised to send a replacement at the end of Alfredo's fifth year in the country. Alfredo then planned to run the legitimate businesses he had purchased. His days with the drug cartel would have ended. He was half way through his fourth year.

"Six more months, Senor Sierramonte. Six more months! Then, my only worry will be the temperature of the yogurt or the price of automobile tires. I can hardly wait. I am grateful to my dear cousin for sending me and my family to this place."

Eduardo smiled.

After dinner, Alfredo drove Eduardo back to the hotel. As they parted, Alfredo assured Eduardo that he would bring the articles Eduardo had requested the next morning. Eduardo slept until awakened by Senor

Espinola the next morning. He carried a small package. The package contained a small pistol, a clip, and a box of ammunition. The men talked briefly. Senor Espinola was late for an appointment. Perhaps if time permitted, they would dine together again. The men shook hands and embraced. They would not see each other again.

Eduardo called Dr. Kevin Pointer's office later that morning. He was told that the doctor was out of the office for the day.

"When will he be in? Do you know where he might be?"

"He's probably down at the Marina." The receptionist replied.

"At the Marina?"

"Yes, he keeps his boat docked at the Marina in Edmonds. If he's not in surgery or not in the office, he's usually at the Marina. I can beep him if it's an emergency."

"Oh, there's no need. I'll call the office in the morning."

Eduardo bought a map of the area from a nearby gas station. He circled the Edmonds area on the map. He drove to Waterview twice during the next several days. The address listed in the Georgetown Directory was on a well-traveled street. The condominium complex sat at the top of a high hill. A winding driveway climbed up the hill. Entrance was by an electronically controlled gate. Eduardo realized that he would not be able to enter or leave the complex without being observed. He would have to try to catch Kevin at one of the other places. The hospital was too risky. Security personnel were always on duty at hospitals. The office building, Eduardo found, had a security guard who sat at a desk in the downstairs lobby. The Marina offered the best chance of escape. It would have to be the Marina.

Using the map, Eduardo drove up Interstate 5. He drove by the Marina several times. He would have to be patient. He would watch Kevin's apartment. If the doctor headed towards the Marina, Eduardo would follow.

It took three days for the doctor to finally drive towards the Marina. During the interval, Eduardo had trailed Pointer as the physician drove from office to home and back to various hospitals. It was Thursday night and Eduardo saw the by now familiar car enter onto the interstate. Following at a safe distance, he followed Kevin's car until the blinker flashed. Eduardo grinned. The doctor was going to the Marina. A fog blanketed the area. More fog was rolling in from the Sound.

Eduardo watched as the doctor turned into the Marina. Parking the rental car not far away, he cautiously approached on foot. The eerie yellow light given off by the mercury lamps tried unsuccessfully to cut through the fog. Kevin was unaware that he was being watched. He was busily loading boxes on the deck of a sailboat that was moored nearby.

Eduardo moved slowly. The gun that Alfredo had given him was in his pocket. He had experienced some difficulty loading the shells into the clip, but after some effort, he had managed to load seven bullets. The weapon was ready. He waited until the doctor had finished loading the vessel. Movement inside the boat had stopped. He waited a bit longer, then began to walk towards the sailboat. He read the name on the transom. "The Spirit." He stepped lightly onto the deck of the vessel. The boat rocked. He thought that he heard a voice from inside the boat's cabin. There was movement from within the vessel. Eduardo pulled the pistol from his pocket. The hatch was opened from inside. The glow of the cabin light exploded from the hatch. A head appeared from inside the hatch. Eduardo raised the pistol and fired point blank at the figure. The man fell back inside the cabin. Eduardo's arm followed the body into the cabin. Spent shells boomed around the boat's cabin. He cursed as he fired the weapon. The smell of gunpowder mingled with the smell of diesel oil.

"This is for Eduardo Junior, you coward!"

It was too late for Kevin to hear. The unseeing eyes of Kevin Pointer were fixed on the legs of his killer. The first bullet had ended his life. Eduardo turned. The silencer had muffled the sound of the shots. He walked quickly back to the car. As he was leaving, he noticed a small blue car driving slowly into the Marina's entrance. Eduardo flattened his body against an adjoining building as the small car drove slowly by his hiding place.

Eduardo drove towards the highway. On the way, he stopped. He tossed the weapon into the waters of Puget Sound. He continued his drive. He had no difficulty finding the hotel. He had traveled this route many times during the last several days. He found a parking space and left the car. He entered the hotel lobby. He walked at a normal pace. He did not want to seem hurried. He took the elevator to the fifth floor. He turned on the late night newscast and as the television droned, Eduardo fell into a deep sleep.

Eduardo still had one more day left in Seattle. He called Alfredo Espinola. He told him that he would be leaving Seattle shortly and would not be able to meet him for dinner. He wished Alfredo luck in his legitimate business pursuits. Eduardo had lunch in a small restaurant in the hotel. He realized that the trip and the recent events had made him very tired. He returned to the room and slept until late that afternoon. He spent the evening watching television. He noted with interest one of the lead stories on the six o'clock news broadcast. A young, blond woman was reporting the details of a murder. Early that morning, the body of a prominent Seattle pediatric surgeon had been found aboard his sailboat. Police had no leads as to the identity of the suspect. Eduardo laughed as the young reporter continued her story. He had one more debt to collect.

Eduardo knew that his last task was to find Catherine Brinks. She was the former friend for whom he carried the most hatred. She had spurned his obvious affection while they were students. She had not heeded his call for help for Eduardo Junior. He took two days to travel from Seattle to Oakland. Upon his arrival in the Bay Area, he drove to an area called Jack London Square. The Square was located on the Oakland Estuary. He found a small hotel that overlooked the bay. Off to the West, he could see the skyline of San Francisco. His heart was too filled with hatred to enjoy the sights that his eyes were experiencing.

As he had done on two previous occasions, he drove around the city of Oakland until he found a sporting goods shop. He left the shop twenty minutes later carrying a package. Inside the package were newly purchased sweatsuits and a stiletto. He spent the next several days locating Catherine Brinks' office and the area in which she lived. On several occasions, he drove into the Oakland hills. One morning, he watched as she hurriedly left her driveway. He decided that he would strike that night.

A fog was settling on the Oakland Hills as he drove up Saroni Drive. He parked his car and was pleased to note that the fog had reduced visibility even further. He had found a well-concealed driveway located approximately an eighth of a mile from the doctor's house. The driveway led to an overgrown, empty lot. The lot had once been the site of a house destroyed by the fires that swept the Oakland Hills some years prior. After parking the car, he cautiously walked down the hill towards Brinks' house. Looking around, he darted into the overgrown bushes that flanked the house. He continued to the back of the house. He noticed a sliding glass door. He pulled on the door handle and the door was locked. He continued around the house, arriving at the front porch. He climbed the several steps and turned the front door knob. To his amazement, the door slid quietly open. Catherine had forgotten to lock the door when she left the house earlier that day.

He entered the darkened building. He had taken several steps inside when he felt something against his leg. He was thrown slightly off balance. He stood still. He again felt something brush his leg. He then heard the meowing of a cat. Eduardo withdrew the stiletto from his pocket and ran his hand slowly down his leg until he felt the fur on the cat's back. Grabbing a handful of fur, he immediately felt the animal's teeth enter his arm. The animal, in all its frenzy, raked his other arm with its claws. Eduardo took the knife and slit the animal's throat. He then flung the cat against the wall of the room.

He walked towards the front door of the house and waited. A short time later, he heard a car pull into the driveway. He stiffened. He heard Catherine pause as she rummaged through her purse looking for the house key. He did not know it, but Catherine always kept her car keys and house keys on separate chains. Oakland had been the scene of many car-jackings.

The doorknob turned and a form entered the room. He heard the doctor calling to her cat. "Lu Lu. Lu Lu. I'm home."

The form passed him in the darkened house. He stepped behind the form and whispered "It is not Lu Lu who awaits you. It is I, Eduardo."

Before the horrified doctor could answer, he cupped his hand over her mouth and plunged the stiletto into her body. He struck her many times. Sweat ran from his body as he completed his last act of revenge.

The ringing of the telephone startled him. He stood motionless while Catherine's voice greeted the caller. A woman's cheery voice was heard leaving a message for her friend while Catherine lay dead a few feet away.

He slowly opened the front door and looked around the area. There were no cars on the lonely road and no neighbors were about. He walked rapidly back to the hidden driveway and started the car. He drove slowly down Saroni Drive. A short distance down the hill from Catherine's home, he noticed a man carrying suitcases out to a car. The man did not look up as Eduardo passed by. Further down the hill, he noticed an oncoming car. The car was a small foreign station wagon. As the other car drove into Eduardo's lights, he could see the driver's face. His features seemed distorted, yet familiar. Eduardo was sure he had seen the driver and the car somewhere else, but he could not remember where.

Eduardo drove back to the hotel near Jack London Square. He parked the car and walked over to the water's edge. Looking around and seeing no one about, he hurled the stiletto into the waters of the estuary. Using the cover of night, he traced his steps back to the car. He unlocked the trunk and removed a small bag containing an identical sweatsuit. He walked to a nearby gas station, went into the men's room and changed out of the bloodied sweatsuit. He placed the bloodstained clothes in the bag. As he walked towards the hotel, he tossed the bag and its contents into a trash filled dumpster.

He slept the rest of the night. The next morning, he noticed that his arm was swollen from the bites and scratches of the cat. He would have to find a nearby drug store and purchase some antibiotic ointment and bandages.

He called the airline reservations desk. He explained that church matters required him to leave sooner than he had intended. Aero Mexicana had a seat available on the flight that left the next morning. Eduardo spent a restless day. His arm throbbed. It was time for him to return to New Savannah. His mission was completed. He had exacted his revenge.

Early the next morning, he drove along the crowded freeways towards the airport. He saw a large car rental return sign, and after signing a few papers, was soon aboard the small shuttle bus. He entered the large terminal and was soon checked in for his flight. He purchased a copy of the Oakland Tribune. In large letters, the headlines read "Oakland Pediatrician Found Slain." In the same edition, but buried among the other news items was a smaller story. The article stated that the body of unidentified white male had been found floating in the waters of the Oakland Estuary near Jack London Square. The unidentified man had apparently died of a self-inflicted gunshot wound.

Eduardo boarded his flight when it was announced. In two days, he was back in New Savannah.

Chapter Twenty-nine

It was Thursday. Alphonso Smith had stayed near his desk for the entire morning. He was expecting a call. He would soon know the results of the FBI print analysis. The laboratory had promised to call him at eleven o'clock. It was a trying morning. Every few minutes, Elza Major or Malcolm Sledge would open the office door.

"Any word yet?"

"No.... None at all. Now will you guys quit bugging me? They'll call us when they have an answer."

It was not the FBI who called later that morning. The caller was Merlin Dobson of the Oakland Police.

"Hello, Smith. Just wanted to tell you that we got a DNA match."

"You're kidding!"

"I kid you not. The laboratory called us first since we had submitted the blood. They have a ninety-nine percent confidence that the match is the Sierramonte guy from the school. I'm going to call the other departments now. What say we do a conference call at two p.m. your time? It is only nine-thirty out here. We'll call you at two your time. We can talk further then."

"Sounds good to me. We'll talk later."

He slowly hung up the receiver. A broad grin covered his face. He immediately went to find the other detectives who had worked on the case. They stood in the center of the booking room and laughed and exchanged handshakes.

Elza Major laughed. "Now all we need is the print comparison and we'll have him nailed to two of the cases."

As they were talking, another detective called out to the group. "Telephone call for Al. Line five. I think it's the Feds."

Alphonso Smith wasted little time in picking up a nearby extension telephone. As the other detectives in the room looked on, he appeared to nod as the caller spoke.

"We certainly want to thank you guys. You really did a number on this one. Thanks again."

The smile on his face told all. The partial prints matched those of Eduardo Sierramonte, taken when he was a student at Georgetown.

At two p.m., the conference call started. Several detectives who had not been assigned to the case listened intently.

The unseen voice spoke. "The DNA and fingerprint matches prove that this guy did at least two of the hits. We may never know who did the other two, but the M.O. was almost identical on the other two. We can hand this all over to the Feds now. We identified the suspect. Now all they have to do is catch the bastard."

Martin Jones, the detective from Oakland spoke. "We still don't know what this guy, Samuel Jones, was doing in the area. He was probably stalking Dr. Brinks. Sure looks like Sierramonte got to her first."

The Seattle detective added, "We know that Sierramonte was up here. I hope they find him."

Smith spoke, "I have been told that he is probably outside the country. His home was listed as the Dominican Republic in school records. But it looks as though that was just a cover. He's actually from a place called New Savannah."

"How can you be sure?"

"Well, a funny thing happened yesterday. I got a call from a guy who claimed to be the college roommate of this Eduardo Sierramonte. Seems he had read about the murder of Mercer when it first happened. He didn't come forward with any information then, but he grew a little concerned when he read in the alumni journal that three other doctors had died and that all the victims were in the Class of 1976. Seems they were all in a study group in medical school while this guy was in law school. Sierramonte shared a townhouse with this guy in Georgetown. All six of them hung out together at times. He told me that he was sure Sierramonte was the killer if the other three died violently. When he called me, he didn't know how the others had died. I filled him in. He talked a long time about this Sierramonte fellow. He said that he was actually from an island called New Savannah. Sierramonte had backed each of the doctors financially when they ran into financial troubles. He had set up bank accounts for them in the Cayman Islands. Each doctor was unaware of the Sierramonte's financial aid to the other members of the group. An old priest from the Dominican Republic evidently laundered the money. I guess they didn't repay him. We'll never know until this guy is caught."

Another voice asked, "Who was this caller? And why do you believe him?"

Smith replied, "He is the attorney for the Venezuelan Consulate right here in Washington. His name is Manuel Augustino. His father was a member of the Venezuelan delegation to the U.N. His father is now the Vice President of Venezuela. This lawyer would not have come forward unless he was reasonably sure of his information. He told me he'd be glad to meet with us if we needed any further information. He gave me no reason not to believe him."

The callers continued talking. It was agreed that the lead homicide detectives from each of the jurisdictions involved would meet with FBI agents in their respective cities. The call ended.

The next day, Detective Alphonso Smith called Dean Avery at the Georgetown School of Medicine. The two men met that afternoon. Detective Smith explained the details of the case to the Dean. Smith was filled with doubts that the murderer would ever be brought to justice. The Dean was satisfied that the identity of the murderer had been discovered. He was equally saddened that Eduardo Sierramonte might go unpunished. He had robbed the medical community of four talented professionals.

The following day, Detective Smith visited the home of Margo Mercer. He spent several hours detailing the findings that implicated Eduardo Sierramonte in the death of her husband. The woman wept openly as the detective read entries from the documents. He explained that the Island of New Savannah had no extradition treaty with the United States and thus, Sierramonte might indeed escape prosecution for the murders.

That afternoon, Margo Mercer called her father at his Langley, Virginia office. He was a senior official in charge of Latin American affairs. The two met in his office several hours later. The older man attempted to comfort his daughter, but his attempts were fruitless.

"He'll get away with it!" she cried. "He murdered James and he'll get away with it! I don't know if I want to live. Knowing that that evil man is free on some island. Oh, Daddy! I'm so sad."

The older man hugged his daughter and escorted her down the long corridor, his arm tightly around her waist. He walked her to her car. "I'll call you this evening, Margo."

The father, Andrew Wilson, was shaken as he walked back to his office. He slumped heavily into the chair behind his desk and was deep in thought. After a few moments, he reached for a green telephone that sat on his desk. He dialed a coded number on the secure telephone. A few seconds passed. There was a sound of static on the telephone line, which soon cleared. A deep voice answered on the other end of the line.

"Hello, Steve. This is Wilson."

The conversation lasted ten minutes. If one had been able to overhear the conversation, they would have recognized words such as "in-country operatives, extreme prejudice, within a reasonable time". The conversation ended and he replaced the receiver.

That night he called his daughter. Things would be worked out.

Epilogue

Samuel sat on a bench near the water's edge. Overhead, the shrill cries of circling gulls filled the air. He pointed a trembling finger at the gulls so that Stacey might better see them. He shook the pill bottles in his coat pocket. There was no more medication. He had gobbled the last of the pills days before. Tears flowed down his cheeks as he sat at the water's edge. He missed Stacey. He missed Claudette.

He placed a hand into the other pocket of the crumbled jacket. He felt the coldness of the revolver on his hand. He gripped the pistol and pulled it slowly out of the pocket. He placed the barrel on his temple and pulled the trigger. The report of the gun was partially drowned out by the shrieking gulls. His body tumbled from the bench into the murky waters of the estuary.

Later that morning, his partially submerged body was spotted by a group of Japanese tourists who had come to the estuary hoping to see the sea lions.

Eduardo returned home. During his absence, the resistance fighters had become bolder. There were scattered skirmishes throughout the island on an almost daily basis. Miguel Aponte was kept busy sending men from point to point on the island. Marcellino suggested that with Eduardo's return, the younger man take a more active role in affairs of the junta. Eduardo agreed to participate without hesitation. His world was here in New Savannah. He had no interests outside of the island.

Eduardo attended the weekly meetings of the junta in Doloresville. These meetings were held every Wednesday morning. He was driven to the meetings by one of Miguel Aponte's heavily armed men, who acted as both a chauffeur and a bodyguard. Four men, including the bodyguard, lived in a small bungalow not far from the main house. Eduardo stood in the entryway of the large house as the bodyguard approached.

A band of heavy showers, the leading edge of a large tropical storm, had passed over New Savannah during the night. The hills glistened as the early morning sun reflected on the verdant landscape.

"Good morning, Senor Sierramonte. That was quite a storm last night, wasn't it?"

"Yes, it was, Pedro. It sounded like the rain would come through the roof."

"The clouds even blocked out the moon."

The two men walked slowly towards the garage, a structure separate from the house. They were still talking when the guard turned the ignition key. A small spark struck a detonator imbedded in two pounds of plastique explosive hidden beneath the car. The men, the car, and the garage all but vanished in the explosion.

Distant revenge!

About the Authors

Edward G. Briscoe, M.D. is a practicing physician. He has published *Dairy of a Short-Timer in Vietnam,* his dairy detailing his experiences as the head of the Anesthesia Department at Da Nang Naval Hospital. Excerpts of this dairy were included in *Exploring America's Past,* a multimedia curriculum published by Holt, Rhinehart and Winston in early 1998. His novel, *Marble Cake,* was listed in the Author Showcase by Authorlink!, an online service for writers, editors, and publishers. His other credits include several medical research papers. Edward G. Briscoe M.D. is a graduate of Howard University (B.S. and M.D. degrees). He was born in New Jersey.

Agatha D. Briscoe is the wife of Dr. Edward G. Briscoe. She is an information systems consultant. Collaborating with her husband and friend on this novel has been very different from the technical writing she has done in the past. Agatha D. Briscoe is a graduate of Texas Southern University (B.S. degree). She is a Texas native.

Edward and Agatha Briscoe have lived in Hawaii and the Caribbean. They have made their home in northern California since 1995. Their adult children live in California, New Jersey, and Maryland.

Delores R. Johnson is a retired Internal Revenue Service official. Her expertise helped bring a sense of realism to this novel, particularly as regards the laundering of money and information concerning overseas accounts. An avid reader, she is involved in many community volunteer organizations. Her collaboration on this work is her first foray into writing. She was born in New Jersey and has lived in California since 1989.